Dead Energy.

The Alex Cave Series Book 1

Written by
James M. Corkill

Chapter 1

PUGET SOUND, WASHINGTON, USA:
The wind had died to a whisper, and ex-CIA operative, Alex Cave, was lashing down the sails of his thirty-five foot chartered sailboat on the last day of his two-week vacation sailing through the San Juan Islands of Washington State. Tomorrow he would return to teaching geophysics at a small college in Montana.

A panic filled voice suddenly came from the VHF radio speaker. "*Mayday*! *Mayday*! Something's happening to the ship!"

He grabbed his binoculars, focusing them on a tanker full of crude oil, now stopped two miles away. He started the engine and headed toward the tanker, when suddenly it was engulfed in brilliant neon blue light. When the light vanished, he started the engine and steered toward the tanker, thinking maybe he could be of some help.

***

U.S. COAST GUARD SHIP, ADLER:
"*Mayday*! *Mayday*! Something's happening to the ship!"

The ship's captain, Commander McBride, and the four men on the bridge stared out through the windows, scanning the area for a ship. When they did not see one, the radio operator pressed the button on the microphone. "This is the U.S. Coast Guard ship, Adler. Who are you, and what's your location?"

"This is the Americrude oil tanker *Defiance*, forty-nine degrees, five minutes south, and one hundred twenty-three west. Get us some help here! There's something … happening to the oil … I think … explode!"

"*Defiance*, you're breaking up. Say again!"

Static erupted from the speaker, and McBride stared at the radio operator. "Try to get him back."

McBride walked to the radarscope and stared at the screen. "It's the only ship in that sector. Let's go see what's going on. Come left to course zero-eight-zero. All ahead flank speed."

***

When Alex arrived at the tanker, it was now riding high in the water, empty. He saw no one on deck, and no one answered when he yelled up from below, so he hung the rubber bumpers over the side of the sailboat and tied off to the rusted rungs of a ladder welded to the side of the ship. With the sailboat secure, he climbed to the main deck and looked around, but didn't see anyone. He went to the open inspection hatches and looked down inside, but there was no oil. He sniffed the air rising from the interior, and then leaned closer and took a deep breath before continuing across the deck and entering the superstructure.

Alex strolled through the dining room, seeing partially eaten meals on the table, and then continued through the sleeping quarters, but didn't find anyone. Through a window, he saw a Coast Guard cruiser pulling alongside and headed down the stairs.

***

The thrumming of the *Adler*'s engines dropped to a low rumble as McBride stared through a set of binoculars at the rust-streaked black paint on the side of the behemoth oil tanker, forty feet away. Thin streams of black smoke trailed from the exhaust stack, but all forward movement had ceased. He scanned her entire length through the binoculars, but there was no sign of an explosion.

When he saw no one on deck or up on the bridge, McBride grabbed the microphone for the public address system. "Ahoy, the *Defiance*. This is the United States Coast Guard responding to your mayday." He waited several minutes for someone to appear, but the *Defiance* looked deserted. "Get the skiff in the water. I don't know what happened here, but I intend to find out."

McBride suddenly saw a man wearing blue jeans and a white sweatshirt appear on *Defiance*'s deck and stand at the railing. He grabbed a bullhorn, stepped through the hatch, and pointed it up at the man. "This is the Commander of the *USS Adler*. What's going on?" The man hollered back, but the rumbling engines drowned out his voice and McBride pointed the horn at the man again. "I'm coming aboard."

***

With the Coast Guard cruiser on the opposite side from his sailboat, Alex realized the Commander would assume he was part of the crew. He dropped the boarding ladder over the side and leaned his forearms across the railing as he watched the procedure. The officer came across in a small launch and ascended the ladder with two of his sailors and continued across the deck to stop in front of him.

McBride realized the stranger was taller in person, about six-foot-four, with a rugged face marked by a few small scars. What stood out were his blue eyes below his thick black brows and wavy black hair. "Where do you get off calling in an explosion?"

Alex folded his arms across his chest and leaned back against the railing. "I didn't. My name's Alex Cave, and I'm not a member of the crew. I heard the distress call and came to help. As you can see, there was no explosion, but there's no one onboard either."

"How did you get onboard?"

Alex waved a hand across the deck. "My sailboat is tied off on the other side. I suggest you look around, Commander."

"Did you see anything from your sailboat?"

"Just a bright blue light."

A sailor with a portable radio interrupted. "We have the information about the ship, Commander."

"Turn that thing up and let's hear it."

The sailor spoke into the radio, turned up the volume, and set it on the table. A moment later, the voice of *Adler*'s radio operator came through the speaker. "The *Defiance*. United States registry, home port, Valdez, Alaska. A three hundred and twenty-six thousand ton universal class oil tanker. It departed Valdez on March ninth, carrying eighty thousand tons of heavy crude oil. Destination, March Point, Washington State. Seven crew members. That's it, Sir."

McBride looked at Alex. "She looks empty to me, but it makes little sense. What made them abandon ship?"

"I don't think they did. All the life rafts are still in the containers along the railing."

"You don't miss much, do you?" Alex grinned in reply. "Just who the hell are you?"

"I'm a geophysics instructor from Montana, but I grew up in the area."

"So, what do you intend to do?"

"I intend to get back on my sailboat and finish my vacation. This ship is in your hands now."

McBride followed Alex across the deck to the opposite railing. "I might need you as a witness in the investigation of what happened here."

"You can contact me at the Montana State Collage."

Alex climbed over the rail and descended the metal ladder down to his sailboat. He started the engine and untied the line, and then waved up at McBride as he left.

McBride stared after Alex for a moment before turning and hurrying back across the deck with the sailors. "We'd better send a message to headquarters in Port Angeles. Tell them to search for an oil spill somewhere off the coast between here and Alaska."

***

Alex's mind kept turning over every detail of the incident, searching for a logical answer. However, by sunset, when his boat was tied in her mooring slip, he had none. He decided it was now the Coast Guard's problem, and after fixing a sandwich in the galley, he retired to the salon with a book.

Three hours later, he bolted upright in bed, his sheets soaked in sweat. It had been a year since the last recurring nightmare, but even now, he vividly saw the stretcher being wheeled out the door of his demolished apartment in Holland, and him raising the sheet, seeing the face of his beloved new bride, Sevi.

He rolled off the bed and grabbed a bottle of water from the refrigerator and thought about that day three years ago. He couldn't quite remember what had happened during the following month, but apparently, he had gone on a killing rampage to get even with the people who tried to kill him. His best friend, Okawna, had extracted him from Russia, and one week after returning to the United States, he resigned from the CIA. He crawled back into bed, but it was an hour before he finally fell asleep.

Just after sunrise, he stepped off his sailboat and walked between the yachts and boats tied in the mooring slips of the marina. He could not stop pondering the fate of the *Defiance*'s crew as he walked up the ramp, past the marina office, and entered the restaurant.

Someone had left a newspaper on a vacant table, and he noticed the article about the tanker on the front page. He sat down to read it and ordered breakfast from the server. The Coast Guard reported there was no oil spill, but the reporter continued about past oil spills and the danger of having tankers enter Puget Sound.

He set the newspaper aside when his breakfast arrived and halfheartedly read the other articles on the front page as he ate, then an article on the lower corner caught his attention. *SKIERS FIND SIX MEN*

FROZEN TO DEATH ON MT. BAKER. The article named the two members of the ski patrol who found the bodies who stated the dead men might have been drunk or part of a prank because five of them were wearing only tee shirts, jeans, and tennis shoes, and oddly, the sixth man was wearing oil-stained coveralls and smelled like diesel fuel. The Whatcom County Sheriff stated one of the dead men was carrying an Alaska driver's license.

Alex set the paper aside while he finished his breakfast, but could not stop thinking about the article. The *Defiance* was out of Alaska, but she had seven men onboard, and they discovered only six men on the mountain. Then again, the crew *would* be dressed like those men. The man in coveralls could be the ship's mechanic. *That's ridiculous,* he thought. *How could they end up on a mountain so far away?*

For his own peace of mind, he decided it was worth a little more investigation and called directory assistance for the number of the Coast Guard, and was connected.

"United States Coast Guard Station, Port Angeles," a young male voice answered.

"The station commander, please."

"Who should I say is calling, sir?"

"Alex Cave."

A moment later, a female voice came on the line. "This is Captain Taylor, Mister Cave. Commander McBride has explained what happened."

"Have you found any of the crew?"

"Not yet."

"Would you have the names of the crew members?"

"Yes. The skipper's name was Joseph Bower." She gave Alex the rest of the names. "Do you need a copy of the report?"

"Not right now. Thanks for the help."

Alex called the newspaper and was transferred to the reporter who wrote the article. He asked the woman if she had learned the names of the six men and was informed the Whatcom County Sheriff's Department in Bellingham wouldn't release the information. Alex thanked her and thought about calling the Sheriff's department himself, but assumed they would not give him the information over the phone. *It's just a coincidence,* he thought again, but something tugged at the back of his mind. He called the local airport and made a reservation on a flight leaving for Bellingham in an hour.

***

The flight took forty-five minutes to the Bellingham airport. From there, Alex took a taxi to the Whatcom County Sheriff's Department and spoke to a deputy at the front desk. "I might have some information which could be helpful in your investigation of those men found on Mt. Baker."

The deputy studied Alex for a moment. "Oh? And who are you?"

"First, I'd like to know the name of the man with the Alaska driver's license."

"I won't give out that kind of information without the Sheriff's approval."

"Fine. Let me talk to the Sheriff."

"The Sheriff's a busy man. If you have anything to report, it's your duty to tell me."

Alex shrugged. "Fine. Solve it yourself." He turned and walked toward the door.

"Wait a minute!"

Alex stopped and turned to look at the deputy, but didn't approach the desk. He just stared at the young man.

"Just hang on a minute. I'll see if the Sheriff can spare a few minutes."

The deputy picked up the phone and spoke. A few moments later, a tall man appeared behind the counter. "I'm Sheriff Ralston. What can you tell me about the men on Mt. Baker?"

Alex took a chance on his gut instinct. "I know where they came from."

The Sheriff studied Alex for a moment. "Come on back to my office."

Once in the office, Sheriff Ralston indicated a stiff wooden chair near the desk and sat on his own padded chair on the other side. "What do you know about all this, Mister?"

"Alex Cave. Have you heard about the oil tanker the Coast Guard brought into Port Angeles?"

"Yes, I read about it in the paper. Why?"

"What the paper didn't say is that the crew was missing. If my suspicions are correct, the skiers found them on Mt. Baker."

The Sheriff stared at Alex for a long moment, a skeptical grin forming on his lips. "Mister Cave, most of those men were young, and this is a college town. It was probably some fraternity prank turned sour."

"The paper said you found identification on one of the bodies."

Ralston reached into the file basket on his desk and grabbed a folder. As the Sheriff scanned through the first few pages, Alex sat up in tense anticipation. "Here it is. An older man had a driver's license."

"Was his name Joseph Bower?"

When the look in the Sheriff's eyes said he was right. Alex sighed with relief and leaned back in the chair. "Bower was the skipper of that tanker."

The Sheriff's jaw went slack. "You're kidding me."

"I'm positive the fingerprints will match the ones taken from the ship. There should have been seven bodies. Did you search the area?"

"The ski patrol did. It was odd, though. They said they found the bodies in soft powder snow, but there weren't any tracks leading in or out of the area. We can't figure out how they got there."

"Have you performed an autopsy yet?"

"Yes, and the coroner is baffled. It seems the blood in all the bodies was dehydrated, and he can't figure out how it was done without heat."

Alex stood up, brought out his wallet, and handed the Sheriff one of his business cards. "I'd appreciate a call once you learn how the blood was dehydrated."

The Sheriff looked at the card. "Why is a geophysics instructor interested in this case?"

"I love a mystery. Thanks for your help, Sheriff."

Rolston accepted Alex's hand and stared after him as he left the office, wondering how a college professor knew the dead men were from the tanker. He tossed the report back into the basket, then grabbed his phone and selected the number for the coroner.

***

Alex's mind kept turning over the facts, but nothing made sense. And what happened to the seventh crew member? He brought out his phone to call his friend Martin Donner, the United States Director of National Security. "Hello, Margaret, Alex here. Let me speak to director Donner, please." He was put on hold for a moment, and then Donner's image appeared on the screen.

Donner smiled at Alex's image on his monitor. "Hello, Alex. What can I do for you?"

Alex gave him a brief account of everything that had happened and everything he knew. "The whole situation is crazy, and I don't have a clue how the bodies turned up a hundred and fifty miles away. The coroner doesn't know what killed them, either."

"Listen, Alex, I've just learned that a tanker ran aground in Brownsville, Texas, and it was also empty and abandoned."

"Do me a favor, Martin. Make this official so I'll get some cooperation and tell the authorities in Brownsville I'll be down to investigate."

"I'll take care of it right away. Let me know what you find out."

"I will."

Alex caught a cab back to the local airport, and after a short delay, he got on a small aircraft for a ride to Seattle Tacoma International Airport. He booked the next flight to Brownsville, which would not leave Seattle until 8:00 AM the next morning, so he took a shuttle to a nearby motel.

Chapter 2

NORTHCENTRAL NEVADA:

At the end of his sermon inside his massive church, Menno Simons stared out over his gathering of two hundred devout followers. Outside, over one hundred more were sitting on the lawn or in chairs, listening to the speakers mounted on the building. *All mine to do with as I please,* he thought. *Only a handful of the thousands who follow my every command.* The incredible sense of power he felt nearly made him giggle with delight, but as always, he kept his expression divine.

He looked at his mother, sitting in the front row. Her thin, straight hair was now gray, and he realized how frail she looked. He watched her bring an inhaler to her mouth and take a deep breath. Her asthma was getting bad, and the air pollution throughout the world was only making it worse for her. He hoped she lived long enough to see his dream come true.

Elizabeth Simons was the only member of the congregation not hypnotized by her son, even though her sense of pride was nearly overwhelming. From the morning she opened the door and found him lying naked on her porch, she felt the power radiating from his little body and knew he was destined to be a prominent leader.

He's so handsome, she thought, since he didn't look fifty-seven. Not a trace of gray showed in his thick blond hair, and his pale skin was still taut over his sharp-boned facial features. His hypnotic gray eyes were still clear and bright; a sharp contrast to his jet-black coat and trousers. She took a deep breath from her inhaler and sighed with pride.

Menno clasped the fist-sized gold cross hanging from a heavy gold chain around his neck; his signal, the meeting was finished. He turned and left the pulpit, disappearing through an ornate wooden door behind him.

His private chamber was sparsely furnished, as a constant reminder that he must maintain a humble image, though his wealth was staggering. He sat in a wooden swivel rocking chair behind a plain wooden desk and leaned back, placing his feet on the scarred surface before closing his eyes. The sermons always drained so much of his energy he needed some time to relax before taking care of business.

He heard a soft rapping at the door, but ignored it. *Too soon.* The door opened, and Menno looked to see who dared enter without being asked.

When Elizabeth stepped into the chamber, she saw the fury in her son's eyes and left the door open. "I'm sorry, but Desmond, Gary, and Peter have returned. I thought you might want to see them right away."

The fury faded from Menno's eyes. "Good news, I hope?" He asked in a smooth baritone voice.

"I think so."

Menno watched her step back through the doorway before three young men stepped through, closing the door behind them. He gave them a questioning stare, and when all three men grinned, he clasped his hands together with a sharp clap. "Wonderful! Marvelous! I want to hear all about it."

Desmond told his tale about the oil tanker in Washington. "One man was vaporized, and we dropped 'the rest of the crew in the snow on a mountain. Trying to figure out how they got there should drive them crazy."

Menno listened to Peter's story about the Arco tanker in the Gulf of Mexico. "Are there any witnesses?"

A smirk formed on Peter's lips. "Not anymore."

Gary Darven hesitated only a second and then explained what had happened with the Alaska pipeline. "I didn't have much time, but everything's fine."

Menno stared at Darven for a moment. He caught the hesitation and knew there must be more to it, but was so elated his dream was coming true, he decided not to press him for the moment. "Then it begins," Menno announced as he clasped the gold cross hanging from a chain around his neck. The meeting was over.

The three men left the chamber, and a moment later, Elizabeth stepped through the door, closing it firmly while staring at her son. "Well?"

Menno smirked. "It has begun." He watched his mother's smile create more wrinkles on her lined face and saw her eyes sparkle for the first time in years.

***

Two hours later, Menno and Elizabeth arrived at his private research facility twenty miles south of town. They stepped out of the limousine, entered the two story cement building, and walked to his office. A few minutes later, the director of the facility entered and Menno grabbed the frail-looking man by the shoulders. "It's started! They did exactly what I expected, Gerard. Well done."

Gerard smiled. "Thank you. The genetic engineers will be pleased. Your instructions were pure genius and you should make millions selling these granules to the oil companies."

Menno's smile faded. "I already have millions, Gerard. I will tell no one about this discovery, and neither will you."

Gerard was puzzled. "I thought you wanted to clean up the pollution?"

"Oh, I do, but not that way. I have a much broader plan."

Gerard wasn't sure what his boss was getting at, but let it drop for the moment. He reached into his coat pocket and brought out a round, flat, three-inch crystal. "When can we experiment with these?"

Menno stared at the crystal and then looked into Gerard's eyes. "Not until I've proven my point to the world. In the meantime, I'm shutting down this facility. We have enough to do what I want done."

Gerard was shocked. "But we do not know what these are! We have to . . ."

Menno grabbed the gold cross, and Gerard instantly stopped his protest. "I know what they are. You may go."

Gerard hesitated for a moment and then left the office.

Menno looked at his mother. "This is it! I will gather my followers in three days and put an end to the pollution." Menno was puzzled when Elizabeth didn't smile.

"What about the director and his engineers?" she asked. "If they tell anyone, the government will try to stop you."

Menno smirked. "Don't worry. Come. We must leave."

***

Gerard returned to his office and stared at the crystal while he thought about what Menno had said. He thought it was wrong, not telling the world what he created. If Menno didn't want the fortune they could make from selling this new technology, why shouldn't he have it?

Gerard looked up at the wall safe. All the information about their research was on the flash drive, and he could take it to another company and make millions of dollars. He walked to the safe, dialed in the combination for the door, and grabbed the electronic storage devices. "To hell with Menno, that religious fanatic. I want to be rich!"

***

At that same moment, the limousine was ten miles away, and Menno instructed the driver to stop. Menno grabbed his smart phone and stepped out of the limousine. "Come, Mother."

Menno helped her out of the car and pointed back the way they came and then entered a number into the phone. A brilliant flash appeared in the distance, and a few moments later, they heard a muffled explosion as an enormous cloud of dust soared into the air above the flash.

"I don't think we'll be bothered by the government, Mother." He helped her into the limousine, and then got in and they drove away.

Chapter 3

TEXAS:

The morning sun flashed off the Gulf of Mexico, as the Boeing 777 jet airliner circled Brownsville International Airport. Alex stared out the window at the sprawling city below, where luxurious hotels lined the white sand beaches for miles on both sides of the city, and small boats skimmed across the light blue water. South of the city, the behemoth oil tanker looked obscenely out of place with its bow so close to the shore in front of the million dollar homes lining the beach. *What's happening to the tankers? Six men are dead with no explanation of how or why.* He sincerely hoped the crew from *this* tanker escaped whatever had taken the lives of the *Defiance*'s crew.

***

AIR TERMINAL:

Alex looked at a television screen inside a bar as he strolled along the walkway and saw the outside temperature was in the upper seventies, with a promise of climbing higher. He walked directly to the men's room and changed into shorts, a polo shirt, and white tennis shoes. His next stop was the car-rental desk, where he received the keys to a vehicle and a map of the city. When the young man handed him a small envelope, Alex tore it open and retrieved the government identification card Director Donner had sent him.

While he drove south along a two-lane road following the shoreline, the air smelled of seaweed and the blue water of the gulf stretched away to the horizon. He continued past several mansions toward the tanker, and as he got closer, saw several police vehicles and television news vans parked on the asphalt driveway of a two million dollar home.

He found a pace to park and climbed out of the sedan, then strolled over to the police officer keeping the public at bay. He showed his identification, then continued past the barricade and walked around the side of the house, emerging on the white sand one hundred feet from the water. The tanker was another one hundred feet from shore, as if trying to make it to the small wooden boat dock in front of the house. Bold blue letters across the black bow stated the ship belonged to the West Gulf Corporation.

Alex approached one of the two men near the shore, who was dressed in a tan police uniform and matching cowboy hat. The other was tall, but exceedingly overweight, and dressed in dark blue shorts and matching lightweight shirt, but Alex extended his hand to the police officer, a lean man in his late forties. "I'm Alex Cave. I believe you're expecting me."

"I'm Sheriff Jackson, and this is Kirt Hendrick, the representative from West Gulf."

Alex accepted Hendrick's handshake, but cringed at the limp grip and turned to face the sheriff. "Fill me in on what you've discovered so far."

Hendrick interrupted before Jackson could speak. "I can't figure it out, Mister Cave. Yesterday evening, she left the offshore oil rig with fifteen thousand tons of crude, but she was empty when she ran aground here eight hours later."

"What about the crew?"

"There were eight, but there's no sign of them. They must have abandoned ship out in the gulf."

Alex looked at the sheriff. "Did the residents in the area see anything unusual?"

"These folks aren't home, and the neighbors said they saw the tanker for the first time yesterday morning."

"Did the tanker radio in that they had problems?"

"The Coast Guard received a short mayday, but no one answered when they replied. They've been searching the gulf by helicopter all night, but only found an overturned pleasure boat with a man and woman sitting on the hull. The Coast Guard had a shrimp trawler pick them up."

"I'd like to ask them some questions later. Have you been down in the cargo hold?"

Hendrick grinned. "Now, why would I want to go down there? You can see she's empty. The Coast Guard has been searching for an oil slick and the crew."

"I'd like to go onboard."

Hendrick led Alex and the sheriff down the dock and onto the nineteen foot motorboat belonging to West Gulf Corporation, fired up the outboard engine, and drove them out to the tanker. To Alex, the ship looked twice the size of the *Defiance*, at about one hundred feet from deck to waterline.

When they tie off to the boarding ladder hanging down from the main deck, Alex was the first to climb up, followed by the sheriff. Both of them thought Hendrick might not make it to the top of the ladder, and when he finally crawled onto the deck, the big man spent several minutes catching his breath. Alex spent the time walking around the open deck and noticed all the inspection hatches were open. A few minutes later, Hendrick led him and the sheriff into the crew quarters.

The bunks were made, but belongings lay scattered around the room. They continued to the galley, which was orderly, and Hendrick waited below while Alex and the sheriff climbed the stairs to the bridge, which was also in perfect condition. "This is a new twist, Sheriff. Apparently, someone stole thousands of tons of crude oil with no resistance from the crew."

Alex and the sheriff rejoined Hendrick on deck, and Alex pointed toward the long, capsule-shaped objects fastened to the railing. "Doesn't it strike you as odd they didn't use the life rafts?"

Hendrick studied the capsules. "Doesn't make sense, does it?"

Alex led Hendrick and the sheriff over to the nearest inspection hatch and peered into the hold, and then looked up at them and grinned. "Care to come along?"

Hendrick chuckled. "No, thanks."

The Sheriff shook his head no. "I'll take your word on what you find down there."

Alex disappeared down the ladder, and several minutes later, the two men stared at him with looks of astonishment when he returned without a trace of oil on him or his clothes.

"What the hell?" Said Hendrick.

Alex smirked at him. "I've seen enough."

***

Once back on shore, the three men stared at the tanker for a moment, and then Alex had a hunch and turned to the sheriff. "I imagine you have a helicopter at your disposal. I'd like to use it for a search, if you don't mind."

"The Coast Guard is already searching."

"So you've told me, but they're searching the gulf. I want to search the desert."

The sheriff squinted and put his hands on his hips. "You seem to have a lot of pull, Mister Cave. Just who the hell are you, anyway? The governor called me personally and said to delay them from moving the tanker until you arrived. Told me to give you whatever help you need."

"Once in a while, the government asks for my help."

The sheriff stared at Alex for a moment and then spoke into his portable radio. "I need a chopper to pick up me and a passenger on the road near the tanker. Tell them to make sure the fuel tank is full because we'll be searching for a while."

Hendrick waved a hand toward the water. "What about my ship? It'll be high tide in two hours. I need to get it towed back out to sea."

"I'm through with her, but I'd like a list of the names and addresses of the crew. Have it sent to the sheriff's office as soon as possible, and I'll pick it up when I get back."

"No problem."

When they heard the helicopter approaching, Alex and the sheriff walked to the road. They shielded their eyes from the billowing sand as the blue police helicopter set down, and then Alex sat in front with the pilot, with the sheriff in the back seat.

The pilot looked over at Alex. "Which direction?"

"Inland, about a hundred miles."

The helicopter leapt from the ground and swung northwest, as mile after mile of green farmland passed below. Half an hour later, they were flying over brown sand and sagebrush while Alex and the sheriff stared out opposite sides of the helicopter. They flew back and forth, north and south, each time extending farther west and deeper into the desert, until an hour later, when the pilot informed them there was only enough fuel for the return trip.

The sheriff told the pilot to head back. "I gave you the benefit of the doubt, Mister Cave, but we're just wasting time. Ain't no way those sailors are out here."

Alex was sure he would find the crew from the tanker on land, just like up in Washington, but he had to admit the idea sounded crazy to someone not familiar with the incident. He stared out the window at the miles of barren desert and realized it would be sheer luck to find them.

As they approached the homes along the coast, Alex saw the tanker being towed away from the shoreline by a large tugboat. The helicopter set down on the road, and Alex and the sheriff jumped out of the side door. When it departed, the two men stared at the receding tanker for a few minutes while Hendrick approached.

The sheriff turned to Alex. "Look, Mister Cave. It's been a long night, and I'm leaving."

"Thanks, Sheriff. Sorry for the inconvenience. I appreciate the help."

When the sheriff walked away, Hendrick moved into Alex's view. "Any luck, Mister Cave?" The look in Alex's eyes was his answer, so he smirked at him. "I didn't think you would."

Alex looked at him and grinned. "Yesterday, there was another tanker incident similar to this one. They found the crew in the snow on a mountaintop, one hundred and fifty miles away."

When Hedrick's jaw dropped open in bewilderment, Alex walked back to his car. As he drove away, he looked in the rearview mirror and saw Hendrick staring after him.

***

Alex was heading back to town when his phone rang, but he didn't recognize the number. "Hello?"

"Sheriff Jackson here, Mister Cave. I, uh, I owe you an apology. It seems you were right. A rancher found the eight men from the tanker on his ranch just outside Austin. Seven of them are dead, but one's still alive. Busted up pretty bad, but the hospital says he might make it."

"Where are the bodies now?"

"At the General Hospital, in Austin."

"I'm on my way."

"I'll call and let them know you're coming."

***

AUSTIN:

Alex hurried into the hospital to the woman at the front desk. After showing his ID, she gave him directions to the emergency ward. A man in a tan police uniform was standing outside the door to the intensive care room, and Alex introduced himself as they shook hands..

"I'm Sheriff Earl Bowdy, Mister Cave. Sheriff Jackson said you'd be coming, so I wanted to be here."

"I appreciate it. How's he doing?"

"Damned if I know how he's even alive. The doctor says his whole spine is a bunch of fractured bones. Early indications are he's paralyzed from the neck down. They have him heavily sedated, and the doctor says he probably won't regain consciousness for a while."

"Was he conscious when you arrived at the ranch?"

"Nope. They were already loading him into the ambulance by the time I got there. The old man who found them said the man was mumbling when he first found him, but we didn't find a single sign of how they got there. No footprints, no tire tracks, nothing."

"Have you identified the bodies?"

"Yeah, they were all carrying identification, and they match Sheriff Jackson's list from the oil tanker."

"I'd like to talk to the rancher."

Bowdy gave him directions. "His name is Gus Tilman. He's an ornery old cuss. Wouldn't say much when I spoke to him."

Alex gave him his card. "If he regains consciousness, I'd appreciate it if you would call me at this number."

***

The air smelled of sage brush as Alex drove along a dirt road across the desert, leaving a cloud of brown dust in his wake. Half an hour later, he saw the faded name Tilman on a battered mailbox. He parked next to an older model pickup truck in front of a doublewide mobile home sitting on cement blocks and climbed out, and behind it was a large wooden structure that might have been a barn.

When no one came out of the mobile, he shut off the engine and climbed out of the car. He walked up the rickety wooden steps and pushed the doorbell button, but no one answered, so he knocked loudly.

When no one came to the door, he walked around the mobile toward the wooden building behind it. Dust from the dry dirt swirled around his tennis shoes as he walked past several pieces of rusted farm equipment partially hidden by overgrown weeds. The building was old and gray with a flat-sloped roof and had several additions crudely built onto both sides, but every part of the structure needed of repair.

"Anybody here?" Alex hollered as he approached the weathered building.

The door on the first addition opened, and a short, skinny man appeared. He was dressed in oil-stained jeans, badly scuffed cowboy boots, and a tee shirt that might have been white at one time. He was also wearing an old, sweat-stained cowboy hat. As Alex walked closer, he saw the man's face was as weathered as the building, and his deep wrinkles give the impression of a prune with the texture of rawhide.

Gus Tilman stared up at Alex. "What can I do for ya?"

"My name's Alex Cave, Mister Tilman. I hope I'm not interrupting anything."

Tilman pulled a rag from his back pocket, lifted his hat, and wiped the tattered cloth across his bald head. "Nothing that can't wait. What's on your mind?"

"It's about the men you found. The sheriff said one of them was mumbling."

Tilman gave Alex a quizzical stare. "You don't look like a lawman, not dressed in them duds."

Alex grinned. "You're right, I'm not. I'm a teacher at a college in Montana."

Tilman's leather face looked as though it would crack when he smiled. "Montana," he said wistfully. "I always wanted to move there. Seen pictures of it when I was a boy. Gaud almighty, that's pretty country."

Tilman took on a faraway look as he stared into the distance for a moment before looking back at Alex. "A teacher, you say? I have a lot of respect for teachers. Never made it past the tenth grade, myself. Lied about my age and joined the Army when I was sixteen. Anyhow, why's a teacher interested in those men?"

"It's a long story, but basically, I'm just curious."

Tilman stared at Alex for a moment. "Yeah, the man was hurting something fearful. Kept mumbling about a bright light."

"Do you remember his exact words?"

Tilman rubbed his jaw as he thought about it. "Seems to me he said something like, 'Stay away from the blue light. I have to hide.' He must have been delirious."

"Anything else you can remember, Mister Tilman? Anything at all?"

"Not in particular."

Alex extended his hand. "Thanks for your help."

Tilman smiled. "You keep on teaching, you hear?"

"I will."

Alex turned and headed toward his car and reached the corner of the mobile home when he heard Tilman yell his name. He stopped, turned around, and saw Tilman shuffling toward him with small clouds of dust swirling around his boots.

"Come to think of it, he said something about a ship. Must have been delirious, though."

"Thanks again."

Alex continued to his car, Climbed in, and waved at Tilman as he drove away. On the drive back to Brownsville, Alex kept repeating the words the injured crew member had mumbled to Tilman. And where did the crew member see a second ship?

Alex looked at the small monitor in the dashboard of the sedan and saw he had an incoming call, so pressed accept. "Hello?"

"Sheriff Jackson here, Alex. I got a preliminary autopsy report, and the coroner is baffled. It seems the blood in all the bodies of the crew has been dehydrated. Must have been the dry desert air."

"It was the same in the bodies of the *Defiance*'s crew. I appreciate the call."

"Did you meet Tilman?"

"Yes, but he wasn't much help, so I'm heading home tomorrow."

"Good luck, and let me know if you figure out what happened."

"I'll try. Thanks for your help."

***

It was nearly dark when Alex checked into a hotel room. He tried calling Donner and had to leave a message, then ordered dinner from room service. While he waited, he sat at the desk and wrote the details he had discovered so far, churning them over and over in his mind, trying to come up with some logical conclusion, but an answer eluded him. His dinner arrived, and he ate at the desk, occasionally jotting down his thoughts.

He finished the dinner, and after a quick shower, crawled into bed and turned on the television, switching channels until he found a news broadcast. He wasn't listening too close while his mind churns over the strange events of the past three days until a map of Alaska suddenly flashed on the screen and the camera zoomed in on an oil tanker in Prince William Sound. He grabbed the remote control and increased the volume.

"The *Exxon Valdez incident. This is the way it looked after the spill,*" the female announcer was saying as the picture changed to show work crews in yellow rubber coats and pants cleaning up the thick, slimy crude oil along the rocky shoreline. The picture changed again, and a dotted line ran down across a map of Alaska. "*The pipeline was completed in 1974, using state-of-the-art technology, and it is supposed to be impossible for a rupture to occur. In a statement released an hour ago, authorities said they don't think the pipeline is ruptured, but they refuse to speculate on why the oil from Prudhoe Bay has failed to reach its destination in Valdez. They have shut down the pumping stations and crews have been dispatched to check every foot of the pipeline for any sign of leakage. Some sections can't be searched because of the severe snowstorm that has*" *moved over the area. Our meteorologist, Mike Banner, will explain what's going on."*

His phone rang, and Alex saw Donner's image. "Hey, Martin."

"We have a major problem in Alaska."

"I know. I just saw the news broadcast."

"Listen, Alex. This is no longer just an investigation. The President called a moment ago and informed me the Joint Chiefs think someone is sabotaging our domestic oil supplies. I don't have to tell you what that will do to our nation, and he wants an all-out effort to find who's behind it and stop them any way we can."

Alex didn't reply for a moment as he thought about sabotage. "I'll fly up to Valdez on the next available flight."

"Good, I'm putting you in charge of the investigation, and I'll call and tell them you're coming. What have you discovered there?"

"It's almost identical to the incident with the Americrude tanker." Alex explained all he knew. "We'll know more when the survivor regains consciousness."

"Okay, stay on top of it. Call me day or night if you find out anything."

"I will. I'll send you the names of the crew members, and I'd like a background check on them as soon as possible."

"Okay, I'll see to it."

"Thanks, Martin."

Alex hung up and called a travel agency, and the next connecting flight to Alaska was in three hours, so he booked a seat. He packed his tote bag, grabbed his notes from the desk, and shoved them inside. After checking out of the hotel, he caught a cab to the airport, hoping he could get some sleep during the long flight to Alaska.

Chapter 4

VALDEZ, ALASKA:

Alex managed a few hours of sleep on the flight from Brownsville, and during the two-hour layover in Seattle, he purchased warmer clothing and an additional suitcase. His next stop was Anchorage, Alaska, where he joined two elderly women on a small plane bound for the southern end of the Alaska pipeline in the town of Valdez.

They landed on a runway covered with brown-colored snow and taxied to the small air terminal, where Alex opened the door, allowing the cold air into the plane. When he stepped out, he noticed a sign on top of the air terminal showing twenty-two degrees F.

After helping the women climb out, he entered the small passenger terminal and looked around, then noticed a petite woman standing a short distance away, staring at him. Her long, light red hair hung loosely inside the pulled back hood of her pale blue snow parka as she smiled warmly and walked toward him.

"You must be Mister Cave," she said in a slightly husky voice, and held out her hand. "I'm Christa Avery."

Alex accepted and felt a firm grip. He noticed her eyes were the color of green candy, and small dimples appeared at the corners of her mouth as she smiled. She was not wearing any makeup and didn't need it, and he guessed she was in her late twenties. "Nice to meet you, Miss Avery. Are you in charge here?"

She grinned at him. "No, I'm just part of the hired help for the All Alaska Company."

"Come again?"

"All the major oil companies joined forces to build the pipeline under the name All Alaska Corporation."

"What do you do?"

"Oh, I do the brain work and chemical tests of the oil for the corporation. It's pretty boring, but I think I can help with your investigation."

"Do you know about the tanker incident in Brownsville, Texas?"

"Not all the details. You can fill us in on the way to the loading docks. I have a ride waiting outside."

Alex grabbed his bags, and together they left the terminal and strolled across hard-packed snow through the chilly evening air. White smoke blossomed from the exhaust of a black Chevy SUV, with ALL ALASKA in white letters painted on the door. As they approached, the driver's door opened and an enormous man wearing a heavy orange parka crawled out, and Christa introduced him.

"Mister Cave, this is the head honcho for the pipeline, Jerhamia Peterson."

Judging by his blond hair and light blue eyes, he appeared to be of Norwegian descent, and Alex's first impression was Peterson had just stepped off a Viking longboat. The hand he extended was nearly twice as big as his hand was, and he estimated Peterson stood six foot six and weighed about two hundred and eighty pounds.

"Everyone calls me Bull," Peterson said in a deep voice.

Alex grinned. "I can see why. It's nice to meet you, Bull." He looked at Christa. "Since we'll be working together, let's use first names."

"Fine with me."

Bull opened the tailgate. "Put your bags in and I'll take you to our office."

Alex tossed his bags inside, and everyone climbed into the front seat, with Christa in the middle. On the drive to the office, Alex filled them in on what he had discovered in Brownsville.

"The incident on the West Gulf tanker was the same as the *Defiance*. Not a trace of oil was left in the hold. We lucked out with the crew, though. There's a survivor, and when he regains consciousness, I hope we'll learn what happened. What's bothers me is what happened to the other crew member? We've learned their names, and I've asked for a background check on each of them."

As they drove past the loading dock, Alex saw the *Defiance* moored to the docks. Bull stopped in front of a single story building with the company logo above the door and light gray smoke escaping from a single silver stack on the roof. They climbed out and followed Christa into the building, where it was warm in the sparsely furnished office. They removed their parkas and hung them near the door, and then Bull introduced them to a wiry little man sitting at one of the desks. "This is Herb Bell, our station manager."

Herb was a native Alaskan, with long black hair streaked with gray tied in a long braided tail as he got up and shook Alex's hand. "Everybody calls me Herb, Mister Cave."

"Just Alex, will do."

"I'll show you what's going on."

Herb walked to a large white-board with columns of numbers scrawled across it. When he released a pin and flipped it over, a large map of Alaska was tacked to the other side, and a narrow red line depicted the pipeline.

"Late yesterday afternoon, the engineers at pumping station thirteen reported a low pressure alarm. We called the primary station in Prudhoe Bay, and they were still pumping oil into the line at eighty-three thousand barrels an hour. We knew immediately something was wrong and shut everything down and closed all one hundred and forty-two valves in the line. The problem is here, at pumping station twelve, just west of Black Rapids. They're the only one we haven't heard from. Unfortunately, the storm is stopping us from finding out why."

"And here's the kicker," Bull added. "When we checked the reservoirs here, we discovered they were empty except for a few inches of sea water."

"That's interesting. I found salt water on the floor in the hold of the *West Gulf* tanker. How much oil was in your reservoirs?"

"About six million barrels, give or take, plus whatever was in the pipeline."

"And it just vanished without a trace?" He looked at Herb. "Can you estimate when this started?"

"Already have. We move two million barrels a day through the line, and I figured the sea water began replacing the oil on the twelfth of March."

"That's the same day the *Defiance* was attacked," Bull added. "She was the last tanker to receive a full load of crude. What bugs me is how sea water got into the line from the middle of Alaska."

Alex turned to Herb. "Any idea when the storm will break?"

Herb shrugged his shoulders. "Sometime tonight, if the forecasters are right."

Christa got Alex's attention. "I've made arrangements for you at the hotel. It's just down the street."

"Thanks. It's getting late, and I have a few calls to make. I'll meet you here in the morning."

Christa watched Alex put on his parka and leave the office, and then turned to Bull and Herb. "A good-looking stranger comes to town, and you'd think he could have at least invited me out for a drink."

Herb moved to the coat rack to get his parka. "Maybe he's married,"

"I didn't see a wedding ring."

She grinned and snatched her coat off the hook, sliding it on as she headed for the door. "Maybe he's the bashful type. Goodnight, boys. I'll see you in the morning."

Christa stepped outside and saw Alex pulling his suitcases across the snow. When he walked, it was with an easy stride, as though unconsciously knowing where each step would land. In the office, he seemed so self-confident. Not egotistically, but like he knew who he was, what he wanted, and was at peace with himself. On impulse, she jogged up beside him, but then felt a little ridiculous. "Can I buy you a drink?"

Alex stopped to look down at her. "That's the best offer I've had all day."

They continued without speaking and entered the hotel where Alex checked in and asked for his bags to be taken to his room. Once he had his room card, they entered the dimly lit cocktail lounge and sat at a small table.

"So, Alex. Where are you from?"

"I have a small ranch outside of Bozeman, Montana."

"And you work for the government?"

"Sometimes. I'm more of a consultant now. I spend most of my time teaching at the college."

"Oh? What do you teach?"

"Geology and geophysics."

The server arrived, and they ordered, and Christa's curiosity was driving her mad. She felt strangely attracted to Alex and wondered why. He wasn't exactly handsome, but decent looking, and suddenly she couldn't restrain herself any longer. "Are you married?" She saw a trace of anguish in his expression as he looked away. "Oh, I'm sorry. I didn't mean to pry."

Alex looked back and saw her embarrassment. "Don't be. It's just a sore spot, is all. I was married, but she was killed three years ago."

Christa saw his painful smile and felt a strange urge to share his misery. "I'm sorry. What happened?"

"I met Sevi when I was an agent in Holland, and after a whirlwind courtship, we were married."

Christa saw him smile at the thought and wondered what Sevi looked like. "Agent, like in CIA?"

Alex's smile suddenly turned to a look of hatred. "Yeah. I made a few enemies over the years, and they decided to get even by planting a bomb in our apartment. One with a timer activated when the door was opened. I was five blocks away when I heard the explosion, but I wasn't sure what it was from. When I arrived at our block, I saw the windows blown out of the apartment. The police and fire departments had already arrived, and the ambulance crew was bringing a body out on a stretcher. I had a sinking feeling deep in my stomach, even before I pulled back the blanket. I couldn't believe what I was seeing, and my mind just went blank. I don't remember everything that happened over the next few days, but later I learned I went crazy for a while and went after the men responsible. The CIA finally tracked me down and my best friend pulled me out of Russia, but only after I killed the three men responsible."

"Is that how you got those scars?"

Alex looked at her, smiled, and touched the scar on his nose. "Doesn't help my appearance much, does it?"

"So, what happened?"

"I came back to the states, finished school and got my degree, and got a job at the college in Bozeman." Alex felt a little foolish and changed the subject. "Enough of my rambling on. Tell me about yourself."

"Oh, not much to tell, really. Born and raised in Salem, Oregon. After college, I was hired by All Alaska. Pretty boring, huh?"

"Never married?"

Christa grinned and shook her head no. "Just never met the right man, I guess. I've had a few boyfriends, but can't seem to get into a long-term relationship." She noticed Alex stifle a yawn. "Listen, I imagine you've had a long day, with the flight and all. I'd better let you get some sleep."

"It's been a long couple of days." He reached for his wallet.

"Oh, no," Christa told him as she reached into her coat pocket. "I said I'd buy you a drink. Women's lib and all."

When Christa set a few bills on the table and got up, Alex stood, too. "Thanks. I guess I'll see you in the morning?"

Christa had to restrain herself from reaching up and hugging him. "You bet." When Alex shook her hand, she could swear she felt a mild tingling sensation from his touch.

Alex watched her leave the cocktail lounge through a side door and a picture of Sevi lying on the stretcher flashed through his mind. "Damn! Don't get involved again, Alex," he whispered as he headed out of the lounge and down the hall to his room.

Chapter 5

AMERICRUDE/WEST GULF OIL REFINERY. MARCH POINT, WASHINGTON:

Tony Mancuso had been a roving night watchman at the refinery for thirty years, and bored as he drove through a field of massive oil storage tanks. He parked near a large pipe, got out and looked around, and then grabbed a whisky bottle hidden behind a concrete support. He tilted his head back, took a long drink, and saw neon blue light coming out of the tanks. His skin suddenly felt warm and the whiskey bottle fell from his grip, shattering on the ground before he collapsed onto the pieces of glass, dead.

***

REFINERY CONTROL ROOM.

Edgar Henley, the night manager of the oil tank farm, suddenly heard alarm horns screaming and leapt out of his chair in the office. He hurried into the control room and saw the young woman operator looking at the flashing red lights on the control panel, and touched her on the shoulder to get her attention. "What just happened?"

Gail Sommers was nervous over her first alarm situation. "All the pumps are cavitating and there's no pressure in the lines from the tanks to the refinery."

"Shut everything down until we identify the problem."

As Gail began flipping switches, Henley watched the lights on the panel return to green and the alarm became silent, then he looked at the computer monitor. "How can they all be empty?"

***

VALDEZ, ALASKA:

At 5:00 A.M, the cellphone on the nightstand rang and Bull fumbled for it. "Yeah?" he answered as he wiped his eyes and listened to the caller. "Okay, Herb, I'll be there in a few minutes."

He turned to look at his wife, who was snoring softly, and then he rolled out of bed and shuffled to the bathroom. After splashing cold water on his face, he dressed and grabbed his heavy orange parka, pulling it on as he walked out the door.

The sting of frigid air on his face helped him gather his senses as he walked in the half-light of morning toward the office. Bright light escaped through the windows in the entrance, and Bull saw Herb moving around inside. When he walked through the doorway, Herb turned to greet him, a deep apprehension etched on his face.

Herb handed Bull three sheets of paper. "This is a copy of the report from the refinery at March Point."

Bull read the report and stared at Herb. "Has this been verified?"

Herb nodded yes. "I just got off the phone. After the alarms went off, they sent a man into the tanks and he said the only thing in them was a little water."

"That's over ten million barrels."

Herb nodded in agreement. "They said there's no oil in the harbor, and the retaining areas around the tanks haven't been contaminated."

"What about the night watchman? Have they questioned him yet?"

"They found him, but he was dead."

Bull walked to the desk and sat down, then looked over at the clock and saw it's after 11:00AM on the east coast. "This whole damn thing is getting ridiculous. I'm calling the company president to recommend we suspend transporting any more crude on the west coast until we find out what's going on."

Herb listened to Bull argue with the man on the other end of the conversation for several minutes. He was shocked to hear Bull use such powerful language with the president of the company.

Bull slammed the receiver down. "That asshole doesn't know what's at stake here. He's going to keep loading tankers from the Kenai Peninsula oil wells and the offshore rig at Cook Inlet, and wants us back online as soon as possible."

Herb had an idea. "Maybe Alex can get someone in Washington, D.C. to intervene?"

"I'll ask him, but I doubt it. What's the weather report, Herb?"

"The storm's moving east, so you should be able to get to the pumping station in a couple of hours. You won't have much time, though. Another storm is supposed to be coming in."

"I'd better wake Alex and Christa. Have you eaten yet?" Herb indicated no. "We'll meet them for breakfast in the hotel restaurant. I have a feeling it's going to be a hectic day."

*****

In the restaurant, Bull explained what had happened at the refinery. "Listen, Alex. Against my recommendation, they're going to keep sending oil south. Do you know someone in Washington D.C. who can stop them until we find out what's happening to the oil?"

"I'll try, but let's check out the pumping station first. Maybe it will give us more ammunition."

"All right. I'll round up a pilot. We have a small plane at the airport, and there's a big landing area near the station."

Alex grinned. "I'm a pilot. Mind if I fly us in?"

Bull shrugged. "Fine by me."

"I'd like to go, too," Christa told them, and Bull indicated she could.

"I'll monitor the radio from the office," said Herb.

They left the restaurant and Bull drove the three of them to the airport. Alex and Bull shoved the single engine craft, which was equipped with huge skis that could be locked down over the tires for landing on snow, out of the hangar. Alex climbed into the pilot seat and began his preflight check, while Bull helped Christa into the rear seat before climbing in front next to Alex.

Fifteen minutes later, they were airborne, headed north up the southern slopes of the Alaskan Mountain range. Blue skies and sunshine enhanced the spectacular view of the desolate, snow-covered mountains as they followed the route of the pipeline. Small areas of the huge pipe were occasionally exposed, but most of it was underground or covered with snow.

As they neared the summit, Bull pointed to a pass in the mountain range, and a large, snow covered meadow just below it. As they circled the clearing to assess the landing area, Bull suddenly leaned forward in his seat and stared out the side window. "There's a section of the pipeline missing! Take us around again."

Alex did as instructed, and Bull pointed out the window. "See that shadowed area? That's the entrance to the underground pumping station. There is supposed to be fifty feet of pipe coming out of the building before it drops underground, but it's not there."

Christa was also looking out through the widows. "Maybe it's buried under the snow?"

"Not possible. That section of pipe is twenty feet above the ground. It's gone, I tell you! Take us down, Alex, and we'll find out what happened."

Alex brought the plane down in a smooth landing and taxied to the northern edge of the meadow before shutting down the engine. One hundred feet directly ahead, a large shadowed arch rose above the snow, marking the entrance to the underground facility.

Bull pointed over his shoulder before getting out of his seat. "The snow shoes are in the rear compartment. Stay on the plane's skis until you put them on or you'll sink to your waist in the snow. We'd better find the crew first, and then we'll check what happened to the pipeline."

Bull led them to the covered entrance, where a flat cement wall separated the entrance chamber from the interior of the facility. White light illuminated the windows built into large double doors in the center of the wall. "At least the generator is still working."

They removed their snowshoes and leaned them against the wall before Bull led them through one side of the doors. They immediately felt the warmth of the interior walkway, which ran to their left and right.

"Anybody here?" Bull yelled down the concrete tunnel as he removed his gloves and unzipped his parka. No one answered, so he waved a hand to the right. "Down there are the pumps and the generator." He turned left. "Let's check out the living quarters."

The first room they entered was the dining and recreation area, with cooking equipment along one wall. Several plates of partially eaten food were on the table, and the air had an acrid, burnt smell. Bull immediately spotted the large pot on the stove and grabbed a dishtowel to slide it into the sink. Steam hissed and billowed from the inside as he turned on the water to fill the pot. "This doesn't look good."

Bull walked across the room to another opening in the concrete wall. "There are three bedrooms down this corridor and a bathroom at the end. Let's check them out."

Bull opened the door to the first room on the right and looked into the bedroom, while Christa and Alex look into the open doorway of the room across from it. The furnishings were comprised of two beds on either side of a single desk in the center of the wall directly ahead. All the rooms were unoccupied, as was the bathroom.

Bull met them in the walkway. "Let's check out the rest of this place."

They walked back down the main tunnel, past a door directly across from the exit, and Christa stopped. "What's in here?"

"Just a storage room,"

They entered the pumping facility, hearing the muffled whine of the gas turbine driven generator filling the massive room. In the center, two gigantic pumps rose above the floor, and at both ends of the room, the forty-eight inch pipeline entered through the wall into the pumps and exited through the opposite wall. The pumps were motionless and quiet, and the large control panel appeared dead.

Bull tried flipping on some switches, but the panel remained dark. "Come on. Let's go back to the living quarters and I'll call Herb."

Bull led the way back through the tunnel, and out of curiosity, Christa opened the small door to the storage room across from the main entrance to see what was inside. She flipped on the switch and gasped in surprise. "In here!" she shouted, and rushed through the opening.

Alex and Bull ran back and stepped inside, where they found Christa kneeling next to a man huddled against a stack of cardboard boxes. The man was shaking uncontrollably, his face a mask of terror and his eyes staring straight ahead, as if no one else was in the room with him. The air was frigid, and the man was only wearing jeans and a tee shirt.

Bull cradled him in his arms and stood as if the man was light as a feather, then carried him into the first bedroom and laid him on the bed. Christa stripped two blankets off the other beds and spread them over the man, who continued to shake uncontrollably, his eyes wide with fear, still staring into space.

Christa noticed Alex wasn't with them. "I'll go make some coffee."

When she entered the kitchen, she still didn't see Alex, but filled the pot with water from the sink. She looked back along the hallway for him, and then dug through the cupboards until she found the coffee and filters.

***

Alex remained in the storage room, staring at the stacks of cardboard boxes lining three walls directly ahead and on both sides of the doorway. Something bothered him about the way they are stacked, so he grabbed the top box in the center and pulled it down. There was a wide gap between the stack and the back wall, so he set the box to the side and dragged the next box down from between the others and set it on the floor. When he bent over to look behind the bottom box, two faces stared up at him through open, sightless eyes. They lay head to head on their backs, and below them were two more bodies.

***

Christa saw Alex returning to the living quarters. "I was wondering where you went."

"I've found the other engineers. They're all dead."

"Oh, my! How?"

"I don't know. How's this one doing? Has he said anything?"

"No, he's still in shock."

"Christa! Alex! Come quick!"

Christa and Alex ran into the room, where Bull was leaning over the engineer. "He's coming around."

When Christa and Alex knelt next to Bull, they heard the engineer mumbling, '*The light! Stay away from the blue light!*'

"What's his name?" Alex asked.

"I don't know. These guys rotate through, and I rarely get to meet them."

"See if he's got any ID."

Bull rolled the man onto his side and felt the back pockets of his jeans, but there was no wallet, then let him back down. Christa pulled on a thin chain around the man's neck and a small medallion slid out from the collar of his tee shirt, so she leaned close to read the inscription on the back. "His name is Mike Broden, and he's allergic to penicillin."

Alex leaned closer to Broden. "What happened, Mike?"

Broden tried to get out of bed. "I can't let them find me!"

Alex held him down. "It's all right. This is very important, Mike. Do you understand?"

Broden's eyes spread wide with fear and he thrashed like a madman. It took Bull's help to hold Broden down for several moments before he passed out.

Christa placed her hand on Broden's forehead, and it was warm. "I think we'd better take him out of here. He needs to be in a hospital."

Alex stood. "I agree. Let's get him on the plane."

Bull leaned back from the bed. "We'd better tie him up. If he thrashes like that on the plane, we won't be able to control him."

Alex remembered seeing a stretcher in the pumping room, and while Bull tried to call the office in Valdez, Alex went to get it. When he returned, he saw the frustrated look in Bull's eyes. "What's going on?"

"The phone lines are dead and so is the radio. We'll have to use the one on the plane."

After they wrapped Broden in several blankets and tied him securely into the stretcher, Alex and Bull carried him out to the entrance area and the trio put on their snowshoes. Christa led the way over the snowdrift at the entrance out to the airplane, and then she removed one of the rear seats so Bull and Alex could slide the stretcher inside.

"What should I do with the seat?"

"Leave it," said Bull. "We don't have room for it."

When Christa tossed the seat onto the snow, everyone turned and stared when it made a loud thud. Alex slipped his foot out of one of his snowshoes and gently stepped onto the snow. His foot sank through the small white flakes for two inches before it was stopped by a solid surface. He knelt down, brushed the surface snow away, and then looked up at the others. "It's solid ice."

Alex stood and looked around the meadow. "Christa, you stay here with Broden. Let's take a walk, Bull. I'd like to know how big this sheet of ice is."

"Okay. Let's split up so we can cover more area."

Alex agreed, so they stepped out of their snowshoes and set off in opposite directions. Both men took slow, careful steps, testing the snow ahead as they moved. Two hundred feet out, Alex's foot suddenly dropped off the ice into deep snow. He turned to see where Bull was, and saw him kneeling in the snow, about one hundred feet away. When Bull stood and looked at him, Alex indicated they should follow the edge.

Bull waved acknowledgement and followed in one direction, Alex in the other, and it was an enormous circle. Bull waved him over, and both men walked to the area where the pipeline came out of the pumping station.

Bull stopped and stared at the open hole of the forty-eight-inch pipe. "Good grief! What happened to it?"

Alex removed his glove and touched the outer edge of the metal pipe. "This was melted."

"Yeah, but what could have done it? And where's the rest of it?"

Alex noticed a small amount of clear liquid at the bottom of the pipe. He reached in and touched it, wetting his fingers, and then sniffed the liquid on his fingertips. "It smells like salt water. It must have a heavy mineral content or it would have frozen by now. How can there be salt water way up here?"

"I don't know, but maybe Broden can tell us. Let's go."

Alex led them back to the airplane. "We'll need to do an autopsy on the four men hidden in the storeroom."

Bull stopped at the side entrance. "There should have been five men in there. Where is the sixth man?"

"This is too much of a coincidence. There has to be a connection with the missing men from the tankers."

***

Fifteen minutes later, they were airborne again, and Bull stared out the window, watching the snow-covered mountain range pass below them. He kept searching for the missing section of the pipeline, though he knew it was useless. The mountain range turned to foothills, then to valleys, as the city of Anchorage appeared against the deep blue water.

Alex radioed the hospital as soon as they were within range, and an ambulance was waiting at the airport when they arrived. Christa and Bull waited at the air terminal while Alex rode with Broden in the ambulance until they arrived at the emergency room.

Alex showed his identification to the hospital's director, explaining Broden was a government witness, and insisted Broden was not to leave the hospital without his approval. Alex gave him his phone number and asked to be called the moment Broden regained consciousness and then took a cab back to the airport.

***

When Alex walked into the air terminal, he saw Bull pacing the floor, a scowl distorting his features. "What's going on?"

Bull stopped pacing. "I got a call from Herb while you were gone. Those assholes on the board of directors sent two more tankers of oil down to the refinery in Washington, and now they're missing. They pay me to run this end of the business for them and then ignore my advice. They just don't realize lives are at stake here. All they care about is the almighty dollar!"

"Let's go. I'll see what I can do about it."

***

Herb Bell was waiting when Bull, Christa, and Alex arrived at the airport in Valdez and told them the latest news as they walked toward the SUV. "The two tankers left early this morning from Cook Inlet, and I just got word a Japanese fishing trawler found one of the tankers running in a circle out in the Pacific Ocean, but nobody's seen the second tanker. All we know is we can't raise either of them on the radio."

Bull suddenly stopped. "That's just great. I told them what would happen. Have you sent a new crew out to the tanker the Japanese reported?"

"Yeah, they called and said the tanker was empty and the crew was missing. The Coast Guard said it's an enormous area to search, and it would be blind luck if they find the second tanker."

***

When the group entered the office, Alex used his phone while the others shrugged out of their parkas and explained the situation to Donner. He listened for several minutes before ending the call, and when he looked up, Christa, Bull, and Herb were staring at him. "Director Donner is ordering the Navy to help with the search and asking for the P-3 Orion submarine hunter aircraft from the Whidbey Island Naval Air Station to assist us. Also, it appears we're not the only country losing crude oil. There's more bad news. Our witness in Texas died this morning, so it looks like Broden is our only hope of finding out what's going on. I'm wanted in D.C. as soon as possible for a briefing, and it's crucial you talk to Broden the moment he comes around. I just booked a seat on the next flight out of here, which leaves in fifteen minutes. Can I get a ride to the hotel to get my luggage?"

Herb handed Alex the keys to the truck. "I'll get it later."

"Great. Thanks."

***

Christa was standing on the bridge of the *Defiance,* talking to an engineer working on the ship's control panel, which appeared dead. "Were the instruments damaged when the ship was attacked in Washington?"

"Yes."

"What caused the damage?"

The young man scratched his head and looked bewildered as he stared down at the panel. "Near as I can figure, it was an electrical short or a sudden power surge or something. You know, if I didn't know better, I'd swear somebody waved a giant magnet over the control panel. Every gauge is magnetized."

"Then how did the new crew drive it back here to Valdez?"

"Oh, that wouldn't be too hard. All the electronic gear was added three years ago. The compass is still working, and the speed selector has a mechanical backup. Same with the steering."

"I see. Thanks for the help."

Christa made her way down to the main deck and saw Bull getting ready to climb down through the inspection hatch into a section of the oil hold. "Mind if I come along?"

"Not at all."

When Bull dropped out of sight, Christa stepped over the electrical cable and climbed down the ladder after him. The interior of the hold was dark and gloomy until she was about halfway down, when suddenly the area was filled with bright light. She stopped, looked down, and saw Bull adjusting a large spotlight mounted on a tripod. She continued down the ladder and stood next to him as they looked around the vast hold.

Bull shook his head in wonder. "It's hard to believe this room was full of crude oil only a few days ago."

"So, what are you looking for?"

"Just curious, I guess. We pumped all the salt water out this morning."

Bull and Christa strolled along the port side of the hold between the massive baffling plates, concentrating their attention on the steel deck. When they reached the far end, they continued to the starboard side and followed it back.

As they moved past the last baffle, Christa looked up at something sparkling high up on the side of it and stopped to point up at the sparkle. "What's that?"

Bull was a few paces past her and turned to look at where she was pointing. "I don't see anything."

Christa moved beside him, but the angle of the light changed and she couldn't see the sparkle, so she moved back a few paces until she saw it again. "Move over here."

Bull moved behind her and looked up. "Whatever it is, it shouldn't be in here."

"Let's get a ladder so I can take a closer look."

Bull leaned his back against the steel baffle. "Here. Stand on my shoulders."

Christa stood on his knee and then stepped into his laced fingers as Bull hoisted her in the air as if she weighed nothing at all. She stepped onto his shoulders, and the sparkle was just above her head. "It's coming from a flat object, about the size of a lemon. It's some type of crystal."

When she reached up to touch it, her fingers barely grazed the surface when the crystal suddenly fell free. As she reached out to catch it, she lost her balance.

Bull felt Christa's weight shift on his shoulders and reached up to steady her, but it was too late. The motion made him lean too far out and he toppled face-first to the deck.

Christa heard a loud swoosh of air as she landed on something softer than the steel deck and listened to Bull moan beneath her. "Oh, crap, I'm sorry!" she said, and rolled off him. "Are you all right?"

Bull grunted softly as he rolled onto his back. "Yeah," he said between deep gulps of air. "Just knocked the wind out of me for a second."

Christa sat up, leaned against the baffle, and realized she was still clutching something in her right hand. She opened her fist and saw the crystal. "I got it!"

Bull rolled to a sitting position and stared at the crystal in Christa's hand. "What do you think it is?"

Christa placed the crystal on edge between her thumb and finger and held it in the spotlight. It was nearly transparent, with a multitude of cracks running through it. "I'm not sure. I'll know more when I put it under a microscope."

Bull got up and helped her stand. "Okay. Let's get out of here."

They left the ship and walked along the pier. "Thanks, Bull. I could have broken my neck."

"Don't mention it. I've been carrying this extra weight around for years. Glad it was finally useful for something."

They stopped at a small cinderblock building, where Christa used a key to unlock a door, and then turned on the lights and stepped inside. Two small tables sat in the center of the single room, and laboratory equipment was set up on a long table fastened to the far wall. This was Christa's laboratory, where she tested the oil from the pipeline for contaminates.

Christa gently placed the crystal under the microscope. At first, she thought the light was affecting what she saw, so she moved the optic lens to a lower position and looked into the microscope again. "This is incredible! Look at this."

Bull placed his eyes over the lens and saw thousands of minuscule cracks, except they were not cracks, he realized, because they were changing shape inside the crystal. "It's moving!" When he looked up, Christa was staring at him. "What is it?"

Christa shook her head in dismay. "I have no idea, but I'm going to stay here until I find out."

Chapter 6

SEATTLE, WASHINGTON:
The red taillights of the car in front of him flashed on, and Harold Woolly stepped on the brake to stop his little station wagon. He looked at his reflection in the rearview mirror, unconsciously pulling his thin brown hair over the bald area in the center of his forehead. He reached down, turned up the volume on the radio, and hummed off key with the gospel singers. The brake lights in front of him flashed off, and he got a break when a trucker was late to respond.

Harold stomped on the accelerator and darted into the right lane, receiving a loud blast from the trucker's horn. *It's like a war zone on the freeway. Everyone's in a hurry, and as inconsiderate as possible. Even the air is deadly while stuck in traffic.*

Twenty minutes later, he eased onto the exit ramp into the parking lot beneath the Corporate Bank Building and stopped, hurrying to get out and running to the elevator. The elevator took him to the thirty-eighth floor, and as he rushed past the receptionist, she hollered his boss wanted to see him first thing.

"This is not good!" Harold mumbled as he tossed his briefcase onto his desk and hurried to the manager's office. He drew a deep breath and stepped through the doorway.

"You're late again, Woolly!"

"I'm sorry, Mister Stuckford," he said to a pompous man in a tailored suit sitting behind the desk. "It's the traffic, sir. It's getting worse every day."

"That's no excuse! I don't have a problem getting here on time."

Harold stared at the desktop and knew better than to say he couldn't afford a nice big house on Lake Union like his boss. As it was, he left two hours early to make it on time, and added another two hours to his workday just to get home. "Yes, sir, I'll do that."

"Good. What's the status on the bank merger?"

"I'm having a hard time convincing them, Mister Stuckford. Their board of directors thinks their stock will double by next year."

Stuckford glared at Harold. "You're not aggressive enough, Woolly! Now either you threaten them, or I'll get someone else to handle the merger and you'll be looking for another job. Is that clear?"

Harold indicated it was and returned to his desk. He spent the better part of the day, including his lunch break, on the phone. When he finally left the office, he wished all the other cars on the highway would run out of gas so he would be the only car on the interstate.

***

By the time he finished the commute home, he was mentally exhausted as he parked on the street. He retrieved his briefcase from the backseat and shuffled along the sidewalk to his front porch, and then entered his three-bedroom, rambler-style house. "I'm home, Cally," he hollered toward the kitchen.

Cally Woolly wiped her hands on a dishtowel as she stepped around the wall from the kitchen and smiled at her husband. "Hi, dear. Dinner is almost ready. Why don't you change clothes now, so we'll be ready to go to choir practice as soon as we're through eating?"

Harold sighed deeply at the thought of more work. "I really don't feel like choir practice tonight."

Her normally soft hazel eyes harden into fierce orbs in a scowling face. "It's only two weeks until the concert, Harold!"

"But Cally, I can't even carry a tune. You've told me enough times, and I get tired of just mouthing the words."

"Well, if you don't practice, you'll embarrass me by mouthing the wrong words!"

Harold released a frustrated sigh. "You go ahead without me. I'll go next week."

Cally stormed back into the kitchen and Harold walked down the hallway, pausing at the open door of his daughter's room.

He saw his seventeen-year-old daughter Pamela sitting at her desk, but she didn't notice him standing in the doorway. He studied the posters on the walls, and they were all of professional women soccer players.

He continued down the hall to his son's bedroom, but fifteen-year-old Mark Woolly was not there. Paintball competition posters covered the walls, and camouflaged clothing lay scattered on the floor below the replica guns and rifles hanging from a pegboard on the wall.

He continued to his bedroom and changed clothes, and when he returned to the kitchen, Cally was standing silently at the stove with her back to him. "Did we get any mail?" he asked, hoping she might have calmed down.

"It's on the counter," she said without turning.

Harold grabbed the small stack of envelopes and sat at the table. He saw bills, bills, and more bills, and they never seem to stop coming. At the bottom was an official-looking envelope addressed to Mark, with A.O.S. printed in the upper left corner, and a Post Office box number in Idaho. He thought about opening it, but knew his son would probably enjoy opening it himself.

The back door suddenly burst open and Mark Woolly rushed through, slamming it closed and peering out the window. A bright yellow substance was splattered on the left shoulder of his camouflaged shirt, and he was holding a long-barreled paint ball gun in his right hand. With a serious expression, he glanced over his shoulder at Harold. "I'm all right, Dad. It's just a shoulder wound."

"Go wash up for dinner," Cally told him.

Mark spun around, devastated, as though about to be executed. "But Mom! Brian is hiding behind the fence and I can sneak out the front door and nail him!"

"You can nail him tomorrow. Now, go wash up for dinner."

"All right," he said, and shuffled across the kitchen, disappearing around the corner.

Cally set plates and silverware on the counter. "Fix your own plate," she snarled to Harold as she took hers into the living room.

Harold stared after her. *So, it's going to be one of those nights. Pamela will come in and fill her plate, and disappear into her bedroom. Cally will sit in front of the television, and Mark will join him at the table.* A moment later, Pamela appeared.

"Hi, Dad," she said as she walked to the stove and piled the stroganoff onto her plate. "You upset Mom again, didn't you?" she continued as she walked past him, disappearing from the kitchen without waiting for a response.

Harold watched Mark walk to the stove. He was tall for his age, like his sister, and still growing, and had no problem piling a mountain of stroganoff onto his plate. He was glad his son liked to buy clothes at the thrift store instead of demanding new clothes, as his daughter did.

Mark grabbed four slices of bread before sitting at the table. "Mom's really pissed."

"Hey, watch the language," Harold said with a grin.

"What's the matter with her this time?"

It always amazed him how his children could be so observant. *This time is right.* It seemed he and Cally were arguing a lot lately and she was getting even more demanding, and he usually gave in to her demands. He fell head over heels in love with her in high school, though she always ignored him. She was one of the most attractive and popular girls in his grade level and always dated the jocks, but in their senior year, he caught her on the rebound from a doomed affair with a macho football player who dumped her for a cheerleader from another school. He gathered enough courage to ask her to the senior prom and was elated when she accepted.

That night, she talked on and on about wanting a more sensitive kind of guy, and on impulse, he asked her to marry him. When she said yes, he was shocked with elation, but she also stipulated they would have to elope to Nevada that night or the deal was off. He was so happy he could hardly control himself and took her to her house so she could grab some clothes. He didn't even bother stopping at his place and drove straight through to Nevada, and she has continued to tell him what to do since that night.

Harold and Mark both looked up when they hear the door into the garage slam shut and heard Cally's car starting. *It's getting worse. Now she isn't even saying goodbye when she leaves.*

Harold lost his appetite and sat watching Mark shovel bread and stroganoff into his mouth, as though he was starved. "This came in the mail for you, Son."

Mark quit eating and tore open the envelope, then brought out a letter and started reading. "This place is amazing!"

"What does AOS stand for?"

"Army of Survival," Mark replied, and dumped two brochures onto the table.

Harold picked one up and studied the information. The brochure had pictures of men and women in camouflaged clothing, posed in various stages of combat. One picture was of a group of men and women standing at attention in front of a raised cabin. On a porch behind them was a tall, dark-haired man with a black patch over one eye. "Where did you learn about this?"

"From Brian Essex's older brother, John. He heard about it when he was in the Marine Corps."

"That's strange. Max Everex never told me he had another son."

"He's from Mister Everex's first marriage, but he doesn't come around much. Brian says it's because neither of his parents like him. I think he's a neat guy. He let Brian and me hold the awesome guns and weapons he carries around in the trunk of his car."

Harold was suddenly alarmed. It was one thing for his son to play with toy weapons, but quite another for him to play with real ones. "Where is Brian's brother now?"

Mark held up a brochure. "Here, I think. That's where he was headed when he left."

Harold relaxed a little. *That's a relief.*

Pamela appeared and set her plate in the sink before sitting at the table, looking very serious. "When you and mom get divorced, I want to live with her."

"Not me," said Mark. "I want to live with you, Dad."

Again, Harold was surprised how astute his children were to have noticed the rift forming between their parents. "Now, wait a minute, both of you. Who said anything about a divorce?"

Pamela looked at him, her expression one of forbidden knowledge. "I heard mom and Miss Stoker talking, and she told mom to get an excellent attorney and take you to the cleaners."

Harold's jaw hung open. He did not know Cally was planning on a divorce, and looked at Pamela. "Uh, how long ago was this?"

"About three weeks ago."

"What does take you to the cleaner's mean?" Mark asked.

Pamela smirked. "It means mom is going to get all of dad's money and property and put him in the poorhouse."

Harold's mind was reeling with the information. *How could Cally do this to him without even talking about it?*

Pamela interrupted his thoughts. "I just wanted you to know what I want, Dad, so it will be easier in the custody battle."

Harold stared after her as she stood and left the room, and then looked over at Mark, who was finishing his stroganoff as though nothing was wrong. Mark got up and put his plate in the sink, and then walked toward the back door. "I'm going to find Brian so we can finish our game."

After the door slammed shut, Harold remained seated and tried to cope with the devastating news. *I don't want a divorce. Why didn't she talk to me about it? Maybe she really isn't going through with it? Maybe it's just talk?*

Harold remembered accidentally discovering where Cally hid old love letters from her high school flings, and slowly got up and shuffled down the hall to their bedroom. He opened her bottom dresser drawer and dug around beneath her lingerie until he found the ribbon-bound stack of letters.

On top was a copy of a petition for divorce, and he sat heavily on the bed, as though in a dream, then opened the document and read the demands. Cally wanted custody of the children, the house, child support, and maintenance payments. He stared in the dresser mirror in shock. *It's all true. She's taking me to the cleaners.*

His fingers felt numb as he replaced the bundle in the drawer. His mind was whirling, and after the mental stress of work and the commute home, it was more than he can take. He just didn't have the willpower to confront Cally when she came home.

He felt as though he couldn't breathe and needed some fresh air, so he slowly got up and walked down the hall. He glanced into Mark's bedroom and saw all the guns hanging on the wall, and took two steps past the door before turning and entering the room.

He stood in front of the guns, carefully studying each one. Most of them were obviously plastic, but near the lower right corner was a real-looking silver pistol. He gently removed it from its peg, feeling the weight of the metal as he lovingly ran his hand along its smooth barrel. *This one will do. So beautiful. Yes, this one will be perfect.*

He carried it back to his bedroom and sat on the end of the bed so he could see himself in the dresser mirror, but the man reflected back looked like someone else. An old man with sunken eyes and an enormous nose. An old man with hardly any hair. He watched the old man in the mirror raise a beautiful silver pistol with his left hand. *Ha!* He exclaimed inwardly. *It's someone else. The man in the mirror is left-handed, and I'm right-handed.*

Harold stared in fascination as the old man turned the pistol and placed the end of the barrel against his temple. The old man in the mirror grinned at him, and Harold watched him pull the hammer back with his thumb and pull the trigger. The hammer fell as if in slow motion, and he heard a quiet click. In the mirror, the old man's grin changed into a mocking grimace, and Harold decided he needed to leave for a while.

Without thinking about it, he walked to the garage, retrieved an old suitcase, and returned to the bedroom. In something of a dream state, he packed a few clothes and his suit, and unconsciously tossed the silver pistol on top of the clothes and shut the lid. He didn't notice Pamela staring at him as he walked past her bedroom, then he mechanically grabbed his briefcase by the sofa and left the house.

Chapter 7

SOUTHCENTRAL IDAHO:

FBI agent George Pickowski sat in his unmarked sedan while watching a driveway leading up a hill to Menno Simon's private home. A tall chain-link fence surrounded the five acre parcel and kept prying eyes from viewing the mansion, but Pickowski had been following Menno's limousine all day and knew he is there.

The explosion of Menno's research facility was more intense than even Menno expected. Plastic explosives caused the initial explosion, but an extremely volatile explosive must have been manufactured at the facility to cause so much damage. Menno's Federal Registration License stated it was a genetic research facility, and the FBI was called in to investigate and find the person or persons responsible. Menno denied any knowledge of the incident, but the FBI kept him under surveillance.

Pickowski saw the ornate steel gates open and started the sedan's engine. A limousine came through, and Pickowski followed it for nearly three hours before it turned off the main highway onto a dirt road winding through thick evergreens. He dropped back and lost sight of the limousine to keep from being spotted. He nearly missed the side road the limo took, but a lingering cloud of dust caught his attention, and Pickowski slammed on the brakes.

He backed up to follow and was about to stomp on the accelerator to catch up when he saw the red flash of taillights through the trees just around the bend. He waited, thinking he had been spotted, but the taillights didn't move. He grabbed the small binoculars sitting on the seat beside him and eased the door open, then stepped out and focused the lenses on the taillights. He heard muffled voices, but the words were indistinguishable.

He heard laughter before the taillights blink out and the limousine drove off. He knew trying to get past the checkpoint would be useless, and he didn't want to tip them off that Menno was being followed. He wasn't dressed for hiking, but the underbrush didn't appear to be too thick.

Pickowski climbed back into the car and backed out to the main dirt road, but now the problem was where to hide the car. He continued past this turn off so anyone going to the same place wouldn't spot his vehicle, and a quarter mile farther, he found an abandoned road and backed the car into the trees. As he stepped out, he realized how quiet it was in the forest and decided he could hear a car coming for quite a distance, and could duck into the trees if he heard one approaching. He climbed out and grabbed the binoculars, then began jogging back to the turnoff.

After the quarter mile jog, Pickowski was sweating in the eighty degree heat, his white shirt sticking uncomfortably against his back and chest. He was slightly out of breath as he approached the turnoff the limousine had taken, and when he heard the noise of an engine growing louder, he jumped over the culvert and ducked into the trees. He stifled a groan of pain as a small stick poked into his left ankle just above his street shoes, and when he was sure he could not be spotted, he stopped and listened.

The engine noise changed pitch, and he heard it change direction, so he followed the sound. He saw several flashes of bright light through the trees, caused by the sun's reflection off the chrome on the vehicle. A few moments later, the engine noise dropped to an idle, and he heard voices at the checkpoint, sixty feet to his right. He continued in the same direction, occasionally stifling a groan of pain as his ankles were subjected to more pokes before he saw the vehicle was still stopped.

When the vehicle drove away, Pickowski continued through the trees until he was well past the checkpoint, and with a sigh of relief for his tortured ankles, he stepped back onto the road. Another car approached, and he ducked into the trees again, and stayed concealed until it stopped on the edge of a vast meadow, and then he moved out of the trees.

The perimeter was lined with cars and recreational vehicles, and a large crowd of people were sitting on the grass in front of an elevated platform. There were no chairs, speakers, or microphones on the stage, and no one was standing on it.

Below the stage and to the left was a long table, where two young men were setting large trays on top of it. Whatever was on the trays seemed to sparkle in different colors, but as the sun disappeared behind the mountains, the meadow got dark and he could not tell what the objects were.

He worked his way through the woods to sit with the others on the grass so he could see and hear what was going on and stepped out from between the cars and RVs. He found a place to sit forty feet from the front of the stage, hoping no one would see the blood on his socks around his ankles.

The man sitting next to him asked for the time, and Pickowski told him. He wanted to ask the man what this is all about, but knew it might make him suspicious, but it turned out he didn't have to.

"So, where are you supposed to take your seeds?" The man asked.

Pickowski thought quickly. "Pennsylvania."

"I'm headed for Florida." He pointed at the girl sitting in front of them. "She has to go all the way to Kuwait. She and about fifty others have to catch a chartered flight first thing tomorrow morning. A friend of mine is Russian, and he's taking a bunch of seeds to his friends over there. Man, people are taking seeds all over the world."

Pickowski looked at the tables and trays, wondering about the seeds, when the rumble of voices suddenly died out, leaving the pitch-black meadow in eerie silence. Up on the stage, a beam of pale blue light suddenly appeared in the center. Pickowski tried to see where it was coming from, but could not spot any light fixtures around the stage or in the trees.

The light grew wider by the second, but only reached a height of ten feet above the stage. When it was five feet wide, it ceased to grow and looked as though something was materializing in the center. At first, it was just a white silhouette, and then the outline of a body took shape. A moment later, a person stepped out.

With the blue light behind the body, there were no discernable features, only a white-robed figure standing with its arms at its sides. The figure extended its arms and rose into the air until it was four feet above the stage and stopped. A voice suddenly echoed across the meadow, as if amplified through a huge speaker system, which Pickowski didn't see.

"The time has come, my children," Menno began.

Pickowski found the baritone voice soothing, and he could not take his eyes off the robed figure floating in blue light. He felt like he was in a dream.

"The age of the machine is about to end," the voice continued. "We will once again breathe clean air and the war machines will cease to threaten our planet with global destruction, and we will live in peace once more. I command you to spread these seeds of peace throughout the world."

The voice droned on, and Pickowski felt lightheaded. *Yes, it makes sense.*

"And when you have fulfilled my command, you will once again live in a world full of love for all the life forms on our beautiful world. Come forward, my children, and gather to your bosoms the seeds of world peace and begin your journeys to the far corners of the planet."

As Pickowski watched, the figure appeared to float back into the blue light and seemed to disintegrate. He felt sad, as though someone precious had been taken from him. When nothing was left of the figure, the blue light shrank to a thin line and vanished.

Pickowski heard the meadow erupt in muffled conversation, as flashlights were turned on throughout the crowd, and they all got up. The man next to him turned on his flashlight and stood, but now that the person in the blue light was gone, Pickowski felt empty and remained seated.

"Are you coming, brother?" the man asked.

Pickowski looked up and smiled. "Yes! Oh, yes!"

The man reached down and Pickowski took his hand, but when he stood, a searing pain shot through his ankles. His mind suddenly cleared, and he realized where he is. The man was frowning with concern, and Pickowski realized he must have flinched. "I guess my legs fell asleep," he said, and smiled.

The man grinned, and Pickowski joined him as lines formed back and forth across the meadow. He looked toward the stage and saw a steady line of people passing in front of the table with the trays.

That son of a bitch hypnotized me! Pickowski realized as he followed in line. He saw the people who had already been through walking toward the vehicles. In their hands, held close to their chests, were small glass vials of sparkling colors. Some had several of them, others only one or two.

He didn't notice it before, but there was a crescent moon straight up above him. He thought it strange he couldn't see any craters on its surface, but dismissed it as an optical illusion created by the atmosphere.

As he passed in front of the table, he saw the trays held thousands of the small glass ampules, all sparkling in rainbow colors. He watched the man in front of him take one ampule and clutch it against his chest, so he did the same and followed the crowd back to the vehicles. He made his way to the last car, and when he was sure no one is watching, dashed back into the trees.

There was enough light from the vehicle headlights filtering through the woods for him to see his way around the underbrush as he made his way in the direction he figured the main road was. His sense of direction was correct, and half an hour later, he emerged from the woods onto the main dirt road.

When he found his car, he climbed in and started the engine, and with the lights off, drove down the road until he was close to where the headlights were emerging from the side road. He waited for a break in the traffic, pulled in behind a large recreational vehicle, and turned on his lights. A moment later, another set of headlights pulled in behind him, and he sighed with relief at not being discovered as an imposter.

Chapter 8

IDAHO:

Retired Army Colonel George Blackwood stood before the bathroom mirror in his private cabin, examining his naked body, and noticing a slight bulge around the waist. *Not bad for a man of fifty-six.* He ran a hand through his short-cropped salt and pepper hair and adjusted the black patch over his left eye. With a grin of satisfaction, he turned and went into the bedroom, opened the closet door, and grabbed a crisply pressed olive green uniform.

Once clothed, he turned sideways to the mirror to check his profile. On the left sleeve of his shirt was a custom patch with a circle of gold leaves and three lightning bolts coming together in the center to form a 'Y'. In gold letters around the circle were the words, ARMY OF SURVIVAL.

When he heard the short array of bugle notes from the camp's public address system, Blackwood peered out the window at the crowd of two hundred men and women assembling in neat rows on the parade ground. He waited for his second in command, Major Robert Conrad, to give a subtle signal that everyone was in place, and then threw back his shoulders and stretched his body ramrod straight. He yanked the door open and strutted out onto the large front porch overlooking the parade ground, and at the top of the steps stopped and slowly turned his head to study his troops.

Conrad snapped to attention. "All personnel present and accounted for, Sir!"

"Thank you, Major," Blackwood began, his voice deep and slightly raspy. "At ease. Men and women of the Army of Survival, we are under attack!"

Muffled conversations of surprise erupted from the crowd, and Blackwood waited a few moments before continuing. "The civilians in the surrounding cities have turned against us and have cut off our supplies to shut us down. This cannot be allowed, and the time has come for us to make our presence known. We will show them we will not be dictated to by a bunch of cowardly civilians, and we will acquire the fuel and supplies we need to survive by any means necessary. Report to your company commanders at thirteen hundred hours for instructions. All company commanders report to headquarters at eleven hundred hours."

Blackwood studied the faces of his troops for several moments, and when he saw most of the people give their approval, felt a great sense of pride and hope for his army. He snapped to attention and gave a smart salute, spun on his heels, and marched back into his cabin.

Conrad turned to the men and women on the parade ground. "Dismissed."

As the crowd broke up, several of the company commanders approached him to ask what was going on, but Conrad was as much in the dark about Blackwood's plan as the rest of the troops, and frustrated, he wasn't consulted ahead of time. "You'll all be briefed at eleven hundred hours."

Conrad hurried across the parade ground and up the steps of Blackwood's cabin. He reached out to rap on the door, but before his knuckles hit the wood, Blackwood hollered to enter, so he opened the door and stepped inside. Blackwood was leaning over a desk in the corner of the room with his back to him, and he closed the door. "What the hell's going on, Colonel?"

Blackwood continued studying the maps. "We're broke, Robert. Or damn near it, anyway."

"I knew we were losing contributions, but I thought we still had enough coming in to keep the camp going."

"Not anymore."

"What are you planning to do?"

"Come over here and see for yourself."

Conrad moved across the room and looked down at the maps, and Blackwood pointed to the one of Idaho, indicating two red lines drawn from east to west. "Interstate 90 to the north and Interstate 84 to the south of us." He slid a map of Nevada below the one of Idaho and pointed at the red line near the center of Nevada. "And Interstate 80. These will be our battle grounds."

Conrad looked up at Blackwood. "I don't follow you, Colonel. What do you mean by battle grounds?"

"These are the three key transport routes to and from the west coast, and every commodity imaginable is trucked across these roads. Food, dry goods, and fuel. Everything we need to survive. These roads are where we are going to get our supplies."

Conrad's jaw dropped. "Are you talking about hijacking?" He watched Blackwood grin in reply. "That's crazy." Conrad stopped when

Blackwood's stare turned savage. "But Colonel, the police would be onto us in a heartbeat."

"Not if we have a plan. Where there are truckers, there are truck stops. We hit them hard all along the interstates. Just one night and we'd have enough supplies to last us a year. Maybe more, if luck's on our side."

"It's still an enormous risk."

"Damn it, Robert! Would you rather risk losing our army? Everything we've worked so hard for?"

Conrad didn't like the idea at all and hesitated to answer. "If some trucker suddenly finds his rig gone, he'll be talking to the highway patrol before we're ten miles down the road."

Blackwood smirked. "Not if he's dead,"

Conrad's eyes went wide with shock. This wasn't his army. It was Blackwood's, and he did not intend to kill some innocent trucker. "Look, Colonel. When I joined this army, I did not sign on to become a cold-blooded murderer."

Blackwood's face turned red with anger. "This is survival, damn it! I've worked for years to build this army, and I'll do whatever it takes to keep it together!" Blackwood moved his face to within inches of Conrad's. "Now, are you with me?"

Conrad stared back and slowly shook his head no. "You're completely mad, Colonel. Count me out." He turned and walked toward the door.

Blackwood shook with rage. "You're a coward!" he snarled, but Conrad didn't respond and reached for the doorknob. Blackwood yanked open a drawer, grabbed a pistol, and pointed it at Conrad's back. "No one desserts my army!" he yelled, and squeezed the trigger.

The explosion echoed throughout the camp as Conrad was hurled against the door and slid to the floor. He rolled onto his back and stared up at Blackwood, stunned disbelief in his eyes. He tried to speak, but only a gurgled moan escaped his crimson-stained lips and his head lolled to the side.

Blackwood stared down at Conrad and realized what he had done. He didn't feel remorse, but realized now he would have to explain what had happened. "Damn!" he swore softly and paced across the room as he tried to figure out what to do.

If anyone finds out about this, I might have a mutiny on my hands. What can I tell the rest of my officers? Conrad was sent on a mission? Yes, that will work! But how do I get rid of the body? Wait until late tonight and take it deep into the woods? No, that's no good. The sentries will see me. I'll have to get somebody else to do it. But who could I get? None of the officers will do it. Possibly an enlisted man. A recruit. Yes, if he gets caught, I'll deny everything. He'll take the blame. What is the name of the recruit I met three weeks ago? There was something cynical about the man. He had a dead, cold look in his eyes. What the devil was his name?

***

John Everex, a thirty-five-year-old dishonorably discharged Marine and hardened criminal, was walking past Blackwood's cabin when he heard the shot, and ran up the steps to beat on the door. "What happened, Colonel?"

***

Blackwood grabbed Conrad by the arms and dragged him into the bathroom, leaving a long smear of blood on the floor. He heard the frantic beating on the door again as he spread a throw rug over the pool of blood.

"An accidental discharge!" he yelled back. He opened the door two inches and saw the man he was thinking about and remembered his name is Everex. He already knew about the man's background and indicated he should enter.

Everex strolled into the room and stared at the blood on the door and floor. He didn't wait for Blackwood as he followed the streak of blood into the bathroom and saw Conrad's body, and then turned around, smirking sadistically at Blackwood. "It seems you need a new second in command, Colonel."

Blackwood studied the man standing before him. Everex was short, but muscular, and might have been good-looking at one time, but several thick facial scars had taken that away, and the crooked nose showed evidence of being broken several times, but it was the eyes told him what he suspected about the man. They were nearly black, and as cold and evil as he had ever seen.

"That's right. And someone to dispose of the Major."

Everex realized the Colonel needed someone to get him out of this situation and saw how desperate he was, so he leaned against the doorjamb. "What's in it for me?"

Blackwood's posture stiffened. He hadn't expected Everex to want something in return. "A promotion to sergeant."

Everex smirked at Blackwood for a moment. "Sorry, Colonel. You'll have to do better than that."

Blackwood's face flushed red with rage. "How dare you, you little son of a bitch! One word from me and you're out of this army!"

"And one word from me and your whole damn army would lose their respect for you, Colonel. I have."

Blackwood's hands formed into fists at his sides. This wasn't going the way he hoped, but he needed someone to get him out of the situation. "What do you want?" he said through clenched teeth.

Everex grinned evilly and indicated Conrad. "I want his job." He watched Blackwood's eyes flash with anger and pushed him to the limit. "And two friends of mine to be promoted to sergeant major."

Blackwood's eyes blazed with bitterness as he stared at Everex, then he shifted his gaze to Conrad's body on the floor of the bathroom. *If I don't agree to Everex's terms, I'll have to kill him, too. Can I find someone else willing to get rid of two bodies? What about the raid on the truckers? I need someone who isn't afraid to get their hands bloody. Someone who can kill without remorse and Everex definitely fits the bill.*

Blackwood's rage slowly faded, like the red flush on his face. "All right, but under two conditions." He waited to see if Everex would back down, but the man stared back almost mockingly. "First, get rid of Conrad's body so no one will find it and clean up this mess. Second, you follow my orders to the letter, no matter what. Understood?"

Everex remembered what he had learned in the Marine Corps before being dishonorably discharged. Always agree to a direct order, but do what you want and plead you must have misunderstood, then he grinned at Blackwood. "Whatever you say, Colonel." He straightened from the doorjamb and walked toward the door. "I'll be back in a few minutes."

***

Blackwood was sitting at his desk when the cabin door suddenly burst open without a knock. He jumped out of the chair and spun around, ready to chew somebody's butt, and saw Everex grin at him as he stepped inside. A green duffel bag was draped over his shoulder and two men follow him in, both looking nearly as nasty as Everex. One carried a mop bucket, the other a mop.

Everex closed the door and stood next to his companions. "Colonel, I'd like you to meet your new Sergeant Majors. Davis and Chapman." Everex saw Blackwood's scowl and smirked in satisfaction. "Just carry on with what you were doing, Colonel. We'll be out of here in no time."

Blackwood stared at the two men. Davis was short, with bad acne scars and a crooked nose. Chapman had dirty brown hair, and an ugly scar from his forehead, across his right eye, and down past the corner of his mouth.

As Davis and Chapman mopped up the blood, Blackwood followed Everex into the bathroom. Everex tossed the duffel bag onto the toilet seat, knelt, and lifted Conrad's body off the floor without the least sign of straining and dumped it into the bathtub. With a speed that surprised Blackwood, a ten-inch knife suddenly appeared in Everex's hand.

Everex stared at it for a moment, as if studying a fine instrument, and then stared at Blackwood with an evil look. "Now the fun begins."

Everex's tone of voice sent a shiver up Blackwood's spine as he stared in stunned disbelief. Everex dismembered Conrad's body, holding each piece over the tub until the blood drained out before tossing it into the duffel bag. The coldness of Everex's actions sent a shiver of fear through Blackwood as he realized he had probably just made the biggest mistake of his life by agreeing to this monstrous animal's demands.

The reek of shit, piss, and bloody guts added to the disgust he felt toward Everex and the flood of memories from the POW camp were more than he could stand. He broke into a cold sweat as a scene from his past took over his last shred of self-control. In his mind, the man who had tortured him looked just like Everex, and his inner voice cried out, *I have to escape!*

Blackwood bolted from his quarters and jogged across the parade ground, oblivious to the salutes and voices as he passed through his troops and broke into a desperate run down a well-worn path through the woods. How far he ran or where he went, he couldn't remember, as he stumbled through the brush behind his cabin. His uniform was ripped to shreds and soaked with sweat and he felt like he had just awoke from a nightmare, as he staggered up the steps and opened the door of his cabin.

He was suddenly frozen with shock when he saw Everex leaning back in his chair, feet propped on his desk, and a folded map in his hands. He stared slack-jawed at the demon from his nightmare before regaining his composure.

Everex smiled, but it was scorching. "You look like shit, Colonel. Better take a shower before you explain your plan to me."

Blackwood glanced at the closed door to the bathroom, and a flood of horrible memories rushed through his mind again. He felt like he was still fighting with his nightmare as he hesitantly approached the door, expecting to find the mocking remnants of the grisly scene. He grabbed the knob, held his breath, and opened the door. The bathroom and tub were spotlessly clean and smelled strongly of disinfectant. Without a backward glance at Everex, he stepped into the bathroom, closed the door, and released a great sigh of relief.

As he stood under the cold water, he realized he must take command of the situation and show Everex he was still in charge and a man to be reckoned with. When he emerged from the bathroom twenty minutes later, completely naked, he looked at Everex, still leaning back in the chair. "Get your damn feet off my desk!" He commanded as he hurried across the room to his bedroom.

A few minutes later, wearing a clean uniform, Blackwood strolled out of his bedroom and saw Everex had not moved, so he shoots him a menacing glare. To his relief, Everex slowly removed his feet. *I'm still in command*, he thought with satisfaction as he continued to desk. "Here's what I want to do."

***

11:30 P.M. INTERSTATE 90, IDAHO:

It was a moonless night when the van pulled off the interstate at a truck stop/restaurant on the outskirts of a little town called Silverton. Identical to the rest of the twelve-person team inside the van, Blackwood was dressed in black pants and a black sweatshirt. He glanced over at Everex, who had the same evil grin as when he dumped Conrad's body in the bathtub.

Everex smirked at Blackwood. "Now the fun begins."

Blackwood felt a chill run up his spine and looked away, and the headlights of the van flick off as they approached the restaurant. Five civilian cars were parked in front of the glass windows, and saw the server pouring coffee to two tired looking men sitting near the door.

The van drove past the restaurant into the parking lot behind it, where several large tractor-trailer rigs were parked in parallel rows. The street lamps illuminated two fuel tankers, a refrigerated grocery carrier, and four freight carriers without markings.

According to plan, the van stopped long enough for ten people to jump out, and then it made a U-turn and headed back onto the interstate. Everex and Blackwood ran to the front door of the restaurant and waited while the other eight people ran toward the trucks. Blackwood's plan was to wait for each trucker to leave the restaurant and grab them as they entered their rig, while he and Everex stood guard in case a highway patrol car stopped for coffee.

Blackwood suddenly heard a diesel engine rev up and turned to Everex. "What the hell's going on?"

"Change of plans, Colonel. We don't have time to wait around."

Blackwood watched Everex swing a backpack from his shoulders and reach inside. "What are you doing?"

"I'm putting them to sleep for a while," Everex said as he removed two small metal canisters.

Before Blackwood could respond, Everex leaned against the door to hold it open, pulled the pins on the canisters, and tossed them into the restaurant. The door swung closed, and Blackwood and Everex stared through the glass. The two canisters rolled part way down the aisle between the counter and the tables, but didn't appear to be doing anything.

The server walked down the aisle and accidentally kicked one of the canisters, and the air in front of her became distorted by the escaping gas. She bent over to pick it up and continued falling forward, sending her tray of dishes crashing to the floor. A tall man at the counter stood to help and collapsed beside her. The other occupants turned and stared uncomprehendingly at the two bodies and within seconds of each other, slumped into their chairs or fell forward onto the tables and counters. Blackwood felt a hand on his shoulder and looked at Everex, who was smiling.

"Let's go, Colonel."

Blackwood looked back into the restaurant, wondering if they were just sleeping, when a hand grabbed his arm and spun him around. He looked into Everex's anxious eyes. "Are they dead?"

"I said, let's go!"

Blackwood followed as Everex ran toward the trucks. More engines roared to life as the small squadron of soldiers climbed into the trucks and drove around the building, heading onto the interstate for the drive back to camp.

***

AOS CAMP:

Blackwood bolted upright in bed, his sheets soaked with sweat from the nightmare of his time in the POW compound and the torture from the camp's commander. In his dream, the commander looked just like Everex.

Someone was knocking on his cabin door, and he squinted at the clock on the nightstand. 10:13 A.M. "Oh, shit!" he moaned. Again, someone knocked. "Just a minute!" he hollered as he rolled out of bed and shuffled to the door. When he opened it, Everex was standing on the other side, and he jumped back, stifling a scream of terror as he cowered against the wall.

Everex studied the Colonel for a moment. He wasn't sure what it was, but Blackwood seemed scared to death of him. He realized the once forceful composure and domineering attitude seemed to disappear, which was fine with him.

Blackwood realized it was a bad dream, but he wasn't dreaming now and knew from the grin on Everex's face, he had better regain control of the situation. He drew himself up and stepped in front of Everex. "What is it, Major?"

Everex waved a hand toward the parade ground. "A good night's work, Colonel."

Blackwood stared at the rows of trucks filling the area. "How many did we get?"

"Six have arrived and seven are still making their way here."

Blackwood smiled. His army would survive. Then another thought occurred to him. "We're going to need more room."

"I've already thought of that. Several crews are clearing out sections of the forest just enough to drive the trucks through, but keep them hidden from anyone flying over the area."

Blackwood admitted to himself even though Everex was sick in the head, he was clever. Maybe it wasn't such a big mistake promoting him after all. "Very good, Major. Carry on."

"When we have enough room in the forest, I'll set up another raid on the truck stops."

Blackwood stared at him. "Do we need more?"

"All we can get, Colonel. We don't have enough room in our cold storage lockers, so we'll concentrate on fuel tankers next time. We'll need fuel to keep the refrigerated trucks running."

When Everex stepped out of the cabin, Blackwood closed the door. *Yes, promoting Everex was an excellent idea, indeed,* he thought as he walked toward the bathroom.

Chapter 9

SEATTLE, WASHINGTON:

Harold Woolly grabbed the television remote control and leaned back against the pillows propped against the headboard in the motel room. The announcer on the eleven o'clock news broadcast was explaining how the disabled pipeline in Alaska might influence the availability of petroleum products in Washington State.

"Authorities tell us there should be enough reserve gasoline and heating oil to carry us through a temporary shutdown of the pipeline, and there is no reason for anyone to panic. The same situation has occurred many times over the past several years, when the pipeline is shut down for routine maintenance, and it has never created a shortage. We are not the only ones dependent on the supply of oil from the pipeline. Oregon and California also receive most of their crude oil from Alaska, and the refineries on the west coast ship the products to Idaho, Montana, Wyoming, Utah, Colorado, and Nevada. In a statement released to the press early this morning, our Governor has asked that nobody panic over the news from Alaska."

Harold shook his head at the stupidity of the media, thinking the people at the news stations were idiots. Nobody would even think about panicking if the broadcasters hadn't planted the idea in people's heads.

His thoughts turned to his family, and what Cally thought of all of this. Since she didn't work, she probably cared less about a gas shortage. The school busses would still run, so the kids would be okay, but it might interfere with her social life.

He grinned as a mental picture of Cally upset because she couldn't get to her precious choir practice. Wouldn't it be funny if they had to cancel the whole concert? That would really fry Cally's butt.

Harold's smile slowly faded as his thoughts returned to his situation. Sure, his boss was happy he made it to work early the past two mornings, but he really missed his family. What good was it to have such a short drive when he had nothing to do with all the extra time? All he could do after leaving the office was return to this tiny room and stare at the television.

He desperately wanted to call Cally and ask if it was all right to come home, then had second thoughts about it. *Wait a minute. I left her. She didn't kick me out. Why should I have to ask permission? She's the one filing for a divorce, not me.*

He thought about packing his suitcase and going home, but the idea of a confrontation with Cally changed his mind. He decided maybe staying away for a while might be good for their marriage. He would give it a little more time, and perhaps Cally would change her mind about divorcing him.

"Why me?" He mumbled softly in the dark as a tear slowly rolled down his cheek. A soft sob escaped his lips, and suddenly he could not hold back the stream of tears and let them flow.

Chapter 10

THE WHITE HOUSE.
The President inserted a video disk into the player, returned to his chair, and pressed play on the remote. He ate a piece of his club sandwich while he watched the news broadcast from Washington State, recorded earlier that morning. The picture was of a young male news broadcaster sitting behind a desk.

"The Governor has been forced to call in the National Guard to stop the fighting in the gasoline lines. Once again, until the refineries are distributing gasoline, he is asking you to not drive and use the metro bus system. For those of you with oil heating systems in your homes, please try to stay with friends and relatives until this crisis is over."

"A man and a woman were shot while robbing a grocery store in Lynnwood yesterday. The owner of the store said he has to keep himself armed at all times because of the constant robbery attempts. This is just one of the many incidents caused by the lack of transportation to bring food supplies into this part of our state. We go now to our reporter, Jan Smith, who is live with a representative of the Teamsters Union in Tacoma."

The picture changed, showing Jan talking to a gray-haired man, both standing in front of a large tractor-trailer rig. *"What seems to be the biggest problem with delivering supplies here to the West Coast?"* Jan asked. *"We have reports that transportation is continuing in Eastern Washington."*

"Once the trucks come over the mountains to bring in supplies, there isn't any fuel available for them to get back. The trucking industry on this side of the mountains is at a standstill until more fuel is available. If we don't get any diesel soon, even the trucking in Eastern Washington will stop."

"Is it true that trucks are being hijacked from the interstate highways?"

"Yes it is, and I've asked the Governor to have the National Guard patrol the interstates, but he says he doesn't have enough people. I'm hoping he'll ask the President for military support."

The President switched recordings to one from Los Angeles and pressed play. On the screen was a view from a helicopter flying over the city, showing live pictures of burning buildings and fighting in the streets, as the broadcaster narrated.

"It's a war zone in Los Angeles as people panic. They are literally fighting their way to the gas pumps, and our latest report is over three hundred people have died because of domestic shootings over gasoline."

The picture changed, showing the broadcaster sitting behind a desk in the studio. *"One of our biggest concerns is agricultural production. Without fuel for their equipment, farmers cannot operate, and even the early harvest won't make it to market if the trucking industry can't get fuel. People are lining up outside grocery stores to buy anything they can before commodities run out. If this oil crisis continues, California's economy will be devastated."*

The President shut off the player, picked up the phone, and waited a moment until Martin Donner answered. "Hi, Martin. Oscar here."

"Yes, Mister President. What can I do for you?"

"Have you heard anything from Mister Cave?"

"Not yet."

"I see. The Chairman of the Joint Chiefs says the Navy has a submarine standing by off the southern coast of Alaska. When you hear from him, tell Mister Cave to inform his people to send the tankers."

"Yes, sir."

The President stared at his half-eaten sandwich. "Less than a year in office and this has to happen."

Chapter 11

ALASKA:

Alex entered the small cement building near the pier and saw Christa leaning over a microscope. "Anything new?"

Christa turned to face him, her eyes slightly bloodshot. "No!" she snapped at him.

Alex raised his hands, palms out. "Sorry."

Christa grinned. "Oh, it's not you, it's this crystal. It doesn't conform to any mineral standards I know of, and it doesn't fit any biological standards, either."

"How about taking a break? I've just learned Mike Broden is coherent, and I'm about to fly up to Anchorage."

"Give me a few minutes to change clothes."

"No problem. I'll give you a ride home."

Alex walked her out to his rental SUV and drove through the little town of Valdez to Christa's small apartment complex. It was built during the boom days of the pipeline's construction, but cosmetically had been neglected.

"It's not much, but the rent's cheap," Christa told him as he parked in front of the building. "You can come up, if you like."

Alex followed her up one flight of stairs and into her unit. Her apartment was a living room/kitchen combination, with one door leading into a bedroom with a bathroom, but it was tastefully decorated.

"Make yourself at home. I'll be out in a moment," Christa said over her shoulder as she walked toward the bedroom.

Alex felt his phone vibrate in his coat pocket and answered. "What's up, Martin?"

"The Navy has a submarine standing by to escort the tankers. Tell All Alaska to get them moving. Things are getting nasty on the west coast, so the sooner the better."

"I'll tell him. I'm flying to Anchorage in a few minutes to talk to my witness, so I'll call you back in a few hours."

"Good. Call me at home if I'm not here."

"I will."

Alex hung up and called the All Alaska office to inform Bull about the escort. A few moments later, Christa walked into the living room, dressed in light blue slacks and a matching sweater. They left the apartment and drove to the airport, and Alex used the All Alaska airplane to take them to Anchorage.

***

ANCHORAGE:

The hospital director escorted Alex and Christa through the hallways. "I'm not sure he's really all that coherent. He insists we're all going to die when some ship returns. Here we are."

When they entered the room, Mike Broden was sitting up in bed, staring through the window at the fir trees in the small park, and the director stopped next to Broden's bed. "You have some visitors, Mike."

Broden didn't acknowledge their presence and continued staring out the window, so Christa walked to the foot of the bed and studied his face. When they found him in the storeroom, she thought he was much older, but now it was apparent he was actually in his early thirties. "We need your help, Mike."

Broden slowly turned to look at Christa, a sad smile forming on his lips. "It's too bad someone as pretty as you has to die."

"See what I mean?" said the director.

Broden shot a menacing look at the man. "I'm not talking to you anymore!"

Alex had an idea and looked at the director. "Perhaps you'd better leave us alone."

"All right. You're getting farther with him than anyone else."

When the director left the room, Alex faced Broden again, who was staring at him suspiciously. He just needed a way to put Mike at ease.

Broden's gaze didn't waver as he looked into the stranger's eyes. "Are you a doctor, too?"

Alex smiled. "No, actually I'm a teacher at a College in Montana. My name's Alex Cave, and this is Christa Avery." Alex extended his hand.

Broden hesitated before accepting. "I'm not crazy. I know what I saw."

Christa moved around the foot of the bed until she was standing next to Broden. "Would you mind telling us about it?"

Broden chuckled. "Why should I? You'll think I'm crazy."

"Mister Broden. Mike. When you hear what I'm about to tell you, you'll think *I'm* crazy."

Broden said nothing, so Christa continued and told him about the oil tankers. When she finished, Broden looked out the window for a moment as he let out a deep sigh of relief. "That's the best news I've heard since I woke up. For a while there, I thought maybe I really was crazy." He looked at Christa and Alex. "Okay. I'll tell you what I saw."

"Start from the beginning," said Christa.

"I was in the bathroom," he said, and felt his face blush. "I could hear the rest of the guys in the kitchen talking and joking around, and then they started yelling. I thought maybe they were yelling at Roberts. He's always playing practical jokes on everyone, but they didn't stop yelling. I felt the toilet shake and heard Marvin scream to get out of the building. I thought it was an earthquake and hurried as fast as I could. When I got to the kitchen, everyone was gone, so I ran down the tunnel to get out of the building. I remember thinking about the light coming in through the windows in the doors, because it was too early for sunrise. I saw the guys standing outside, staring at the light, but it scared me, so I ducked into the storage room, and that's when the door opened and I saw it. Scared the shit out of me and I ducked behind some boxes!"

"What did you see?" she asked.

"The, ah." Broden looked down at the bed. When he looked up, his eyes were begging for understanding. "The spaceship." He saw Christa and Alex exchange looks. "You think I'm crazy, but I know what I saw. I didn't know for sure. I mean, not at first. Just that it was huge. Then they came out, and I knew what it was."

"Who came out?" Asked Christa.

Again, Broden's eyes pleaded for understanding. "The spacemen in white suits." This time, Christa and Alex restrained the urge to look at each other and let Broden continue. "They tossed the bodies of my friends into the storeroom, and that's when I realized, I mean, the way their eyes were open and all. I didn't want to look, but I couldn't stop. I've never seen dead people before, but I just knew it. I felt like a coward, but I didn't want them to kill me, so I stayed behind the boxes. They just kept staring at me, my friends, I mean. I couldn't stand to keep looking at them, so when I thought it was safe, I stacked a bunch of boxes up in front of them. Later, I don't really know how long it was, I felt the ground shake again, but I wasn't about to come out. The next thing I know, I'm here, in this hospital."

"Can you describe the spaceship for us?" Alex asked.

Broden looked baffled for a moment. "It was a gigantic chromed hockey puck. Must have been at least forty feet across and twenty-five feet high."

Broden saw Christa's skeptical smile. "You think I'm crazy, don't you?"

"No, Mister Broden," said Alex. "That would explain several mysteries."

Christa glanced at Alex, wondering if he really believed Broden's fantasy. She was about to ask Broden a question when she saw the change in his expression.

Broden's mood lightened as he stared at Alex. "Then I can leave the hospital?"

"If the doctor thinks you're physically fit, I don't see why not?"

Broden smiled. "Thank you, Mister Cave!"

Alex's expression turned serious. "One man from your station is still missing. Gary Darven. Do you have any idea what happened to him?"

Broden's brows bunched together in thought. "You know, come to think of it, he wasn't in the storeroom with the rest of the guys."

"What do you know about him?"

Broden shrugged. "Not much. Kind of a weird guy, though. He'd only been there for two weeks and didn't talk all that much. He did some strange things, too."

"Such as?"

"Well, I don't know how to explain it exactly. He just did things somewhat different and wasn't friendly, but mainly it was what he did the night before all this happened. I got off watch, and as I was walking past his room, I heard him talking on the other side of the door and stopped to listen. It sounded like he was praying, then I saw a bright blue light under the door. It's common courtesy not to invade someone's privacy, but I couldn't help myself."

Alex saw the regret in Broden's expression. "Then what happened?"

"I opened the door a crack and peeked into the room. Gary was kneeling in front of the desk, saying a prayer or something, and staring at what looked like a blue light bulb, but it wasn't connected to a lamp. I couldn't hear his words clearly, but I heard him repeat the word 'messiah' a few of times as he held up a small glass tube full of colored, sparkly stuff. He held it close to the blue light and I know it was just my imagination, but the sparkles looked like they were moving around in the tube. A moment later, the light got dimmer until it blinked out. I didn't want him to catch me, so I closed the door. Of course, I couldn't tell anyone. Then they would know I was spying and no one would trust me anymore, so I just went to my room and read for a while."

"Do you know where he came from?"

"Not really."

"Just one more thing, Mister Broden. Do you have any idea how this spaceship stole six million barrels of oil out of the pipeline?"

Broden looked bewildered by the question and slowly shook his head no. "I didn't know anything about it."

"Okay. You've been very helpful and I'll tell the director you're free to go. By the way. You shouldn't tell anyone else about the spaceship, if you know what I mean."

Broden chuckled. "Damn right, I won't. They'd put me away in a loony bin for sure. Wait. How am I going to get home?"

Christa reached into her purse and handed Broden a company business card. "Call them when you're ready to leave, and they'll arrange transportation for you to get home."

***

The director was standing near the nurses' station and approached Alex and Christa as they strolled down the hall. "Well? What do you think?"

"If he's physically ready to leave the hospital, release him."

"What? You can't be serious! He's been in a delusional state since he was admitted. I want to run a complete psychological evaluation, and that takes time. Our staff psychologist, Dr. Brandstrom, can't fit him in until tomorrow afternoon."

Christa handed the director one of her cards. "I'll see he gets the help he needs. Send the bill to the All Alaska Company."

Alex and Christa left the hospital, and during the taxi ride back to the airport, Christa looked over at Alex's calm expression. "Do you believe all what Broden told us?"

Alex hesitated while he mentally compared Broden's story with the events of the past week. "I think I do."

"What?"

"I don't think it was spacemen, but people wearing protective suits. I'm not sure about the spaceship. Perhaps he saw a reflection off the chrome of an airplane."

"What are you going to tell Bull and the people in Washington D.C? Surely you don't think they'll accept Broden's story."

"Nothing for the moment. At least, not until we have proof. Are you with me on this?"

"Okay. Where do we start?"

"I think the crystal you found could be very important, and I'd like you to take it to a more sophisticated lab for further testing. I'll arrange it at the College in Montana, and you can stay at my ranch while you're there, if you like."

"All right," she answered, and smiled at the thought of staying with Alex at his ranch and having a great opportunity to learn more about him. She hesitated to bring up another option, thinking he'll cancel his invitation to the ranch. "Since you work for the government, why not have them check it out?"

"I don't actually work for the government. I'm more of a consultant. That being said, I know how it works and it will take too long. The equipment at the college is top rate, so you'll be fine. How soon can you leave?"

"I can be ready for the first flight out in the morning."

"Good. I'll pick you up and give you a ride to the airport."

She suddenly realized he wasn't going with her. "What? Where will you be?"

"I'm going on a cruise on one of the tankers."

She suddenly felt a deep, sinking feeling in the pit of her stomach. She just knew if Alex left on one of those tankers, she would never see him again. "How about dinner?" she asked softly.

Alex was staring out the window, absorbed in thought, and turned toward Christa. "Sorry, what was that?"

"I said, how about a last dinner together?"

"You make it sound so final. I'll be joining you in Montana in a few days."

"You, of all people, should realize what will happen if you're on one of those tankers."

Alex saw the anguish in her eyes. "Listen, Christa. Now we know what can happen, so we'll be ready. I'm not suicidal."

Christa realized it was useless to argue, leaned back in the seat, and stared out the window. She felt Alex gently grab her hand and realized he must think she was pouting, and looked at him and tried to smile. "So, how about that dinner?"

"I'd like that."

***

VALDEZ:

That evening, Alex was waiting in the hotel restaurant when Christa strolled in, wearing a black satin cocktail dress, cut in a deep V at the neckline, with thin shoulder straps. She wore silver and diamond earrings and a matching choker necklace. He stood and slid her chair to the table, then smiled and moved his lips close to her ear. "You look ravishing."

Christa smiled at his boyish manner and obvious approval. After dinner, Alex walked her out to her car. "I'll see you in the morning."

"No wait! I mean, would you like to go to my place for a nightcap?"

A picture of Sevi's body on the stretcher flashed through his mind. *No! I'm already becoming too emotionally attached to her. I can't let it happen again.* "I don't think I should." He saw Christa's hurt expression. "I'm sorry."

Christa wondered if he didn't like her, then had another thought. *He must miss his wife.* She forced a smile. "Okay. I'll see you in the morning."

Alex walked her to the front door and helped her into her coat. When they stepped outside, he opened her car door and Christa climbed in. "Have a safe drive home."

Alex waited until she drove away, and then headed to his room. *I did the right thing. It has to be this way.*

***

The next morning, Alex carried her suitcase to the check-in counter at the airport, and the attendant informed her to board immediately. Christa impulsively threw her arms around Alex's neck and hugged him fiercely. "Be careful," she whispered in his ear.

Alex felt the moisture of her tears on his neck. When she released him, he wanted desperately to kiss her, but smiled instead. "I'll meet you in Montana. I promise. You'd better get on the plane, or they'll leave without you."

Christa tried to smile bravely as she wiped the tears from her cheeks. She walked toward the door, glancing over her shoulder once before stepping through. She saw Alex smiling confidently and felt he meant what he said, and then she got into the airplane.

Alex's smile faded as soon as the door closed behind her, for he had a premonition he might never see her again. He swore to himself he would, as he walked through the terminal.

Chapter 12

SEATTLE, WASHINGTON:

"Oh, dear God! I should never have left home!" Harold Woolly mumbled as he staggered along the street. He stumbled and fell, gashing his knee on the asphalt as his rubbery legs gave out beneath him.

When he arrived at the office this morning, he was the only one there and waited around until Cally called him, screaming in panic she heard gunshots and saw a group of young people breaking into houses up the street. He had left immediately and drove as far as he could on what little gas he had left in his car.

He had passed hundreds of abandoned vehicles on the freeway before his car sputtered and died. Then he had grabbed his briefcase and ran until his chest heaved and his muscles ached. That was an hour ago, and since then, he had been walking, occasionally seeing tall columns of black smoke in different parts of the suburbs.

He quickened his pace as he rounded the corner and saw his house half a block away. He heard gunshots and looked further up the street at a group of ten young men and women dragging an elderly man out the front door of a house. They tossed him onto the lawn, kicking him viciously, and Harold heard the man screaming for help and begging not to be killed. He felt sympathy for the man and wished he had the courage to help him.

A sense of foreboding suddenly filled his thoughts as he pictured Cally and his children lying on the lawn in front of his home. His heart felt as though it was about to explode, but he ran the rest of the way and beat on his front door. "Cally! It's me. Let me in!"

The door opened a few inches, and someone shoved a shotgun barrel in his face and it took a moment before he saw his son's face appear in the opening. "Open the door!"

"Dad?"

"Yes, it's me! Let me in!"

The rifle barrel withdrew through the gap, and Harold heard the familiar sound of the chain lock being unfastened. The door opened, and Harold rushed through as Mark slammed it shut behind him. When he turned, Mark bent down and threw his arms around him. Harold felt him shaking and tried to sound confident. "It's going to be okay." He felt his voice quivering. "Where's your mom? Where's Pamela? Is everyone okay?"

"Yeah. They're in the back room, but they're scared."

"Oh, Harold!" Cally hollered from the hall and rushed toward him. "Thank God you're home!" She threw her arms around his neck and hugged him tightly. "I've been so scared!"

They heard a gunshot and Harold felt her flinch. "It'll be all right," he told her, then looked at Mark. "How long has this been going on? Did you call the police?"

"Yeah, I heard the first shots early this morning, but the police said they were too busy and would come when they could. They still haven't come by. There isn't any food in the stores anymore, and everyone is robbing and killing each other for whatever they have."

Harold eased Cally away and looked into her tear-swollen eyes. "I'm sorry I left."

"No. I'm sorry I drove you away. It's my fault for being such a nag. You work so hard, and all I do is complain about everything."

"Shush. It's both our faults, okay? Do we have any food left?"

"Just some canned stuff."

Harold looked toward the hallway and saw Pamela standing with a baseball bat slung over her shoulder. She walked over, bent down, and gave him a kiss on the cheek.

"I'm glad you're home, Dad."

Harold looked up and saw the tears in her eyes, and then another gunshot echoed through the neighborhood. "Listen, those thugs are headed this way. I think it's best if we pack some clothes and food and leave the area."

"But this is our home!" Cally blurted. "Everything we own is here!"

"Cally, it doesn't matter anymore. We can't fight those people out there. We wouldn't stand a chance, and I couldn't stand it if something were to happen to any of you."

"I've got my guns," said Mark.

Harold studied the plastic shotgun in Mark's hand. "Those are just toys."

"Yeah, but they don't know that. I had one real gun, but I don't know what happened to it."

Cally was shocked and nearly screamed at her son. "What? You had a real gun? You could have hurt yourself!"

Harold tried to keep his voice calm. "Where did you get it?"

"From Brian Everex. He got it from his brother, and I traded some stuff for it. It was really neat looking. Sort of like what the Lone Ranger used."

The breath caught in Harold's throat as he remembered staring at the old man in the mirror. He regained his composure and opened his briefcase, and on top of his papers was the silver pistol. "Is this it?"

"Yeah! Where did you get it?"

"It's a long story. Do you have any bullets for it?"

"Yeah, they're in my bottom drawer. I knew better than to keep it loaded."

"Okay. Get those and pack some clothes while you're there. Not much, just two changes." Harold looked at his wife and daughter. "You two do the same. Try to pack light, because I don't know where we're going, or how long it will take. I just know we have to get out of here, and fast." He looked at Cally. "Is there any gas left in your van?"

"A little over half a tank. Once the rationing started, I walked whenever possible."

"Okay. Pack some clothes for me, Cally, and I'll stand guard until we're ready." He turned to Mark. "Better bring me the bullets for this gun first."

Ten minutes later, the minivan in the garage was loaded. "Okay, everyone," said Harold. "Those people are only a couple of houses away. Cally, I want you to drive. Pam will be in the car with you, and Mark and I will be out in front of the house. I want you to back out into the street and be ready to drive away from those people as soon as we get in, okay?"

Cally had a moment of panic. "Shouldn't you and Mark be in the car with us?"

"No. It would be better if those people see we're armed. Otherwise, they might shoot at the car. All right, is everybody ready? Let's go."

Harold and Mark went back into the house and waited. As soon as they heard the car on the garage start, they stepped out into the front yard with their guns clearly visible. The people up the street don't notice them until the garage door opened, and then they all stared at Harold and Mark. As the car backed out into the street, two of the boys ran toward it.

"They've got gas!" One boy yelled.

Harold had never been so frightened in his life. He took a deep breath and pointed the gun at the two boys, and could see the sight of the barrel shaking. The gun suddenly exploded and nearly tore his wrist off, and one of the boys flew backward from the shot and crumpled to the ground. The other boy staggered to a stop, and no one made another move, while Harold kept the gun pointed in their direction.

Cally pulled forward and stopped next to Harold and Mark. "Get in!"

Harold heard the door open and backed toward it. "Get in, son."

Mark did as instructed. "Come on, Dad!"

Harold kept the gun pointed at the crowd as he slid on to the seat. He left the door open, leaning out so he could watch the other people in case they tried to shoot at him and his family. "Okay, Cally. Drive away, nice and easy."

Harold watched the crowd looking smaller, and no one attempted to stop them. When Cally turned the corner, Harold leaned back inside the car and closed the door. He collapsed against the seat and sighed with relief, still holding the gun on his lap. "Oh, my goodness! I just killed that boy!"

Pamela looked back over her shoulder. "You didn't have any choice, Dad."

Harold looked at her, feeling like he had turned into some kind of savage beast. "I know, I know."

The Woollys drove east on Interstate 90 out of Seattle, and the road was crowded with abandoned vehicles, and occasionally, Harold and Mark had to shove cars out of the way so they could continue. They passed several people walking with their thumbs out for a lift and eyes imploring for sympathy.

Cally noticed a woman with two small children sitting on a suitcase beside the road. When the woman stood and shouted for help, Cally pulled over.

Harold sat up and looked at Cally's face in the rearview mirror. "What are you doing?"

"Look at them, Harold. Those poor children must be exhausted, and that woman is all alone."

"No, Cally."

"Oh, Harold, don't be so selfish. There's room enough to squeeze them in," Cally told him in her familiar, domineering tone as she slowed the car to stop.

"I said, NO!"

Cally glanced in the rearview mirror at Harold in the back seat and a chill ran through her body. She had never seen that look in Harold's eyes before, and sighed in frustration. As they got closer to the forlorn mother, something slammed into the side of the car. Startled, Cally swerved across the road, nearly slamming into the guardrail before regaining control.

Harold flinched and looked out the back window, and saw a man was running after them, heaving large rocks at their car.

Cally glanced at Harold's face in the mirror. "What was that?"

Harold was shaking, more from rage than fear. "Those were rocks! It was a trap, Cally. Probably that woman's husband was hiding nearby waiting to carjack us! We can't trust anyone. Understand. The world's gone crazy!"

Harold stared at Cally's reflection in the mirror, her eyes showing stunned understanding. Pamela turned in her seat to look at him, and he patted her soothingly on the shoulder, trying to hide his own fear of this new reality. "We'll be all right, honey. We just have to be careful."

Mark leaned forward in the back seat. "We have guns, so nobody will mess with us!"

Pamela scoffed at her brother. "We have one gun and that stupid toy. What if somebody has more guns? What do we do then, dummy?"

"Don't call me a dummy, you wart hog!"

"That's enough, both of you!" Harold snapped. "Listen, all we have is each other. We're a family and we have to work together or none of us will survive. Is that clear?"

Pamela turned and stared out the front window, and Mark did the same out the side window. Silence filled the car until Cally spoke a few minutes later.

"We're getting low on gas, Harold. We're down below an eighth of a tank."

They passed a sign advertising three major gas stations in North Bend a mile ahead, and Harold knew it was the last stop for gasoline until they made it over Snoqualmie Pass. "Take the next exit. Maybe they still have some gas left."

Cally continued up the grade, and as they came around a sweeping turn, they saw thick black smoke drifting across the highway, and a few moments later, they saw the source. Two cars were burning on the off ramp into North Bend, with half a dozen people standing off to the side, staring at the carnage.

"Stay on the Interstate, Cally. Get as far over to the left as you can. Keep the speed up or go faster."

The group of people stared at them as they passed, but no one tried to stop them. The highway continued to climb, and Cally kept glancing at the gas gauge. There were fewer abandoned vehicles along the road, and they didn't see any more people walking. The gas gauge was touching the red line when they reached the summit and the sign for Snoqualmie Ski Resort, and the exit looked clear.

"Harold? We're on empty."

"All right, take this exit. It will be better than being stranded on the highway."

Cally took the off ramp and followed the road to the ski lodge. A large sign announced it was closed for the summer, so she drove past it into the little community. Everything appeared abandoned, and from all the broken windows, it was obvious the buildings had been looted.

Cally looked at the rearview mirror. "What are we going to do now, Harold?"

"I'm not sure. Pull in here at the motel, and we'll think about it."

The parking lot for the motel was empty, except for a long fifth-wheel RV trailer attached to a one ton pickup truck parked at the far end. Cally parked at the opposite end and shut off the engine, then the four of them remain in the car, and no one spoke as they listened to the ticking of the engine as it cooled down.

Harold sighed in resignation. "It's getting late, and I think we should hold up here for the night."

"Do you think it is safe, Dad?" Pamela asked.

Harold shrugged. "Safe as anywhere, I guess. At least we'll have beds to sleep in. I wouldn't want us to have to sleep in the car on the highway." Harold grabbed the gun sitting on the seat next to him. "I'll look around first."

Mark grabbed his toy shotgun. "I'll go with you."

Harold smiled at his son. "No, you stay here and protect the women."

"Yeah, right!" Pamela said and stared out the window.

Harold opened the door and slowly climbed out to look around and listen, hearing only the wind and faint traces of music. He tucked the pistol into his belt, cupped his hands around his ears, and tried to locate the source. It seemed to come from the RV trailer, and as he stared at it, one of the curtains slid back and a man stared back at him for a moment before the curtain closed.

Harold wondered why the man didn't come out and then realized he must be as leery of strangers as he was. He walked to the front doors of the motel and the glass from one side lay scattered on the carpet inside, so he walked through and the reception desk looked unscathed. Even the little bell still sat on the counter, so he tapped it and heard the little ding. When no one came to the desk, he walked past it and stopped in the corridor, looking left and right, with only the setting sun streaming through the windows for light. Most of the doors were open, and the nearest one had been kicked in.

Harold's heart beat faster, and he grabbed the pistol from his belt as he walked down the left corridor, wondering if someone might still be lurking around. He stopped at each room and took a quick look inside, and except for a few unmade beds, all of them look as though they hadn't been stayed in for quite a while. He stopped at the glass exit door at the end of the hall and looked out at a cement walkway curving around the building back to the parking lot.

His nerves settled down a little as he walked in the opposite direction and saw the same thing in the rooms down the right corridor, and again, he looked out the exit window. The door suddenly flew open, and a huge rifle barrel was thrust in front of his eyes. Harold's heart leaped into his throat and he staggered backward, tripping and crashing to the floor. He stared up in stunned disbelief as a tall, slightly overweight man with gray hair stepped through the doorway and shoved the rifle barrel against his chest.

Chapter 13

AIRPORT. BOZEMAN, MONTANA:

After grabbing her suitcase from the small carrousel, Christa strolled out of the air terminal and found Alex's silver SUV in the parking lot. She stowed her suitcase in the back seat, got in, and followed the directions on the map Alex had drawn for her. On the drive to the ranch with the widow partially open, she enjoyed the aroma of pine filled the air and marveled at the beautiful scenery of huge green meadows surrounded by trees and the rugged mountains reaching up to a deep blue sky.

Alex had not described the ranch, but as she drove through the timber and meadows, she pictured Alex's home as a quaint log cabin with a rustic old barn near a meandering stream. She turned off the main road as directed, and was slightly disappointed when she drove into the circular driveway and saw a modern rambler style, with a barn made of steel instead of a wood.

She shut off the engine and stepped out of the car to look around, and at the end of the cement walkway was a deck on the back of the house facing a magnificent view of the valley and rugged mountains in the distance. She grinned when she saw a stream farther down the hill.

She turned to walk up the sidewalk to the house and froze in mid-stride when she saw a huge brown bear standing a few feet away. She took a step back and bumped against the car, fumbled behind her for the handle, and eased the door open. She felt a sense of relief when the bear just stared at her as she backed on to the driver's seat and closed the door. Even though it served no purpose, she pushed the lock button.

As she stared out the window, the bear slowly plodded toward the car, rose on its hind feet, and placed its massive paws on the door as it stared inside. Her heart pounded in her chest as she scooted across the seat, forcing herself against the opposite door as she stared at the huge head filling the window. She suddenly saw movement beyond the bear and heard a woman's voice.

"Barney, get down."

The bear's head turned away and dropped from view, and Christa watched a tall, attractive young woman with long brown hair approach the window. The woman tried the door handle, but it was still locked, so

Christa slid across the seat. She could see the bear standing a short distance away and rolled the window down a little.

The woman bent over to look at the stranger. "Who are you?"

"I'm a friend of Alex Cave. I thought this was his ranch, and I'm sorry if I disturbed you. I must have taken a wrong turn."

"No, this is Alex's place. He told me someone would be staying here, but he didn't say it would be a girl."

Christa thought she saw a hint of jealousy in the woman's eyes. "I'm sorry. I didn't expect anyone to be here. I'll be doing some work at the college."

The woman stared at Christa for a moment, like one cat sizing up another. "I'm a friend of Alex's, too. Come on in and I'll show you around."

Christa looked at the massive beast a short distance away. "What about the bear?"

The woman chuckled. "That's Alex's dog, Barney. Don't worry. He likes women."

Christa eased the door open and slowly climbed out. "Alex said he had a dog, but he's huge!"

"He sure is." The woman turned toward the dog. "Come here, Barney. Say hello."

Barney's tail wagged back and forth as he trotted up to Christa, sat, and lifted a big paw. Christa reached down, which wasn't very far, and shook it, feeling the massive callused pads on the bottom. She stroked Barney's head and smiled up at the woman. "He seems friendly."

"He's a big baby around women, but if you were a man, he wouldn't let you out of the car unless Alex told him it was okay."

Christa stood and extended her hand to the woman. "I'm Christa Avery."

The woman accepted. "I'm Judy Kerns. Grab your bag and come inside. I'll show you the guest room."

Christa retrieved her suitcase from the back seat and followed the woman up the sidewalk. She noticed Judy was much taller than she was, with a nice figure filling her blue corduroy shirt and blue jeans tucked into her well-worn cowboy boots. Christa guessed she was probably in her late twenties, and suddenly felt a little depressed. Alex hadn't mentioned he was living with another woman. *That must be the reason he didn't want to come into my apartment last night. Damn! And I just threw myself at him like some kind of what? Bitch? Slut? No. Just like a lonely woman attracted to a handsome man. No, it's his fault for not telling her about Judy.*

Judy led Christa through the living room and pointed out the bathroom in the hallway. As they passed an open door, Christa glanced inside the office and saw the walls were lined with books, and a computer sat on a large desk under the window.

At the end of the hall, Judy indicated the room on the right. "You can stay in there. Make yourself comfortable. I'll be in the living room."

Christa entered and set her suitcase on the bed of the sparsely furnished room, with a small dresser and two nightstands. She hung part of her clothes in the closet and put the rest in the drawers, and then on the way to the living room, she stopped to look in the other bedroom.

A king-size bed with an ornately carved headboard dominated the room, with a massive dresser and mirror against the opposite wall. The two nightstands matched the headboard, and she saw a door which probably led to another bathroom. She smelled slight traces of aftershave in the room, but no trace of perfume.

She began to grin, but suddenly stopped and turned to leave the room. When she entered the living room, Judy was sitting at a breakfast bar separating the large kitchen and joined her. "This place is newer than I imagined it would be when he said it was a ranch."

Judy studied Christa's body for a moment, noting the slim figure. "Would you like something to drink?"

"Yes, thank you. A beer, if you've got one."

Judy walked to the refrigerator and returned with two beers. She handed one to Christa, then opened her own and took a sip from the bottle.

Christa opened her bottle and looked around the kitchen. "Where do you keep the glasses?"

"Oh. Up there, in the last cupboard."

Christa received a cold feeling from Judy as she walked to the cupboard and brought back a glass, then thought about what to say as she poured the beer. "Listen, Judy. If it's going to be a problem, I can stay at a motel instead. I mean, Alex didn't tell me he was living with someone." Christa glanced up and saw a flash of bitterness in Judy's dark blue eyes.

Judy stared at the bottle she was turning in her hands. "I live a few miles away and take care of Barney and the ranch while Alex is gone." Judy looked up and gave Christa a warning look. "But we're really close, if you know what I mean."

So, he's not living with her. Christa felt relieved and restrained from laughing with joy, though she smiled. "Yes, I see."

When Judy saw Christa smile, the hair on the back of her neck stood up at the thought of this woman invading her territory. She had been trying to get a serious relationship going with Alex since he bought the ranch two years ago, and even though they dated and a few times, she couldn't get him to make a commitment. She accepted the fact that Alex was not the type of man to be possessed by any woman. Still, this attractive little gal might nudge her out of Alex's life, and she needed to know just how much competition she was up against. "So, are you and Alex, ah, close friends?"

Christa knew to play it cool with this woman and shook her head no. "I've only known him a little over a week. We're just working on the same project together." Christa noticed the tension between them ease up as Judy relaxed a little.

"That's good. I mean, that you're working on the same project. What is it, anyway?"

Christa did not want to say too much about what was happening to the crude oil. "We're working on a way to solve the oil problem on the west coast."

"Yeah, it's been on the news a lot lately. All those people rioting over gasoline and food. It's affecting us, too. It's getting harder to get some things at the stores."

"What about gasoline? Any shortage yet?"

"It's getting worse. Smaller stations have closed, but the bigger companies still have gas. You just have to wait in line longer." Judy glanced at the clock on the stove. "I have to get going before it gets dark. Help yourself to whatever you need."

"Thanks." Christa watched Judy chug down the rest of her beer. "How are you getting back? I didn't see your car."

"I'll walk. It's only a mile."

"Can I give you a ride?"

"No, thanks. I live just across the valley. It's about thirty miles by car, so I can walk it faster than you could drive me there. I'll stop by tomorrow and see if you need anything."

"Thanks."

Christa walked Judy to the door and stood on the porch, watching Barney wagging his tail as he followed Judy until she walked through a gate beside the barn and headed across the meadow. *So that's the type of woman Alex is interested in dating. The rough-edged cowgirl type. Then again, maybe not. Judy seemed to be the outspoken type, and if she and Alex were serious, she was sure Judy would have said so.*

Christa stared Barney, standing at the gate until Judy disappeared over a small rise, then he turned and headed across the driveway, wagging his tail as he walked up the sidewalk and sat at her feet. She petted his head for a few moments and then walked into the house.

She took her glass of beer into the living room and sat on the curved sectional sofa, picked up the remote control from the glass coffee table, and turned on the television. She flipped through the stations until she found a news broadcast, where the meteorologist was explaining his forecast for the next day. Sunny, with the temperature reaching sixty-five.

After a commercial, the picture showed a slender, serious looking man standing behind a podium with a presidential seal on the front. A newswoman's voice announced she was broadcasting live from the White House pressroom for a special announcement from the Director of National Transportation, Sam Barnsworth.

"Ladies and gentleman," Barnsworth began. "I've been asked by the President to announce the implementation of a temporary nationwide rationing of petroleum products."

The pressroom resounded with questions shouted at Barnsworth, who patiently waited for everyone to quiet down. Several long moments passed before the room was quiet again, and he continued. "The rationing process will begin immediately. Every citizen will be mailed a ration card, based on last year's income tax records. The amounts of gasoline and oil each person will be entitled to will be based on employment, types of business, and priority needs. We feel this will be the most honest and fair way to decide how the rationing should be distributed."

Again, questions were shouted at Barnsworth, who waved his hands to quiet them down. "Ladies and gentleman, please! I'll answer your questions one at a time!" As the voices quieted down, Barnsworth pointed to a man in the audience, who stood to ask a question.

"Mister Barnsworth, are you saying big business will be allotted more gasoline than the private citizen?"

"Not necessarily. Some key industries will be allotted more if their products are an integral part of the national welfare, such as hospitals, food manufacturers, and portions of the trucking industry." Barnsworth pointed to a woman reporter.

"What about the military? Will the Government be rationed along with its citizens?"

"To a certain extent, yes. However, we still need to ensure national security."

"What about the airline industry?" The woman continued.

"We've ordered them to cut back on the number of flights to ensure the planes carry a full complement of passengers." Barnsworth pointed to a man in the back row.

"How are people supposed to get to work? Does the President realize how many businesses will go bankrupt?"

"Like I said, this is only temporary. We will give financial aid to companies specializing in mass transit. We know this will be a burden for a while, but we're confident the citizens of the United States will pull together to curtail the waste of petroleum products." Barnsworth indicated another man standing to the right side.

"Mister Barnsworth, you're telling us what we have to do, but you're not telling us why this is happening."

"I'm not at liberty to give you specific details, but let me say we are not the only country forced to implement a rationing system. Canada is following our lead, as will other countries around the world."

"You can't expect people to accept this rationing without telling them why!"

Barnsworth talked quietly with a man standing next to him and then faced the audience. "Okay. I'll tell you why. For years we've squandered our crude oil, and now it's time to face the consequences. To put it bluntly, for the time being, we're running out of oil."

Again, the room erupted with questions, but Barnsworth didn't reply and walked away from the podium as the newswoman's voice replaced the sound of the pressroom. "We don't have all the details yet," she explained, "but we will fill you in once we've read the press release they are handing out right now."

Christa turned off the television and stared at nothing in particular, lost in thought. If Broden was right, this rationing could just be the beginning of a serious situation, which would only get worse.

She slowly stood and walked to the bathroom, took a shower, and crawled into bed. By the light on the nightstand, she stared at the crystal she found in the tanker, now enclosed in a small, clear plastic box. "What have you got to do with all this?" she asked, as if it was alive and could answer. She sighed, set it on the nightstand, and turned off the light.

Chapter 14

SNOQUALMIE, WASHINGTON:

Harold stared up at the man holding the shotgun against his chest, both looking gigantic. He had never been so scared in his life.

The man studied the intruder, thinking the little fella looked like he would piss his pants if he said boo. "Well now. If you lay that pistol off to the side real gentle like, I'll move this scatter gun off your chest."

Harold extended his arm and let the pistol slip from his hand. "I, ah. I don't want any trouble, mister."

"Neither do I, but I'm tired of people stealing from my motel."

"Oh, no, no, no! I wasn't trying to steal anything. We're just looking for someplace to spend the night. Honest, Mister. I mean, this *is* a motel."

The man stared at Harold for a moment and then grinned. "Yeah, I guess you're right. Might as well use it." The man switched the shotgun to his left hand and brought it up, pointing over his shoulder, while reaching down with his right hand. "The name's Jerry Monroe."

Harold reached up and Monroe hauled him on to his feet. "I'm Harold Woolly. My wife and kids are out in the car."

"I noticed. No sense letting them worry about what happened to you."

Monroe indicated the corridor, and Harold looked down at his pistol. "I shouldn't leave that laying there."

"Sure. Do you even know how to use it?"

Harold thought about the boy he had shot and felt a deep sense of remorse. "Yeah, I'm afraid so."

Monroe noticed the sadness in Harold's eyes. He knew people were having serious problems now that the old ways had changed, so he didn't ask Harold for an explanation as he watched him pick up the pistol and shove it under his belt.

Harold turned and led Monroe down the corridor and out the front door, then saw the fear on Cally's face when she saw the big man with the shotgun. "Everything's okay," he hollered as they approached the car, but his wife and kids did not get out when he waved to them. "It's all right, everyone. Come out and say hello to our host, Mister Monroe. This is his motel, and he said we can stay here tonight."

Mark climbed out first and walked up to Monroe, eyeing the shotgun. "Is that a Remington twelve gauge?"

"That's right. You seem to know your guns."

"I collect them. I have twenty-eight handguns and rifles."

Monroe looked at Harold for confirmation. "Twenty-eight?"

"Plastic replicas. Except for this one." He touched the one in his belt. "He shouldn't have had it in the first place, but I guess it saved our lives once already. This is my son, Mark."

Harold turned when he heard the car doors opening and watched the girls haltingly climb out of the car. "This is my daughter, Pamela, and my wife, Cally."

Cally stared at the shotgun. "Hello, Mister Monroe,"

"Nice to meet you. You'll have to pardon the weapon, ma'am, but as you can see, I've had some problems here."

"Yes, I see that. We're all pretty tired, Mister Monroe. If you don't mind, we'd like to move into one of your rooms and try to relax. It's been a terrible day."

Monroe studied his new guests. "You look hungry. Have you eaten anything today?"

Pamela leaned back against the car. "Not since breakfast."

"And I'm starved," Mark added.

"We have some canned food in the car," Harold told him. "I'm sure we have a can opener someplace."

Monroe looked at each of them and his general feeling was they were probably decent folks thrown into a world gone mad. "You're welcome to sit in my trailer and use the stove. It beats eating it cold."

The Woollys traded looks. After what had happened earlier, it seemed strange for someone to be hospitable, but Harold knew his family would appreciate a hot meal. "That's very kind of you. We accept."

"Put your things in a room or two and come on over when you're ready." Monroe suddenly chuckled. "I guess there's no need to fill out a registration card."

Harold smiled at the irony. "Thanks again."

Harold insisted they share one room with two beds, much to the disgust of his children, who argued they could not possibly sleep together. He grabbed enough canned food for Monroe to join them, and then the group strolled to the trailer. Monroe hollered the door was open before Harold knocked, and his family followed him in.

As he stepped through the doorway, Harold looked around. To the right was a small hallway with doors on both sides and steps leading up to a large bed. To the left was a dining and kitchen area, and at the far end was a small living room with a sofa, coffee table, and a swivel chair. An entertainment center with television, DVD player, and a stereo was mounted on the wall across from the sofa.

Monroe was sitting in the swivel chair, with a drink in one hand and a remote control in the other. "If you'd like a drink, the liquor's above the sink. Make yourselves at home."

"Thank you, Mister Monroe," said Cally, "but we don't drink."

"I'll have one," Harold told him, receiving a shocked expression from Cally, and shrugged. "After the day I've had, I could use one."

Cally started to argue, but Monroe interrupted.

"It's been one hell of a week, hasn't it?"

Cally stared at Harold for a moment before she turned to make him a drink. Harold was changing, she realized, and she wasn't sure if she liked it. She fixed his drink, glaring at him as she set it on the kitchen table.

Monroe noticed Harold hesitate to grab the drink. "Come and sit down for a spell, and I'll fill you in on the news I just saw on TV."

"I'll join you in a minute," said Cally. "I want to get dinner started. We brought enough for you, too, Mister. Monroe."

"Thank you. And call me Jerry."

Harold grabbed the drink and led the rest of his family into the living room, and then he sat on the sofa. His children sat on the floor, staring at the snowy picture on the television of a news announcer sitting behind a desk.

Monroe looked at Harold. "The reception's not that great, but it's the only station I can get. Things aren't getting any better, and the military's trying to get control of things, but it looks like it'll be a waste of time. People are desperate and doing desperate things, even shooting people who are just trying to help them. I don't know what started this mess, but I don't think it's going to end soon."

Cally dumped the cans of stew into a pot and turned on the burner, then looked into the living room. "What are we supposed to do?"

Monroe chuckled. "That's a good question. I think I'll head for some part of the country that's more open. Someplace warm, like Arizona or New Mexico. Of course, everybody else is probably thinking the same thing. It might be hard to find enough fuel to get there, though." He studied Harold for a moment. "What about you?"

"I'm not sure. We're out of gas, so I guess we'll have to stay here for a while."

"There's no food left, and it gets cold up here at night. When the power goes out, which it will, you won't make it."

Mark turned to Monroe. "We should head to Idaho and stay with the Army of Survival. I'm sure they have food. The brochure says they've planned for something like this."

Harold saw Monroe looking at him for an explanation. "It's some kind of survivalist group. Like a private army, I guess. I don't know much about it."

Monroe waited while Mark stood and searched through his pockets to find the brochure for the AOS and hand it to him. "Hmm, I'm retired Air Force. Captain, to be exact. I've never heard of this outfit. Sounds like they have their act together, though." He looked at Mark. "Where did you get this, son?"

"My best friend's brother sent it to me. He was headed there after he got out of the Marines."

"It says their mailing address is Osborn, Idaho."

Monroe reached under the coffee table for a road atlas and then studied the map of Idaho and Washington for a few moments. "About three hundred miles, give or take. I should be able to make it on what fuel I have left. That's why it's only a single cab truck. I needed the room for the big silver tank in the back. It holds two hundred gallons, and I always keep it full, because it cost so much to fill up if I ever let it go empty."

Mark felt his heart rate increase. "Are you going to the AOS?"

"I might."

"Can I go with you? I know John Everex, and I know he'll let us stay there. Please, Mister Monroe. I even know the way, sort of."

"That's enough, Mark!" Harold interrupted. "I don't think Mister Monroe wants a boy tagging along. We're a family, and we'll stick together."

Monroe thought about it for a moment. "Oh, I don't know. Actually, I was thinking all of you might like to go with me. There's enough room for all of us in this trailer if one of the kids doesn't mind sleeping on an air mattress."

Cally slid the pot off the stove and moved closer to Harold. "I don't like this idea at all! We have no way of telling what those people are going to be like. You've never been in the military, Harold. From what I know, military people are trained killers! No. I absolutely refuse to go to this army!"

When Cally stomped back into the kitchen, Monroe looked at Harold. "It's up to you, but just consider the alternatives. It will not be pleasant out there on the road, and you'll never make it staying here. You should think strongly about it."

Pamela looked across the coffee table at Monroe. "I think we should go with you."

Cally could not believe her daughter wanted to go with Monroe. "You stay out of this, Pamela! We're not going, and that's final!" She walked into the living room and sat on the sofa, but kept her distance from Harold.

Pamela looked up at her father. "Don't Mark and I have a say in this, Dad? It's our lives, too."

Harold thought about it for a moment. "You're right. Under the circumstances, I accept your offer, Jerry. Thanks."

Cally's face flushed with rage and she leapt up and stormed into the kitchen, sitting at the table with her back to the living room. *Now I definitely don't like the way Harold is changing. Well, if he thinks he can start telling me what to do, he's in for a rude awakening. I'm not going to any army camp!*

Harold watched Cally leave and realized he didn't really care about her being upset. He had decided, and he was going to stick with it. He was suddenly overwhelmed with a sense of pride and smiled. He had never felt so in control before, and he liked it. He finally felt like a real man. A feeling he had never felt in his whole, miserable life. His smile grew wider the more he thought about it. *I, Harold Woolly, am finally in control of my destiny.* He continued smiling as he looked at Monroe. "When do we leave?"

"Tomorrow morning is as good a time as any."

"Yes!" Mark yelled.

Pamela looked at her father and smiled. She suddenly felt respect for him. A feeling she thought she would never have.

Harold saw the look in his daughter's eyes and his heart soared even higher. He would have to deal with Cally next, but he knew he could handle her and would never let her dominate him again.

Chapter 15

PACIFIC OCEAN. THE DEFIANCE:
The ship rolled incessantly in the storm, making walking extremely difficult as Alex moved through the passageway and up the stairs to the bridge. When he stepped through the doorway, he steadied himself against the bulkhead. He looked at Bull and the helmsman, both wearing the life jackets, as he tightened the straps on his inflatable life vest. He pushed away from the bulkhead and moved over to join them, and with one hand on the control panel, he bent his knees to the rhythm of the pitching. "I'd rather be on a sailboat."

Alex looked through the starboard window at the lights of the other tanker. A Shell Oil Company ship called *Mercer*, then turned to Bull. "How long before we enter the Strait of Juan de Fuca?"

"Another day and a half."

"Have you contacted the submarine?"

"Yeah, I talked to the commander of the *Tannen* just before the storm hit. They're going to stay down for a while, but will be right behind us and the *Mercer*. Said they'd make radio contact again when the storm eased up."

When Alex told him he wanted to be on the tanker when it headed to the refineries in Washington, Bull decided to accompany him. He liked Alex immensely and thought he was intelligent, but also found Alex gutsy for wanting to be on this tanker when no one knew exactly what had killed the previous crew.

"*Defiance*, this is *Mercer*. Come in, over."

Bull grabbed the microphone. "*Mercer*, this is the *Defiance*. Go ahead."

"Something's happening in the holds. It's not a fire, but there's a bright blue light coming out of the hatch. Can you see it?"

Bull and Alex stared out the starboard window, watching the blue light on the *Mercer* increase in intensity as it rose above the deck.

Alex spun toward Bull in sudden fear. "That's what I saw happen to this ship in Puget Sound. Tell them to abandon ship immediately!"

Bull saw the fear in Alex's eyes and keyed the microphone. "*Mercer*, this is *Defiance*. Abandon ship right now!"

"*Defiance*, come in. It's too bright. I can't breathe!"

Bull saw the outline of the *Mercer* as the blue light continued to grow in intensity. "*Mercer*, you're breaking up. Say again. What is it?"

A burst of static erupted from the radio speaker for a moment, then ceased. Alex steadied himself as he looked through the window at the *Mercer*, then her deck suddenly erupted in a geyser of sparkling colors, which reached a height of two hundred feet and vanish.

Bull stared at the dark silhouette of the *Mercer* riding high in the water. "Oh, crap!"

"*Defiance*, this is the *USS Tannen*. Come in, over."

Bull regained his composure and keyed the microphone. "*Tannen*, this is *Defiance*. Go ahead."

"What the hell's happening up there? We came up to look around and saw a rainbow."

Alex got Bull's attention. "Ask them if they have anything on their sonar."

Bull keyed the microphone. "Are you detecting any other traffic in this area?"

"Negative, *Defiance*, not a blip or ping."

The helmsman grabbed Alex's arm. "Down there on the deck! Someone is opening a hatch!"

Alex and Bull turned to the forward window and watched the shadowy figure drop something into the hold, and as he turned, another figure ran across the deck and tackled him. Bright blue light suddenly glowed from the open hatch, and they saw the two figures struggling on deck.

Alex grabbed the helmsman's shoulders to get his attention. "Shut down the engines and sound the abandon ship alarm!" He let go and turned to Bull. "Tell the *Tannen* we're abandoning ship before we lose radio contact."

A loud Claxton sounded throughout the ship as the helmsman slammed his palm on the alarm button. Bull informed the sub of their situation and tried to describe what he was seeing while Alex stared through the window at the two men on deck, and then the helmsman ran past him and out the door. The blue light grew in intensity, escaping from the hatch like a searchlight, while the two figures on deck froze in mid-motion, locked in combat, and then they burst into blue light and disappear.

Alex waited until Bull dropped the microphone and then staggered across the rolling deck toward the door. He lost his balance and crashed against the bulkhead, and Bull grabbed his arm and helped him stand.

"We're out of time, Alex! We'll have to jump from up here."

"Okay."

Both men staggered outside and past the stairs to another door leading to the lookout station on the starboard side of the ship and rushed to the railing to look down. The light from the open hatch illuminated the choppy water below, and they stared at the two life rafts holding eleven men drifting past, looking tiny from that height. They saw the helmsman leap over the deck railing and swim toward the rafts.

Bull grabbed the railing to steady himself, then pulled Alex close. "Wait until the ship rolls to this side and then jump. It'll put us closer to the water."

The ship's forward momentum left the two life rafts well past the stern, and both men looked at each other with a sense of foreboding. They felt themselves dropping with the roll of the ship, and with a last nod from Bull, both men leapt over the railing into the freezing water.

Alex felt as though he was falling forever and struggled to keep his feet pointed straight down. The ice-cold water suddenly closed over his head, but he kept going deeper and deeper.

Bull flailed his arms to keep himself upright, but knew it was no use as the water rush toward him. He smacked the surface and his side erupted in searing pain as the air was driven from his lungs. Bright dots of light swirled on the inside of his eyelids, and he could not tell which way is up, then his head suddenly broke through the surface, and he desperately tried to fill his lungs with air. His first gasp caused a sharp sting on his side, and the second breath is easier, but again, he felt the sting and knew something was broken. He rose on a swell and looked around for Alex, whose head suddenly broke the surface a few feet away.

Alex sucked the cold, damp air into his lungs with a great sense of relief, then looked around and saw Bull a few feet away. "Are you okay?"

"Not really."

Alex and Bull turned and saw a large orange raft, with one man reaching over the front and two more paddling vigorously. The raft reached Bull first, and he accepted the hand, but when he tried to pull himself over the side, it felt like he was being stabbed with a red-hot poker. He yelled in agony and fell back into the water.

Alex heard Bull scream and swam up next to him. "What's wrong?"

"I think I broke some ribs."

Alex looked up at the man in the raft. "Get some help!"

A moment later, the two paddlers were leaning over the side. The three men grabbed Bull's arms, and with Alex pushing as best he could from below, rolled Bull into the raft. Two men helped him to the center, while the third man helped Alex over the side into the boat.

"Get us away from the ship!" Alex ordered and grabbed a fourth paddle. Together, they put some distance between themselves and the *Defiance,* while Bull lay stretched out in the middle of the floor.

The sound of the screaming claxon on the *Defiance* suddenly ceased, and Bull struggled to a sitting position, and then suddenly pointed behind them. "Look!"

Everyone stopped paddling and turned around, watching a sparkling rainbow of colors erupting out of the cargo hold. In numbed fascination, everyone watched the rainbow rise two hundred feet into the air and vanish, leaving the *Defiance* a dark silhouette blocking the horizon.

Alex had a gut feeling something else wasn't right and looked up. High above, just under the cloud cover, was a bright crescent moon.

Alex knelt closer to Bull and spoke into his ear. "There's no way the submarine can take all of us onboard, so I think we should row over to the *Defiance*. I learned she doesn't need a computer to operate. Do you think you can climb the ladder?"

"Do you think it's safe?"

"I think so. Whatever happened is over now."

"I can make it."

When the two rafts met up, Alex told everyone they should return to the *Defiance*. Two men objected out of fear, but Alex convinced them he had seen this before and the light would not return. As they battled to row against the rough seas, they were constantly battered by wind-driven rain and seawater. One man in each raft bailed out the water continuously, and to everyone, it seemed like they had paddled for hours before reaching the *Defiance*.

The ship had swung around into the wind, making it easier to grab the rungs near the stern. Still somewhat afraid, the other men insisted Alex go up first, but now empty, the *Defiance* rode high in the water, making the climb much longer. Weary from paddling, Alex found the climb exhausting and wondered how Bull would manage. Once on deck, he spotted a life ring and rope and lowered it over the side.

"Two of you come up and give me a hand," Alex shouted through cupped hands toward the rafts, and waited. A short time later, two men step on deck and Alex gave them a few moments to regain their strength, and then waved his arms down at the raft as a signal to send Bull up.

Bull allowed the rope to be tied under his arms, and then grunted in pain as he stood and grabbed the ladder and began his assent. Each time he reached up for the next rung, he felt a sharp pain in his side, but forced himself to ignore it and kept climbing. As he neared the top of the ladder, he could feel the rope getting tighter and knew he was losing his strength, putting more demand on his helpers. By the time he reached the top, it was all he could do to raise his arm for the last rung.

Several hands grabbed Bull's wrists, dragging him onto the deck. He was more exhausted than he had ever been in his life, and each deep breath sent sharp pains through his chest. He rolled onto his back and stared up at the dark clouds, and they gradually grew darker as the pain in his side seemed to vanish, and he thankfully drifted into the deep black void of unconsciousness.

***

PORT ANGELES, WASHINGTON:
The darkness faded, replaced by a bright white light as Bull opened his eyes, squinting at the face above him. "Hey, Alex."

"How are you feeling, pal?"

Bull saw the concerned look on Alex's face. "Like shit," Bull answered, turning his head to look around, and saw the metal track and white curtain surrounding him. "What happened? Where am I?"

"You passed out, and we took you down to the sleeping quarters. Your men pumped seawater into the holds for ballast and brought the ship into Port Angeles, and I called an ambulance and rode with you to this hospital. You have three broken ribs, and you're damn lucky none of them punctured a lung."

"I guess so. What happened to the *Mercer*?"

Alex shook his head solemnly and looked dismal. "She capsized in the storm. The Navy searched for survivors but didn't find anyone." Alex saw the sorrow in Bull's eyes. "I'm sorry, Bull. There was nothing we could do."

"I suppose you're right, but why is this happening?"

"I wish I knew. Listen, you'll have to stay here for a few days. I'm flying to Washington to brief the President. Things are getting worse around the world, too. A super tanker ran aground in India after leaving Kuwait, and the circumstances are almost identical to our tankers. It was empty before it ran aground, and the crew is missing. Now OPEC is threatening to stop shipping oil from their countries until we find out what's happening."

"Thanks for staying with me until now."

Alex got up. "No problem. I'll see you when I get back."

Chapter 16

SNOQUALMIE, WASHINGTON:
Cally had refused to sleep in the same bed with Harold last night, and she and Pamela went to another room, but during the night, Harold had felt her crawl under the covers next to him. In the morning, she continued to argue she wasn't going to any army camp, and he could leave without her, trying to force him to change his mind, but he decided to leave for the AOS camp and helped his children load their belongings into the trailer.

He felt more self-confident about his new ability to decide for his family and his new sense of individuality. Despite her refusal to go with them, he put Cally's bags inside, too. He waited outside, and when Monroe started his truck, Cally walked from the motel and climbed into the trailer with Pamela and Mark while he climbed into the truck with Monroe.

They made good time along Interstate 90, but when they decided to stop at a rest area, discovered it was crowded with hitchhikers, so they drove through without stopping, all of them painfully aware of the sudden madness forcing people to do whatever was needed to survive.

The interstate bypassed most of the small towns along the way until they reached the outskirts of Spokane, Washington, where the police stopped them at a roadblock. The soldiers from the Air Force base and the National Guard had joined forces with the police to maintain law and order in the city, and no outsiders were allowed in unless they surrendered all their weapons and brought enough food to last them for three weeks, which would be turned over to the community supply to be rationed out.

Monroe explained they were just passing through and refused to surrender their weapons, so they were curtly denied passage and forced to backtrack thirty miles to take narrow winding back roads around the city. They drove across the border, merging with Interstate 90 again in Coeur D'Alene, Idaho.

Back on the interstate, they proceed without further incident and finally made it to the little town of Osborn. It appeared deserted, with familiar signs of looters. Monroe parked on the main street and let Mark out of the trailer to ride in the truck with him and Harold.

Mark tried to remember what John Everex had told him about finding the AOS camp. "He said the road doesn't have a street name, just a number, but I can't remember what it is."

Monroe continued through town, watching the signs on the side streets until they stumble on Route 26 north. "Is this it, Mark?"

Mark shifted uncomfortably in the seat and looked left at the two-lane road of Route 26, which went up the hill. He looked to the right and saw a row of stores with broken windows, but no street. "I, ah. I'm not positive, but the number twenty-six sounds familiar."

Monroe turned to the left, and Mark grew more excited by the moment. His dream of joining an army was about to come true, and he fidgeted between the men.

Fifteen miles farther on, they stopped at a barricade across the road, where four soldiers in olive green uniforms leapt out of a small building and quickly surrounded the truck and trailer. Monroe's hands involuntarily tightened on the steering wheel as the serious-looking soldiers pointed their rifles at the windshield.

***

Cally and Pamela stared out the front window of the trailer at the soldiers, unsure of what would happen next. Cally was uncomfortable with the guns Harold and Monroe carried, and the sight of more guns caused her stomach to tighten in fear.

"I don't like this at all!" she whispered to Pamela. "We don't know what type of people they are. Maybe they're Neo-Nazis or something."

Pamela watched a fifth soldier step out of the guard shack and approach the truck window. "I think it's exciting, Mom! We'll have our own army to protect us, and the one coming toward us looks so handsome in his uniform."

Cally stared at her daughter in surprise. This was the first time she had seen Pamela show an interest in the male species. In another time and place, she would have been glad, but now it didn't ease her tension.

***

Monroe rolled down his window as the soldier stopped beside him and noticed the AOS patch on his sleeve. "It looks like we came to the right place."

The look in the soldier's eyes was one of impatience as he stared back. "You'll have to turn around and go back the way you came."

Monroe glanced at Mark before turning back to the soldier. "We were told we could join your army."

"Not anymore. We have plenty of people. Too many, if you ask me, so just turn around and leave."

Mark leaned closer to the window. "My name's Mark Woolly and I was invited." Mark handed the soldier the brochure he received in the mail.

The soldier glanced at it, smirked, and tossed it to the ground. "I've seen hundreds of these things in the past few weeks. They don't mean shit anymore. Just do what I tell you!"

Mark was devastated. "I know one of your soldiers, and he sent me this letter."

Harold put his hand on Mark's shoulder. "Don't argue with him, son. We're sorry, Jerry."

Monroe smiled politely. "We had to try."

Mark watched the soldier walk away, but he wanted to join this army with all his heart and soul and wasn't about to give up this easily. When Monroe shifted into reverse and backed the trailer away from the barricade, he leaned out the window in front of Monroe's face. "His name is John Everex, and if you call him, he'll tell you it is okay!"

Monroe stepped on the brake and eased Mark out of his face onto the seat. "I don't want any trouble, kid."

The soldier froze in mid-stride and spun back toward the pickup. "Hold it!" he hollered, and ran up to the window. "Did I hear you right? Did you say you were invited by Major Everex?"

This time Mark remained in the center and just looked past Monroe. "Yeah. He sent me the brochure personally."

The soldier suddenly looked nervous and licked his lips. "I, ah. You should have said that in the first place. Wait here a minute while I call this in. What's your name again?"

"Mark Woolly."

The soldier turned and jogged back into the shack. A few moments later, he stepped out and waved to the soldiers to remove the barricade before running back to the truck, grabbing the brochure on his way. He wiped it off on his pants and handed it to Monroe. "Look, I'm sorry about this, but I had my orders, and you didn't tell me you know Major Everex."

"It's all right, son. It was just a misunderstanding."

The soldier grinned. "You go right on through for another six miles and you'll come to the camp. Someone will be there to meet you."

Monroe shifted into drive and passed through the open barricade. The road continued through the forest for six miles and made a sharp left turn, and then the forest opened into a wide clearing with several buildings around the perimeter. Another soldier stood in the road, so Monroe stopped and the man walked up to his window.

The soldier ignored Monroe and looked at Mark. "Hello, Mister Woolly. I'm Luke Ardle, the senior camp instructor. Come with me, please. Major Everex would like to see you." He looked at Monroe. "There's a road just up ahead on the right. Take it and you'll see Tent City. Drive past the camping tents and set your rig up under the trees with the others, but don't wander off. Someone will be there in a little while to explain how things operate around here."

Harold opened his door and let Mark crawl out, feeling nervous about the whole situation. Apparently, Mark didn't, since he was grinning from ear to ear. "See you later, son."

Mark just waved and walked around to the soldier, staring at the man's uniform with adoration. It was neatly creased, and the black belt and holster were impressive, and he wondered how long it would take before he had a uniform.

***

Cally watched Mark climb out and walk to the soldier. Not knowing what was going on was bad enough, but when the truck began to move without Mark, she panicked and rushed to the door, throwing it open and nearly falling through. She held onto the doorknob to regain her balance while she leaned out of the opening. "Mark!" she yelled, but didn't hear a reply. She looked down at the road slowly moving past and was about to jump out when Pamela grabbed her around the waist and pulled her back into the trailer. Rage coursed through Cally, and she spun on her daughter. "What are you doing?" she snarled. "They've got Mark!"

"Calm down, Mom! They don't *have* him. He came here to join them. He's going to come back later, so try to calm down."

"You don't know that for sure. Maybe he'll be tortured for information."

"Just think a moment, Mom. Mark was invited, so he's just going to set things up for us. It's just that we have to park someplace first, that's all."

Cally realized Pamela was probably right, but her sense of fear remained. She was upset with the whole situation, but sat in a chair, nervously wringing her hands in her lap while she awaited the outcome.

***

Monroe turned onto the side road and saw several massive tents, four log barracks, and a large area in the center with tables and benches for sitting around and eating. Just past the tents were two large bonfires, with two dozen men, women, and children standing or sitting around them, all in civilian clothes. As he drove past, he saw dozens of individual tents in a wide variety of styles and sizes. More civilians were mulling around the tents or sitting beside the road, watching him drive past. No one smiled or waved, and the looks he received were more suspicious than curious.

Past the tents were another one hundred feet of forest before the area opened up and he saw six motorhomes and nine trailers parked in areas cleared out between rows of trees. Some had people sitting out front in chairs, most of whom looked up suspiciously as he passed, but Monroe waved and received a couple of nods in return. The last RV in line is a beautiful Road Master forty footer, complete with a satellite dish on the roof, but there was nobody outside.

There wasn't much room at the end of the clearing, only enough for four more trailers or RVs, so Monroe stopped and climbed out to assess where he wanted to park. Harold also climbed out and walked around to Monroe, and then Cally and Pamela joined them.

"I don't like this at all!" Cally moaned.

Monroe decided to try to calm her fears. "I've been taking this trailer to different RV camps all over North America, and it's always this way when you first arrive. People got to get to know you first, that's all."

The door on the Road Master suddenly opened, and the man who stepped out instantly caught their attention. It wasn't so much his immense belly and bald head, but the bright florescent green pantsuit he was wearing. He waved, smiled, and waddled over to them.

"Welcome!" he beamed, and extended his hand. "My name's Chuck Berry. No relation to the guitar player, unless my great granddaddy messed around. HA, HA, HA, HA, HA!"

Pamela giggled and thought the man's loud laugh was as funny as his clothes. She kept grinning as Monroe accepted his hand and introduced everyone, and then it was her turn. "I like you, mister Berry."

"HA, HA, HA, HA, HA. I like you, too, Pamela, so you can call me Chuck." He studied the trailer. "Well, you're welcome to park next to us. It's pretty level, and the Colonel said everyone should stay in line."

Monroe and the Woollys were vastly relieved by Berry's open hospitality. Monroe knew his friends were in good hands, so he climbed into his truck and began maneuvering the trailer into place.

"So, where are you folks from?" Berry asked, keeping up the friendly chatter.

"Just outside Seattle, Washington," Harold answered.

"We're from the Bay Area. Down near San Francisco. We were visiting my daughter in Utah when all this happened."

Cally noticed the sad look in Berry's eyes. "This whole army thing scares me."

Berry shoved his hands into his front pockets. "Just got to take everything in stride, I always say."

Harold indicated the tents at the opposite end. "Nobody seems to be happy here. Except you, I mean."

Berry turned and looked for a moment. "Well, I can't really blame them. Most of them walked here with just what they could carry. They're a little envious, that's all. No, I don't blame them one bit, having to sleep on the ground and all." He smiled. "Shucks! It would kill a fat man like me. HA, HA, HA, HA, HA!"

This time, all the Woollys smiled, and Harold turned to see how Monroe was doing. He admired the way Monroe confidently steered the fifth-wheeled trailer between the massive tree trunks.

Monroe got the trailer in place, unhooked the truck, and spent a few more minutes getting it leveled and supported on jack stands. "That's it," he said as he approached the group.

"Welcome to the neighborhood," Berry said, and smiled. "Let me get my wife out here to meet you. Hey Joyce!" he bellowed. "Come meet our neighbors."

They all watched as the door on the Road Master opened, and when a blond woman stepped out, both Harold and Monroe's jaws dropped open. She could not be over thirty years old, and could have stepped off the cover of a fashion model magazine. Cally unconsciously patted her dirty hair, but Pamela just gawked at the gorgeous woman.

Berry saw their familiar expressions and loved the reaction Joyce got from people, especially men. "She's something else, isn't she? I bet you're wondering why such a goddess would marry someone like me, right." When the Woollys and Monroe stared at him, he smiled. "Money, pure and simple. HA, HA, HA, HA, HA! See, I made my fortune selling explosives. Everything you can imagine. I made several million bucks and retired this last spring."

Joyce walked over and showed her a gorgeous smile. "Don't pay any attention to him," she said in a voice sounding like fingernails across a blackboard. "He's a sweetheart, and it's nice to meet you."

Berry saw the slight grimace from his new neighbors. "You get used to it after a while." He looked around and leaned in close to them. "I didn't turn all my booze over to the soldiers. Let's step into my rig and have a drink."

Monroe didn't hesitate. "Sounds good."

"I'd like that," Harold told him, receiving a venomous look from Cally.

Cally looked at Berry. "Pamela and I will pass, but thank you anyway." When Cally stomped across to Monroe's trailer, Pamela shrugged and followed her.

Joyce walked toward the Road Master with the men tagging along behind, staring at her sensuously moving butt. "So what's it like here?" Monroe finally asked.

"So far, not too bad, but we've only been here a few days. Oh, they have rules. No one is to have any firearms or liquor, and you have to turn all your food over to them to be rationed out. But basically, it's a good place for protection, with things being the way they are outside the camp."

"We were stopped outside Spokane, and they had the same rules."

When they entered the Road Master, Berry offered them chairs in the living area, telling them all he could offer was bourbon and mixers. Joyce expertly mixed the drinks and passed them around, and then sat across from Monroe and Harold. Both men had a hard time not staring at her, and Berry noticed, but merely grinned. "Have any trouble getting here?"

"Just getting past Spokane," said Monroe. "How about you?" Berry's face became a mask of sadness, and Monroe regretted asking. "Sorry."

"That's okay. We didn't have any trouble until we left Utah with my daughter and were ambushed passing through a little town." Berry pointed at a blown out piece of paneling in the wall to the left and behind where Harold was sitting, and on the floor was a dark brown stain. Berry's eyes suddenly filled with moisture. "The bullet hit my daughter in the chest." His lips trembled as tears ran down his cheeks. "She didn't suffer, but I miss her so much."

Berry released a sob, and Joyce put her arm around his shoulders to comfort him. He buried his face against her chest, and she rocked him soothingly for a few moments. He finally straightened and wiped the tears from his cheeks with the back of his hand. "We, ah." Berry swallowed hard. "We were trying to find a place to bury her when we met a convoy of grocery trucks. I flagged them down, thinking they must be headed for a city with sane people in it, and it turned out they were soldiers from here at the AOS camp. The leader, a lieutenant named Luke Ardle, ordered his men to help me bury my daughter and offered to let us come here." He was quiet for a few moments while he regained his composure. "So, how did you folks end up here?"

"Mister Monroe was kind enough to let us ride with him." Harold explained what happened in Seattle.

***

BLACKWOOD'S CABIN:
Luke led Mark across the parade ground and up the steps and then knocked on the door. When it opened, Blackwood looked down at Mark with an appraising stare.

Mark's mind went blank with the thrill of actually meeting the man on the brochure, something he had been anticipating since they joined Monroe and came here. He closed his mouth and snapped to attention. "Mark Woolly reporting for duty, Sir." When Blackwood smiled, Mark was elated.

"Come in, Private Woolly," said Blackwood, and stepped aside.

Mark saluted and entered the cabin and saw John Everex sitting near a desk. Again, he snapped to attention.

Everex extended his hand to Mark. "At ease, soldier."

Mark smiled and grabbed Everex's hand. "Boy, I'm glad to be here! I didn't think we'd ever make it. Do I get a uniform? And a gun?"

Everex glanced up at Blackwood and then stared at Mark. "Not yet. First, you need to prove yourself worthy."

Mark's jaw dropped. *Worthy? This is my dream, my reason for living! How can they not think me worthy?* "What do I need to do, Sir?"

Everex saw the look of disappointment and knew he could count on Mark. "First, tell me about the people who brought you here. How they feel about coming. What supplies they brought. How many weapons, any liquor, and how much, and what you saw on your way here?"

Mark smiled with relief and gladly told them everything they wanted to know. When Mark explained what happened in Spokane, Everex gave Blackwood a troubled look before focusing on Mark. "How many men did you see guarding the highway?"

"Half a dozen that I could see. Maybe more in the tanks and Humvees."

Again, Everex and Blackwood exchange looks. They knew about the Air Force base, but didn't realize the city was so organized. Now they would have to make plans in case the government expanded their realm of control.

"Well, Mark, so far, you're doing great. I think you deserve a uniform."

Everex stood and walked Mark to the door and they stepped out onto the porch, where Luke stood up from one of the chairs. "Take Private Woolly to the gear issue building and fix him up with a uniform." Everex looked at Mark. "My brother is here."

Mark grinned from ear to ear. *This is great! I've been accepted into the AOS, and my best friend is here, too! How can things possibly get any better?* "Thank you, sir. I won't let you down. I'll be the best soldier in camp."

"I know you will, Private." Everex turned to Luke. "When he's in uniform, find my brother and escort him and Private Woolly to his parents. You know what to do."

Everex stepped back into the cabin and closed the door, and then looked at Blackwood, sitting at the desk. "Spokane could give us trouble."

"I agree. Got any ideas?"

"I'll send some scouts to assess the situation. We'll make some decisions when they return." He stood and headed for the door.

Chapter 17

WASHINGTON, D.C:

After a long flight from Seattle, Alex entered the Director of National Security's office in the Whitehouse. When he saw Donner talking on the phone, he sat in a chair in front of the desk and waited.

"Yes, Mister President. I understand, Sir. Yes, Sir. Mister Cave just walked in. Yes, Sir. I'll call you back."

Donner hung up and looked across the desk at Alex. "More oil was stolen from one of the refineries on the East Coast, and OPEC refuses to send any of their oil. The President is ordering a permanent national rationing program, but not just gasoline, all petroleum products. We'll have to rely on our national reserves until we stop this hijacking."

When Alex slowly stood and walked to the window, Donner rotated his chair and stared at his back. "What is it, Alex?"

Alex continued to stare out the window. "I'm not sure, really. I have a feeling we may not be able to stop what's happening. What would you think if I told you the crude oil is not being stolen, but changed into something else?"

Donner chuckled. "You're kidding, of course." When Alex turned to face him, the look on his face said he wasn't. "Good grief!"

"We watched it happen to another tanker, and to the *Defiance*. That's why we abandoned ship." Alex told him about the two men fighting on *Defiance*'s deck. "It looked like the light coming out of the cargo hold incinerated them. Later, when we were on the rafts, we saw billions of crystals, like the one Christa found, flow out of the holds and rise into the air. The strangest part was then they vanished. We got back on the *Defiance*, and a short time later, the submarine arrived. They informed us the other tanker had capsized in the storm, so we searched for the crew, but couldn't find a single person."

Donner saw the sorrow in Alex's eyes. He knew about the warning from the All Alaska manager, but there was nothing he could do to stop the tankers. "The West Coast is in chaos."

"Yeah, I heard. We still don't know who's behind this."

"The Navy is putting its own people on one of the last tankers at Cook Inlet. Vetted crew only, and a Seal team. They'll try to get it to a refinery in Washington."

"No sense me hanging around here, Martin. I'll be in Montana, so let me know if you learn anything."

When the phone rang, and Donner answered, then listened to the caller as Alex moved toward the door. "Hold on a minute, Alex!"

Alex turned, listening to Donner's side of the conversation. The look on the director's face meant something important had just happened.

Donner ended the call and stared at his friend. "Better stick around for a few minutes. The FBI is sending a man over with some important information about the oil."

They heard a knock on the door, and a burly man entered the office. "I'm Bill Pickowski," the man said as he stepped in and closed the door.

Donner indicated the chair in front of the desk, and Pickowski sat down. "What have you discovered?"

"I know who is stealing the oil." Pickowski explained everything he knew about the events that took place in the Idaho meadow. "Menno Simons hypnotized hundreds of people at a time. I was even under his spell for a while, and it was the most amazing thing I ever saw. It was like a scene out of a movie. Menno somehow produced a bright crescent moon, high in the sky."

Alex snapped his head toward Pickowski as he remembered the moon he saw after the tanker incident. "I saw a moon above the tankers, but it was below the clouds"

Donner got back on the topic. "You say you have one of the ampoules?"

Pickowski reached into his coat pocket and handed the two inch long ampoule to Donner. "Menno's people handed out thousands of those things to people taking them to oil-producing countries."

Donner studied the colored granules inside, and then handed it to Alex. Alex held it up to the light from the window and stared at it for a moment. When he noticed the sparkling powder appeared to be moving, he spun toward Donner. "I'd like to take this to the college immediately. We'll see if there's a connection between this and the crystal Christa found on the tanker. The interior also appeared to be moving, just like this powder."

"All right. Keep me informed."

Alex left the room, and as he entered the parking area below the White House, his assigned driver informed him they would have to use the alternate exit because of the crowds of protestors blocking the streets around the Capitol. They drove down a long tunnel for several minutes and exited four miles away. As they approached Washington International Airport, the traffic slowed, and when they were within half a mile of the terminal, the vehicles were at a standstill.

The driver looked out the side window at the rearview mirror. "I'm sorry, Mister Cave, but we're blocked in."

"Okay. I'll walk the rest of the way to the air terminal."

The driver opened the trunk and handed Alex his bag, and Alex walked beside the bumper-to-bumper traffic as he tried to figure out why it was so congested. When he reached the terminal, he found hundreds of people lined up outside the doors, and airport security police standing at each entrance to keep them out of the terminal, and approached one of the officers. "What's going on?"

"Ain't you been listening to the news, Mister? The rationing started this morning and the airlines are cutting a lot of their flights. You'll have to wait in line like everyone else."

"It's very important that I catch the next flight to Montana."

The officer laughed. "You and everyone else out here."

"Look, you don't understand."

"You'll wait like everyone else!"

Alex retrieved the government ID from his coat pocket and showed it to the officer. "I want to talk to your supervisor," he told him and pointed to the portable radio clipped to the officer's belt. When the officer ignored his request, he grabbed the sleeve openings of his florescent orange vest and moved his face within inches of the officers. "Call him!"

The officer grudgingly spoke into the radio, and when the supervisor arrived, Alex showed her his ID and handed her a piece of paper. "Call that number and ask about me. I'll wait."

The supervisor stared at Alex for a moment before stepping away and then dialed the number. When she returned, she looked at the guard. "Let him through, George. Follow me, Mister Cave."

Once inside the air terminal, the crowd thinned out dramatically, and the supervisor led Alex to a ticket counter. After purchasing a ticket, the woman then led him through the sprawling building to a boarding gate where a line of passengers waited. The supervisor spoke to the boarding attendant, who let Alex onto the aircraft, while those in line shouted their protests. A moment later, a steady stream of people passed his seat, and Alex heard an angry man yelling at the boarding attendant just before the airplane door closed.

Chapter 18

BOZEMAN STATE COLLEGE:

Christa was escorted down the hall by a student to a small office with potted plants sitting on shelves under the window and is introduced to the Director of the Science Department. Marcia Story stood and smiled as she stepped around the desk to shake Christa's hand. "Hello, Christa. I've been expecting you."

Christa was momentarily mesmerized by the woman's size. Marcia was the tallest woman she had ever met, but she moved with a bouncy energy you would expect from a twenty-five-year-old, with only a few traces of gray in her light brown hair. Marcia's hazel eyes seemed to sparkle with energy and her smile was warm, and her reading glasses hung from a florescent green string around her neck.

Marcia waved a hand toward a well-padded chair at one end of the desk and then sat in her chair. "Have a seat and tell me about this crystal. Alex didn't go into details over the phone."

Christa sat, retrieved the plastic box from her purse, and handed it to Marcia. "It appears to be a crystal, Miss Story, but under a microscope, it has movement, like living organic material."

Marcia studied the crystal, turning it over in her hands. "Please, call me Marcia."

"Okay. The laboratory in Alaska doesn't have the proper equipment for determining its composition, so Alex sent me to you."

"I see. Well, we have an electron microscope and an excellent computer system. We should be able to get a better idea of what we're dealing with. I'll be working with you on this." Marcia got up. "Let's go to the laboratory and meet my assistant. He's a physics' major, and one of the most intelligent scientists I know."

***

When Christa and Marcia entered the laboratory, two young students and a young man looked up from their projects. Marcia approached the two young women and asked if they could continue at another time before turning to the young man. "David, this is Christa Avery. This is my assistant, David Conway."

When the girls walked away, Christa studied the young man and thought David couldn't be over nineteen years old. "Nice to meet you, David."

A shy grin spread across David's face, and his heart rate increased as he stared at Christa. He couldn't think of anything to say and kept staring at her until Marcia got his attention.

"We have an urgent project, David."

David's head snapped around toward Marcia. "What?"

"We need to discover what this crystal is composed of. And we need to hurry. Are you working on anything that can't wait?"

"Ah, yes. I mean, yes, it can wait." David accepted the crystal and held it up to the light, and then turned to Christa. "Where did you get it? Is it a polymer or mineral?"

"I'm not sure."

"Interesting. We should do a spectrum analysis for composition."

"I agree," said Marcia.

David handed the crystal to Christa. "I'll set up the spectrum analyzer."

When David left the room, Marcia grinned at Christa. "You made quite an impression on David. I've never seen him act like that before."

Christa gave her a quizzical expression. "What do you mean?"

"I think he has a crush on you."

"He's just a boy."

"That *boy* has an IQ of one hundred and seventy-one and spends most of his time with academics closer to my age group."

Christa said nothing as they approached a tall structure nestled in one corner of the room, where a table supported a computer terminal next to the electron microscope. Christa had used one before and set up the crystal, while Marcia programed the computer, and then the video display screen came on, informing them the unit is ready. Marcia typed a command into the computer, and a few moments later, the video monitor showed a magnified picture of the crystal.

The crystal contained thousands of blue spider web veins in different layers, none of which appear to have an end. Marcia entered another command, the magnification increased, and a small section of veins filled the screen. When they saw movement inside, they turned to stare at each other.

Christa indicated the image on the monitor. "That's what makes me think it might be organic. It looks like a cardiovascular system."

"Yes, but I don't see any internal organs. I'll increase the magnification."

The display changed, isolating a crisscrossed group of five veins, and in each one, a luminescent blue substance was slowly moving through the tiny capillaries. Christa and Marcia stared at the display for a moment until they heard footsteps, and then turned as David approached.

David studied the display on the monitor. "What magnification are you on?"

"Ten thousand," Marcia told him.

"Are you ready to increase it?"

"Yes. Going to one hundred thousand."

Marcia typed in another command, and the display isolated a small section of a single vein which filled the screen, and minuscule particles of blue light moved across the monitor. "Let's see what the computer analysis tells us about the composition."

Marcia typed in a command and the display screen went blank for a second, then a short sentence appeared. INSUFFICIENT DATA FOR IDENTIFICATION.

"Interesting," said David. "Increase the magnification. Maybe we can isolate a single particle."

Marcia entered another command, and the screen returned to a view of the blue substance. The picture changed again, and large, glowing blue dots shot across the screen.

"Still picture, please," David asked, and when Marcia entered the command, all movement ceased, leaving two blue dots on the screen. "My first impression is it's some type of chemical. Let's put it in the spectrum analyzer. I've tied it into the mainframe computer, so transfer this computer's information into it, and maybe the spectrum analyzer will compile enough information for an intelligent answer. Bring the crystal when you're ready."

When David left the room, Christa looked at Marcia. "He's a little on the bossy side, isn't he?"

"He doesn't mean to be. I guess it's because people have been asking his advice for most of his life. He's much different when he's away from the laboratory, and spends most of his time hiking and camping in the mountains. He says it's his way of escaping. In the summer, he spends weeks at a time up there."

Christa removed the crystal from the holder while Marcia shut down the microscope, and then they left the laboratory. Marcia led Christa into the hallway and down the corridor to a steel door at the end of the building, and when they entered, saw David standing next to an open section of a ten foot long, cylinder shaped device. It was mounted on a three foot high metal stand which was bolted to the floor.

The spectrum analyzer gathered data by shooting a laser beam at an object placed in the chamber and reading the different colors of light given off when the object burned. Each frequency of light represented a specific element, and the computer could determine how much of each element the object contained.

When David held out his hand, Christa gave him the crystal. "This won't destroy it, will it?"

David shook his head no. "It's set on minimum power, and we'll only shoot a small section of the outside edge."

David slid back the lid on a metal enclosure, inserted the crystal, and adjusted the bracket until a thin red laser beam was shown on the top edge of the crystal. He closed the lid, walked to the end of the device and pressed a series of keys on a computer terminal, and then moved toward the door. "I'm all set, but we need to leave the room for safety. The laser will fire in one minute."

David waited until the two women were in the hallway, closed the heavy steel door behind him, and stared at his watch as he counted down. "Three, two, one, now!"

Everyone jumped when they heard a muffled explosion and felt the floor shake, and David's eyes went wide with fear. "Good grief! That's not supposed to happen!"

David grabbed the doorknob to get back in, but when he pushed, the door refused to move. He pounded his shoulder against the door, and on the third try, it burst open, causing him to stagger into the room. He caught his balance and froze in place, numbly staring at the empty area where the spectrum analyzer had been. Sunlight was streaming in through a gaping hole in the brick wall, and he saw the campus lawn on the other side.

Christa and Marcia stood behind him, neither able to speak as they tried to comprehend what had happened. David regained his composure and walked farther into the room and up to the gaping hole in the wall. He stepped through and stared at the two furrows in the lawn leading to the analyzer, still upright, about fifty feet away.

Christa and Marcia follow him through the hole and stood on either side of him. The enclosure had been blown open, but the crystal was still in one piece.

Bells rang across the campus as someone pulled a fire alarm, and students and faculty streamed from the buildings. The College President ran across the lawn to where the trio and the analyzer stood and saw the hole in the brick wall. "What happened?"

David shrugged his shoulders. "I don't have any idea, sir. I was running a test, and this happened." He leaned forward for a closer look at the crystal, and it appeared unmarred by the event. He hesitantly touched it, and it was cold, so he held it up against the sunlight and it looked the same as when he first looked through it.

David looked first at Christa, then at Marcia. "Let's find out if the computer gathered any information."

The College President watched them walk back through the hole in the building, and then he stared at the analyzer for a moment, wondering how he was going to explain this to the directors. He shook his head in bewilderment and headed back across the lawn, barely noticing the passing throng of curious students.

Chapter 19

BOZEMAN, MONTANA:

Six hours later, Alex landed at the small air terminal, and once outside, the number of taxies was limited, and he had to wait twenty minutes for his turn. The driver told him the cost will be double the normal rate, and Alex asked why.

"Shit, Mister, I have to make a living. They're gouging us at the gas stations, so I have to pass it along."

Alex agreed to pay, and they left the airport. There was little traffic on the highway, and as they passed the outskirts of the city, he saw lines of cars waiting at major gas stations.

"See all those people, Mister? They'll stay there all night until the gas tanker shows up in the morning. *If* it shows up. Rumor has it the tankers are being hijacked before they get here, and soon I'll have to get my gas from the black market. Now, ain't that a trip?"

When they arrived at the college, Alex directed him to his personal car in the parking lot and paid the driver the extravagant fee. He removed the small glass vial from his suitcase and put it in his pocket before tossing the bag onto the back seat and locking the doors.

On his way to the main building, he saw plywood fastened to the outside wall of the Science Department, and wondered what had happened. He entered the laboratory and found Christa and David standing behind Marcia, who was sitting at a computer terminal. "Any luck?"

The trio turned simultaneously. "Hey, Alex!" said David. "Welcome back," Marcia added.

Christa smiled warmly. "You're just in time. The computer is correlating all the information we have on the crystal."

"Good. I almost didn't get out of D.C."

"Because of the rationing?"

"Yes. What happened to the science building?"

David held up the plastic box containing the crystal. "This! It reacts violently to laser light. It released enough energy to hurl a two thousand pound spectrum analyzer nearly sixty feet, *after* it sheered four half-inch bolts, *and* forced it through six inches of brick wall. And that was on the *lowest* setting. I can't imagine how it would have reacted to the full power of the laser."

"Damn," Alex whispered.

David's face became flush with excitement when the computer came on and the analysis of the laser test appeared on the monitor.

Dimensions reduced 0.0000003 percent in comparison with the first electron microscope scan. composition bio-chemical-organic, in crystalline acidic base. Compressed light energy released during laser burst equal to thirty-two billion angstroms per 0.000000021 cubic meters. Six thousand pounds of thrust released during laser burst.

0.0046 parts per thousand of hydrogen gas released during laser burst.

0.0038 parts per thousand of sodium particles released during laser burst.

Insufficient data for further analysis.

End of report.

"It's compressed energy!" David exclaimed.

"But it's also alive," Christa added.

"It's clean energy, too," David continued. "If the hydrogen gas mixes with oxygen, it creates water. Add the sodium, and the byproduct released when the energy is used is salt water."

Christa and Alex looked at each other in understanding, and then Christa turned to Marcia and David. "That explains how the oil in the reservoirs was replaced with salt water."

Marcia was elated. "Just think of the possibilities of using this type of energy?"

Alex set the ampoule on the counter. "This is related." He explained what he had learned from Pickowski. "All the missing men are part of Menno Simon's followers, and this might be what Mike Broden saw when he peeked into Gary Darven's bedroom at the pumping station."

Marcia picked up the ampoule and held it to the light. "I'll find out what it is."

Alex looked at Christa. "Do you have any ideas about why this one crystal was left in the tanker?"

"Not really. It was stuck in a grove in the side of a metal baffle and fell off when I touched it."

"Interesting," David mumbled, and appeared to be deep in thought for a moment. "I'll bet the light coming from the hatch was the energy released from converting the oil into these crystals, and that's what killed the two men on your tanker, Alex."

Alex envisioned the two men who had vanished. "I think you're right, and we may not be able to stop what's happening to the crude oil. And that, my friends, is a scary thought."

Chapter 20

COOK INLET, ALASKA:
When Bull learned about the military support for one of the tankers leaving for Washington State, he had wanted to leave the hospital to supervise the operation himself. When the doctor refused to let him go, Bull snuck out when no one was looking. He had flagged down a cab and was taken to the fuel docks.

When he entered the All Alaska office, there was a message for him to call Alex at the college, so he sat down and entered the number. "Hey, Alex. I just got in. What's going on?"

Alex explained what they had discovered about the crystal. "We don't know who else might have some of these granules, but it could be someone in the military on the ship, and we can't afford to lose any more oil."

"I'll ask around, and maybe one of our people heard something about it. I'll call if I learn anything new."

Bull left the office to meet the military representative waiting at the docks and strolled along the pier. A few moments later, he approached a tall man in a military uniform standing near the boarding ramp of the two hundred thousand ton ARCO oil tanker *Sentry*. The tanker was one of three left stranded in the harbor when the company decided not to risk the loss of any more ships until the oil hijacking problem was solved.

Navy Captain John Parks arrived an hour ago from the *USS Harrison* to inspect the *Sentry* while the eleven enlisted men with him familiarized themselves with the ship's operation procedure. Parks considered commanding an oil tanker one step above commanding a garbage scow, and stared with disgust at the rusty ship, considering this assignment to be far below what he thought he rightfully deserved.

He turned as someone approached, and from the description, recognized the All Alaska representative. "Mister Peterson, I presume. I thought this tanker was supposed to be loaded by now? What's the holdup?"

Bull took an instant dislike to the cocky officer and suppressed a grin, knowing he would screw with the man. "I'm really sorry, Sir. We didn't expect to be pumping any oil for a while, so everything was shut down. It takes time to heat the oil so it will flow through the lines."

Bull held his breath for a moment, hoping Parks was dumb enough to accept the ruse. In reality, they could pump immediately if he ordered it done.

Not wanting to appear stupid, yet show his authority, Parks nodded in understanding. "I'll have my crew assist in the loading operation as soon as you're ready. Time is of the essence, and I insist you have your people pump the oil as quickly as possible."

"I'll stay right on top of them, Captain, don't worry."

Bull turned and strolled up the pier. "In your ass!"

Parks thought he heard the man from All Alaska say something. "What?" he asked, but when Bull didn't look back, Parks walked across the gangway onto the tanker's deck.

***

Bull entered the distribution control center and approached the day supervisor. "Hello, Bruce," he said, and reached down to shake the man's hand.

"Hey, Bull. Good to see you again. What brings you this far west?"

Bull liked the feisty little gray-haired man who had worked for him when they were building the pipeline. He realized Bruce Sullivan must be nearly sixty-five by now and wondered why he hadn't retired. "I need a favor, Bruce."

"Name it."

"Stall off pumping crude into the *Sentry* as long as possible."

"That Navy Captain was breathing down my neck an hour ago."

"I know, but I told him we had to heat the oil first. That should hold him for a few hours, but try to think of something else to delay the operation. I'll take the flak."

Bruce smirked. "What are you up to, Bull?"

"Let's just say it's for the Captain's own good."

"Fine by me. How long should I delay?"

"Until I say it's okay, if possible." When Bruce indicated he understood, Bull left the control center.

***

Eight hours later, Captain Parks was literally frothing at the mouth and bits of spittle splattered Bruce's face as he demanded the old man transfer the oil to the ship immediately.

"It'll only take a few more hours, Captain. If you hadn't insisted we pump so soon, the main pump wouldn't have seized up."

Parks exploded with rage and grabbed Bruce by the lapels of his coat. "Don't you dare try to blame this on me, you sawed off little shit! I'll break you in two. It's been three hours since the pump went down, and that's plenty of time to repair it. Now start pumping!" Parks suddenly felt his shirt collar tighten around his throat.

Seething with rage, Bull ignored the fire in his ribcage as he hurled Parks against the wall, but the twisting motion was more than he could stand, so he released him, and Parks' face slammed into the concrete. When Parks turned around to face him, Bull shoved his palm into the man's chest, pinning him against the wall. "If you ever lay a hand on one of my people again, I'll break *you* in two!"

Parks saw the fire in the big man's eyes and nodded his agreement, so Bull released him, and Parks gently placed his fingers on his nose. It didn't feel broken, but he felt a warm liquid and stared incredulously at the blood on his fingertips. *I'm an officer! How dare this civilian assault me!* With eyes red in bitterness, Parks glared at Bull. "You're in big trouble, Mister!"

Bull didn't reply and stared back coldly. When Parks spun around and stormed out the door, Bull placed his hand over his ribs and bent over to ease the pain. "Are you all right, Bruce?"

"Yeah, I'm fine. How about you? Are you all right? Should I call an ambulance?"

Bull shook his head no. "I'll be fine. I guess I've stalled as long as I can. You'd better start pumping." He watched Bruce pick up the phone to call the workers. "One more thing. Fill three quarters of the load with seawater. I have a bad feeling about those crews, and I don't want to lose any more crude oil than necessary."

Chapter 21

ARMY OF SURVIVAL, IDAHO:
Blackwood stood in the bathroom, looking in the mirror at the dark circles around his bloodshot eyes. It was the same nightmare night after night, always waking when the Everex-POW-officer dropped human body parts on him. He tried not to sleep at all so he would not dream, but eventually, he dozed off and the dreams came. He knew if he could just get rid of Everex, maybe the nightmares would end. He also knew that as long as Everex kept his elite guards nearby, he would never get the chance to kill him.

He heard a knock on his cabin door and stepped out of the bathroom. "Enter," he shouted as he sat in a chair at his desk. When Everex stepped in and closed the door, the look on his face told Blackwood something was wrong.

Everex walked across the room and sat in a chair across from Blackwood. "We lost seven people last night, Colonel. The trucks are getting harder to find, and the damn drivers are armed to the teeth, and always have someone riding shotgun with them."

"Did you get the supplies?" Everex indicated no. "No fuel trucks?"

"We had a chance for one, but it blew up during the gunfight."

Blackwood slammed his fist on the desk. "How can you be so stupid? Don't you realize we need fuel for the refrigerated trucks? If you can't do the job, I'll get someone who can."

When Everex leapt from his chair and grabbed him by the throat, the force knocked the Colonel over backward onto the floor. Stunned and unable to draw a breath because of the hand still around his throat, Blackwood stared into the cold, black eyes and the savage face above him, and knew he was about to die.

"Don't push me, Colonel!" Everex hissed through clenched teeth. "Maybe it's time the AOS had a new leader?"

Blackwood's eyes went wide with fear as the face above him grinned sadistically and the hand tightened around his throat, cutting off his air. Blackwood had seen that look before, and it still sent a chill down his spine. He knew if Everex said, now the fun begins, his life was over. His stomach tightened into a knot of fear as the seconds dragged on, but suddenly he felt the pressure leave his throat.

"What the hell," Everex said in a mocking tone. "I already run this place." He stood and stared down at Blackwood. "You're just a figurehead, Colonel. The people do what I tell them. They kill if I tell them, they steal if I tell them, and they believe what I tell them. Just keep that in mind."

Blackwood remained on his back until Everex sat back down, and then slowly sat up on the floor and massaged his aching throat. Using the chair for support, he pushed himself up and sat across from Everex.

Everex placed one dirty boot on the desk. "Now, Colonel, let's talk about the new recruits."

Blackwood's throat felt constricted, and it was hard to talk. "We got thirteen new arrivals last night."

"I know. Listen, Colonel. We took in more people to build up the size of our army, but they look like homeless families, not soldiers. Too many women and children, and I think we should change the rules around here."

Blackwood knew he would not like the answer, but needed to ask the question. "Like what?"

"If we let them stay, we train the men and strong women. The kids will do all the domestic work, and the soft women will become camp prostitutes."

Blackwood's jaw dropped. "What?"

"Let's face it, Colonel. With the shortage of food and fuel in the outside world, we'll get more families, and they have to earn their keep."

"How are you going to convince them to do that?"

"They'll volunteer on their own."

Blackwood laughed. "Right." He looked at Everex, saw the menacing smirk, and stopped grinning.

Everex stood and headed toward the door. "Come along, Colonel. I'll show you."

Blackwood stood and followed Everex out the doorway and down the steps, then across the parade ground, where he met up with Sergeant Major Davis and the special group of ten soldiers Everex called his elite guards. They were big, mean men, with little or no morals. Men looking for a fight, and each of them had the same sadistic streak as Everex did.

They all gathered in front of the large, temporary tents at the edge of the woods, where most of the new people were sitting around campfires. About two-thirds were family groups, and the others a mixture of young to middle-aged men and women, and Blackwood estimated there were about one hundred and eighty civilians gathered in front of them.

Everex waited for the people in the RV camp, and when he saw them approaching, turned to Sergeant Major Davis, who blew a loud shrill from a whistle. The newcomers left their fires and tents and stood in front of the soldiers. Everex stepped forward and folded his arms across his chest as he stared at the all the people. "Now, listen up. These are the new rules. All children under fourteen years of age will report to Sergeant Major Chapman for work details."

Everex grinned in satisfaction when he saw several children move closer to their parents, their faces masks of fear as the parents tried to comfort them. "The men will meet in the parade ground in one hour, and the women will go with Sergeant Major Davis. Those women physically able to become soldiers will start training, and the rest will be assigned cooking and cleaning responsibilities. As an added benefit to the camp, some of the women will be assigned to the special services tents. Men too, if they prefer to satisfy the other women."

The family groups erupted in mumbled conversations, and Cally and Harold look at each other. Berry wasn't about to put up with the new rules and stepped past his attractive wife to address Everex. "What do you mean by special services?" he asked with a wary expression on his face.

Everex smirked at him. "The special services tents are where any of the men," Everex's grin widened, "or women, if they like, can satisfy their sexual needs."

Berry's face became a mask of incredulous disbelief. "What? You can't order our wives to become prostitutes!"

Everex shrugged indifferently. "That's the way it is. Take it or leave it."

Berry stared in stunned disbelief for a moment, and then spun around and grabbed Joyce by the hand. "We don't have to put up with this!" he snarled over his shoulder. "We're leaving!"

Everex shot a look at Davis, who blew a short blast from the whistle. Chuck and Joyce stopped and look back at Everex, whose expression was as cold as a deep freeze.

"No one leaves this camp!"

Berry hesitated for a moment and then turned and started walking away with Joyce while the rest of the group watched. Everyone flinched at the sudden explosion and watched Berry pitch forward and tumble to the ground. Joyce stood in numb shock for a moment as she stared at the lifeless body of her husband, and then screamed and dropped beside him, sobbing hysterically while Cally bent down to comfort her.

Blackwood stared at Everex in stunned disbelief as the man slowly put his gun back in his holster. *This isn't what I expected*, he thought, but realized he should have.

Everex turned to Davis, who blew on the whistle again. When he had everyone's attention, Everex continued. "Is there anyone who doesn't understand the rules?"

Most of the women looked at their husbands with imploring expressions, as if the men could stop the nightmare. The men looked at the dead man on the ground, his lifeless body in a growing pool of blood, and the woman sobbing over him. They glanced at their wives for understanding before staring at the ground in shame. They had to accept this harsh fate or die.

Everex grinned in satisfaction. "Dismissed!" he hollered, and turned to Blackwood. "I told you they'd volunteer," he said as he watched Blackwood's face flush with rage. He let out a short laugh and strolled back across the parade ground.

Blackwood turned and stared after Everex in disgust for a moment. "I'm losing control of my army."

He watched the ten men from the elite group follow Everex and realized it was too late to stop this insane course of events. He turned back to the group of newcomers and saw a woman trying to comfort the attractive grieving wife, and felt ashamed the poor woman's nightmare was about to get worse.

Harold and Monroe exchanged worried looks, and Monroe knew his best chance of getting out of here alive was to play the game with this colonel and his perverted Major. He decided to tell the Colonel about his career and status in the Air Force and hoped he could have some kind of status in this crazy army. He knew if he has to stay here, he might as well get some kind of creature comforts out of it.

He looked over at Joyce and Cally and wondered what was going to happen to them. There wasn't much he could do right now, but if he got some kind of high rank out of all this, he might be able to help them. He hurried across the tent camp and walked beside Blackwood. "Excuse me, Colonel. I'm Captain Jerry Monroe, retired. Maybe I can be of assistance to you."

Chapter 22

9:48 P.M. MONTANA STATE COLLEGE:

Alex, Christa, and David were standing behind Marcia, who looked up from the electron microscope monitor. "This is incredible. As near as I can tell, these particles from the ampule are microorganism, but unlike anything I've ever seen."

"Could they be some type of enzyme?" Christa asked. "Similar to what I helped develop for the oil companies to consume raw crude oil?"

"Nothing I'm familiar with, but it's an interesting observation. What if these organisms consume the crude oil and become a crystal like the one you found in the tanker?"

"Only one way to find out."

"I agree. The problem is, I don't have any crude oil to experiment with."

Christa turned to Alex. "I'll take the ampoule to my facility in Valdez. I'm sure Bull can bring me some crude from one of the facilities on the Kenai Peninsula."

Alex noticed how red Christa's eyes were. "All right. You all look exhausted, so why don't we get some sleep and we'll make arrangements in the morning?"

Both women nodded agreement, and Marcia placed the ampoule in a padded container, then handed it to Christa.

David looked up at Alex. "I'm too excited to sleep, and there's an experiment I want to try, so I'll stay a while longer."

"We'll be back in the morning."

The three of them left the building, and Marcia climbed into her old blue Cadillac while Alex and Christa climb into his Blazer. They waved to her, and then headed to his ranch.

***

Alex parked in the driveway, and he and Christa climbed out. Barney was standing on the porch, and when he saw Alex, leapt down the steps and lopped along the sidewalk, his tail wagging furiously.

Alex knelt beside the enormous animal and wrapped his arms around the dog's thick neck. "Hello, Barney."

When Barney laid his head over Alex's shoulder, Christa swore the dog was smiling and did the same. After a few moments, Alex stood and grabbed his bag from the back seat, and led Christa up the sidewalk into the house.

***

Alex waited until Christa was inside and then closed the door. "I'm going to take a quick shower and change clothes, so make yourself at home," he told her as he continued down the hall to his bedroom.

Christa opened a bottle of wine and poured a glass before strolling to the large window above the sink to look at the view. She sipped her wine and smiled to herself as she studied the water rippling in the stream below, pleased to be with him again.

She had thought she might not see him again, at least alive, and wondered what had happened on the tanker. She turned from the window when she heard footsteps moving in her direction, then Alex walked into the living room and sat at the counter.

She smiled and lowered herself onto a stool across from him, and they sat in silence for a few moments while sipping the wine, until Christa's curiosity became aroused. "I met Judy yesterday, and she helped me settle in. She seems like a nice girl."

"Yes, she is. A little rough around the edges, but she's a big help around here."

"She gave me the impression you two are. Well, I mean."

"A couple?" Alex shook his head no. "I've taken her to dinner a few times for taking care of Barney for me, but there's nothing serious between us, if that's what you want to know."

Christa felt both relieved and upset at the same time. Relieved by what Alex had just said and upset with herself for being so obvious.

When the wine was gone, Alex stood from the counter. "Well, I think we both could use some sleep."

Christa followed Alex down the hallway, and when they reach the bedroom doors, he stopped and turned to her. "I'll see you in the morning."

As he turned away, Christa suddenly grabbed his neck and pulled down with gentle pressure until he bent over slightly. She stood on her tiptoes and kissed him gently on the lips, and felt his arms slowly wrap around her back. He suddenly stopped and gently pushed her away, so she looked at him. "What's wrong?"

Alex sighed and looked at different parts of the wall as he tried to figure out how to tell her what he felt. Suddenly, the door chimes sounded, interrupting his thoughts. They chimed again and again, so he turned and headed to the door, with Christa following him.

The door suddenly opened, and Judy stepped in. "You're back!" she said and put her arms out to hug him. She saw Christa standing behind him and gave Alex a passionate kiss. Alex didn't respond, but she didn't care. She just wanted Christa to see he was hers.

It was all Christa could do not to show the seething jealousy she felt. When Judy stopped kissing Alex and looked at her with a smug grin, she forced a smile.

Alex noticed the women exchange glances. "What brings you by this late at night?" he asked, trying to ease the situation.

Judy turned to him. "I didn't know you were back, and I came over to see if Christa saw the news tonight."

Alex and Christa exchanged uneasy glances, both wondering what had happened since they had left the College, and Alex answered. "We haven't. What's going on?"

"Some of the major oil fields are going dry."

"Where?"

"California, Texas, and Oklahoma. Do you know what's going on?"

Alex grabbed the remote control for the television and switched stations to the headline news broadcast, and they all listened to the female announcer. "It's very complicated."

We have reports some of the offshore oil wells have suddenly gone dry with no explanation of how or why. Our correspondents in the Middle East report OPEC has called a special meeting and are in contact with our representatives at the White House, but there is no official word yet why. Reliable sources say there is a similar crisis with the OPEC oil wells.'

His phone rang, and Alex stared at the television screen as he answered. "I'm here, Martin."

"No, it's Bull. Have you heard about the new oil crisis?"

"Sorry. Yeah, I just found out. What about the oil wells up there?"

"Not yet."

"Let me talk to him," Christa interrupted.

"I'll call you after I've talked to Martin. Hang on a second."

Christa grabbed the phone. "Bull, it's Christa. Do you have any crude left at all?"

"Yes. As a precaution, I have ten barrels hidden away where no one can get to them."

"Put them under heavy guard and get them to my laboratory in Valdez. It's very important that I have a supply of crude when I arrive."

Bull heard the desperation in her voice. "Okay. It'll take a full day by the time I round up some guards and get them loaded onto trucks. How soon will you be here?"

"I'm not sure. I'll have to catch a flight from here in Montana, but Alex says the schedules are erratic."

"Okay. I'll be waiting."

Christa hung up and handed the phone back to Alex. "Now the problem is getting to Valdez."

Judy put her hands on her hips and stared at Alex and Christa. "Will somebody tell me what the hell's going on?"

Alex reached over and took her hand. "I need a big favor. Do you still have your airplane? Your Cessna?"

"Yes. It's at the airport waiting for an annual tune up."

"Could you fly Christa to Valdez for me?"

"That's a long way, Alex. I don't have the range. Even so, I can't do anything until I talk to the mechanic in the morning."

Alex hurried to his den and returned with an atlas and a ruler. He opened the atlas to the North American continent, and using the scale at the top of the page, he moved the ruler to measure the distance. "Nearly fifteen hundred miles."

Judy shook her head no. "Too far. I'll have to stop somewhere along the way."

Alex studied the map for a moment, gently tapping the ruler against the counter. He abruptly stopped and pointed at Washington State. "What about the Naval Air Station on Whidbey Island? It's halfway there, and they have a flying club. I'll make arrangements for you to land there and refuel."

Judy stared at him for a moment. "That works, but not until you tell me what's going on."

Alex was about to explain when the phone rang again, so he snatched it up and saw Donner's image. "How bad is it?"

"It's turning into a nightmare, Alex. Everyone's running scared because no one knows how or why this is happening, except us."

"We're onto something here, and we suspect the ampoule contains some type of enzyme that turns the crude oil into the crystals. I'm trying to get Christa back to Valdez to make sure, so I need another favor."

"Pickowski said there were thousands of those ampoules passed out!"

"Exactly."

"Is there a way to reverse what's happening?"

"We won't know until Christa can experiment with some crude oil and the enzymes. There is still some crude in Alaska, and my friend from All Alaska is going to get it from Cook Inlet to Valdez." Alex heard a beep on the phone, indicating he had a call waiting, but ignored it temporarily. "Also, we need arrangements for a private plane to refuel at the Navy base on Whidbey Island in Washington State."

"No problem."

"Thanks, Martin. Any word of Menno Simons?"

"He was seen in northern Utah, and then he crossed into Idaho. We lost him near a town called Orofino, but we're still searching."

"All right, I'll call you later." Alex pressed the clear button to retrieve the next caller. "Hello?"

"Alex, it's Marcia. I've been listening to the news, and wondered if there is anything I can do to help?"

"No, we've had a change of plans. We just finished arranging for Christa to fly to Valdez, Alaska, so I'll be taking her and Judy to the airport in the morning."

"Okay. Stop by the College on the way. I'll give her the computer disks with all our information she'll need for her experiments."

"All right, we'll meet you there." Alex hung up and looked at the women. "Okay. Let's try to get some sleep."

As Christa and Alex walked down the hall, Judy grabbed his arm. "I need to talk to you for a minute."

Judy saw Christa had stopped and turned to listen, and smirked at the little woman. "In private."

Christa didn't enjoy leaving Judy alone with Alex, but had no choice. "All right. I'll see you in the morning." She walked into her bedroom, closing the door.

Alex looked at Judy. "What is it?"

"Where am I supposed to sleep?"

"I thought you were going home." He indicated the couch. "I'll get you some blankets."

"Not if you want me to fly that woman to Alaska."

"What?"

"I'm sleeping with you, or no deal."

"Judy, I can't do that. Not now."

Judy folded her arms across her chest and looked him in the eyes. "That's the deal."

"That's blackmail," he said coldly.

Judy shrugged. "Call it what you will."

Alex glanced down the hall and then looked at Judy. "All right."

Judy smiled, grabbed his arm, and led him down the hall. She let him through the doorway first and smirked at the guest bedroom door before closing hers.

Christa lay in bed, listening, and heard the door to Alex's bedroom close, and was about to fall asleep when she heard Judy's voice. Tears slid down her cheeks, and she rolled over and buried her face in the pillow to muffle her crying.

***

In the morning, Christa was the first one up, unable to sleep much during the night. She put on some coffee and sat at the counter, thinking before the door to Alex's room opened and Judy stepped out.

Judy strolled down the hall wearing only a long-sleeved shirt and smiled at Christa. "Sleep well?"

Christa ignored her tone and forced a smile. "Just fine."

Alex stepped into the hall, and when he looked at Christa, felt a deep sense of remorse. His heart raced when she looked at him for a second, then she turned away. When he saw her bags on the floor by the door, he tried to think of something to say to her, but could not think of anything appropriate. "We'd better get going. We can pick up something for breakfast on the way."

***

The trio didn't speak on the way to the college. When they arrived, they found the laboratory deserted, but a quick search discovered David asleep in the faculty lounge. Alex gently shook his shoulder, and David opened his eyes. "Have you seen Marcia?"

"Yeah," he said, and rubbed one eye with the back of his fist. "She woke me a while ago and said to tell you she'll be right back." David closed his eyes and rolled onto his side. "Electricity," he mumbled.

"What was that?"

"The crystal. It reacts to electricity," he mumbled, and fell back asleep.

They walked back to the laboratory and Christa grabbed the crystal off the counter, shoved it into one of her coat pockets, and then placed the box with the small ampoule into the other. The computer disks were lying there, and she tucked them into her purse.

A few moments later, Marcia met them in the hallway. "I'm all set," she told them and smiled.

Alex stared at her. "All set for what?"

"I'm going with Christa to Valdez. They can do without me here for a while, and I'd like to help with the experiments. I put my bag in the back of your Blazer."

"All right, let's go."

On the way to the parking lot, Alex introduced Marcia to Judy and explained the situation and travel plans. "It's going to be a long ride. Are you sure you want to go?"

Marcia stopped at the side of the SUV and grabbed the door handle. "I'm looking forward to a good adventure."

Judy opened her door, but looked across at Marcia before getting in. "Be careful what you wish for."

***

The highway was nearly deserted, as well as was the airport. They parked by the flight office to file a flight plan, and Alex followed Judy inside.

They found one person on duty, and Judy recognized the FAA employee, Bob Fisher. "Hey, Bob. Where is everyone?"

Fisher remained seated behind the desk and shrugged. "The airport's shut down, so everyone went home."

"Will I be able to take off?"

Fisher chuckled. "Sure, Judy, if you already have fuel. There isn't an airport within a thousand miles that will give you any. Haven't you heard? The government put a restriction on the sale of any kind of fuel. Hell, you can hardly buy gasoline anymore."

"Is there anyone manning the control tower?"

"Nope. If you're leaving, you still need to file a flight plan."

Judy filed her plan, using Alex as a contact. They returned to the SUV and drove to the hangars.

Alex recognized Judy's Cessna and stopped beside it. He helped Christa and Marcia load their baggage into the side compartment, and while the ladies climbed into the airplane, a mechanic walked over from outside the hangar and stopped to talk with Judy. Alex heard them arguing and saw the mechanic wave his arms for a second before Judy hurried back to the airplane.

"What was that all about?"

"He said my plane didn't have the mandatory one hundred hour tune-up and certification." Judy shrugged. "It was running fine two weeks ago, so there shouldn't be any problem."

A knot formed in Alex's stomach as Judy climbed the steps into the airplane. He closed the door behind her and stepped back as the engines spun to life, and after a few moments, Judy and the women waved as the Cessna rolled forward to the taxiway. Alex stood next to his SUV and watched the Cessna gain speed down the runway. When it climbed into the air and disappeared over the treetops, he climbed into his car and headed back to the College.

***

IDAHO:

Because of the noise, Marcia and Christa sat in seats near the rear of the airplane while talking about what experiments to perform with the powder. Both abruptly stopped when they heard one of the engines sputter. They sat in silence for a few moments, but the noise smoothed out and they continued talking about what to do when they reached Valdez. Fifteen minutes later, they heard an engine sputter again, smooth out, and then sputter erratically. Both women stood and moved up behind Judy, who flipped a switch on the console.

"What's wrong?" Christa asked.

Judy did not reply and kept glancing out the left window at a thin streak of brown oil blowing over the engine cowling. "Shit!" she swore and flipped the switch to shut down the engine.

Marcia and Christa looked at each other, seeing their fear reflected on each other's faces. Neither felt like returning to their seats and remained standing behind Judy.

"I'll have to turn back!" Judy shouted over her shoulder. "Don't worry. We can make it on one engine."

Judy got through to Fisher on the radio and informed him she was returning, but as she banked the plane, the right engine sputtered for a few moments before smoothing out. She looked over her shoulder at the worried expressions of her passengers, knowing there was nothing she could say to calm their fears. "Better sit down and fasten your seat belts. It might be a rough ride back."

Marcia and Christa returned to their seats, their adrenaline level rising with their sense of foreboding and fear. They fastened their seat belts and nervously glanced at each other. When the right engine sputtered, they stared at the back of Judy's head.

The women felt their stomachs rise as the plane lost altitude. Christa saw the terror-stricken look on Marcia's face and reached over to give her hand a reassuring squeeze, but knew she probably had the same look herself. She tried to smile reassuringly, but couldn't maintain it as the plane continued to drop.

The engine sputtered while Judy stared through the windows, desperately looking for a clear area to land, but seeing only the tops of trees. There was some sort of clearing about three miles ahead and to the left, but she couldn't tell how large it was. A glance at the falling altimeter showed her she had little choice, so she banked to the left and lined up on the clearing.

The treetops appeared to rise up as if to grab the fragile plane, while Judy watched the clearing draw near and realized it wasn't nearly large enough to land in, but she was committed and had no other option. The thought of her passengers flashed through her mind as she concentrated on controlling the airplane. "I'm sorry," she mumbled.

They were within one hundred feet of the small clearing when they felt a thump from a tree top against the bottom of the airplane, followed by several more thumps in rapid succession. At the last possible second, Judy lowered the landing gear as she pulled on the steering yoke. The airplane seemed to drop from beneath them as they cleared the trees, and everyone was forced against their seatbelts when the wheels pounded into the ground.

The right wheel collapsed under the wing, tossing everyone violently against the restraints, and then the wing dug into the ground, throwing the airplane into a flat spin. As the tail swung around, the left wheel collapsed and the nose wheel acted like a rudder, causing the plane to slide tail first. The momentum kept the airplane bouncing backward, its belly sliding across the field. When the tail section reached the trees on the opposite side, it miraculously slid between two massive trunks.

Everyone was violently hurled back into their seats as the wings were torn from the plane in a screech of tortured metal before the plane slid to a stop among the trees.

The speed and intensity of the event left everyone in stunned shock, then Christa heard a moan and turned to look at Marcia. The window beside Marcia's head was shattered, and a small trickle of blood ran down her cheek and dripped off the end of her chin.

She looked forward and saw Judy's head slumped over the steering yoke. She fumbled to unlatch her seat belt, and using the seats for support, Christa moved across to Marcia and grabbed her shoulder. "Marcia? Can you hear me?" Marcia's eyes slowly opened. "Marcia, it's me, Christa. How bad are you hurt?"

Marcia slowly came out of her foggy haze and saw someone leaning over her. The features were indistinct for a moment, and then became more focused, and she recognized Christa. "Umm," she moaned, and reached up to the side of her head. "Ah!" she winced and brought her hand back down.

"You have a nasty cut on your head," Christa told her. "Do you hurt anywhere else?"

"Ah, I don't think so. Just my head."

"All right. Just sit still while I check on Judy."

Christa turned and grabbed the back of the forward seats for support as she moved up the slanted aisle. She knelt next to Judy and looked her over carefully, and the only apparent injury was a large red welt on her forehead, near the hairline. Christa gripped Judy's right wrist, felt a strong pulse, and sighed with relief.

"Judy? Can you hear me?" Judy didn't reply, and Christa shook her shoulder. "Judy! Wake up!" she shouted, but Judy didn't stir.

Christa tried to gather her thoughts. "First aid," she said to herself. "There should be a first aid kit around here somewhere."

She looked all around the walls of the interior, but didn't see it. "Darn," she mumbled as a thought occurred to her. She knelt on the floor and looked under the seats. "Yes!" she shouted, and reached under to release the latches holding the first aid kit. She pulled it out and carried it back down the aisle before sitting next to Marcia. "How are you doing?"

"I'm fine. My head hurts, but otherwise, I think I'm okay."

Christa grabbed a few gauze pads. "Okay. I need to wipe away the blood for a better look." When Christa gently drew the pad across her forehead, she felt Marcia wince, but didn't utter a word. "It's not real bad, and it looks like the bleeding has stopped."

Marcia reached up and held a gauze pad in place as she looked at Judy. "How is she?"

"I think she was knocked out. She doesn't respond and has a nasty bruise on her forehead. As soon as you're ready, we'll get her out of the plane."

"There could be a fire, so we can't wait. We have to get Judy out now."

Fear suddenly coursed through her body, and Christa spun her head around, quickly looking through all the windows. "Not yet," she said, though her adrenaline level continued to rise. "I'll get her out. You stay here and rest a moment."

Christa hurried forward and released Judy's seat belt, grabbing her across the chest as she toppled forward. She didn't have time to consider how hard it might be for a woman her size to drag a limp body from the plane, since her only thought was to get Judy out. Christa wrapped her arms under Judy's shoulders and pulled her from behind the steering yoke, and grunting with the effort, she dragged her down the walkway and gently laid her on the floor.

She tried to open the door of the plane, but it was jammed. She put her shoulder against the door, shoving with all her weight, but it would not budge. "Open, darn it!" she yelled, grunting with pain each time her shoulder bounced off the unyielding metal.

She turned around, put her back against a seat opposite the door, and kicked the metal with her foot, but the door held fast. Frustrated, she brought both knees up against her chest and put every ounce of strength into her thrust, and with a screech of grinding metal, the door burst open.

Christa took a few seconds to catch her breath, then grabbed Judy under the arms and dragged her to the opening. She jumped out and pulled her through the doorway, and Judy's feet drop to the ground with a thud. Christa thought she heard Judy groan and gently laid her on the ground before climbing back into the airplane.

Marcia was already climbing out of her seat. "I'm okay. You'd better get Judy farther away from the plane."

"You sure you can manage?"

"Yes. Just hurry."

Christa checked to make sure the crystal, ampule, and data devices were still in her pockets, and then leapt out of the opening. The plane had stopped about one hundred feet into the trees at the edge of a small, grassy clearing, and when she saw the ground littered with broken branches and toppled trees, she realized she would have to carry Judy over the mess to the clearing.

She remembered watching a documentary on firefighters rescuing victims, and straddled Judy's legs, grabbed her wrists, and pulled like she remembered, but Judy's limp body bent in half at the waist, and Christa had to waddle back a few feet. She pulled on Judy's wrists again, but only got Judy's butt a few inches off the ground before letting her plop back down.

"Darn!" Christa swore in frustration while taking a few deep breaths. "I can do it! I *can* do it!" she growled and gripped Judy's wrists as tight as she could, then pulled with all her might. Leaning back for leverage, Judy's body slowly rose off the ground. Christa bent down to catch her and staggered backward as Judy's weight fell onto her shoulder. Grunting with the effort, Christa headed towards the clearing, barely keeping Judy balanced as she staggered over branches and tree trunks.

***

Marcia moved toward the exit as everything around her was spinning. She suddenly felt lightheaded and clung to the chair backs for support, waiting for several moments before the sensation stopped. She took two faltering steps forward, and the dizziness returned in full force, and she felt as though she was looking down a long, dark tunnel. Darkness closed in around her and she felt herself falling forward, but was helpless to stop it. The dark tunnel collapsed as she fell in front of the doorway.

***

Christa staggered into the clearing, her breath coming in deep gasps. She desperately wanted Judy's weight off her shoulder, but kept going for what felt like hundreds of yards until she reached the trees on the far side. She made it a few yards into the woods, then her legs gave out and she and Judy tumbled to the ground.

Christa laid there for several minutes, pinned to the ground from the waist up by Judy's body. Her breath came in ragged gasps, struggling to draw air into her lungs because of the weight, but she was too exhausted to shove Judy off her chest.

Christa wasn't sure how long she lay there before she heard Judy moan, then Judy's face turned toward her, and Christa watched Judy's eyes slowly open. Judy's vision slowly cleared, and she recognized the face beneath her. "Christa? What are you doing down there?"

Judy tried to push herself up, but her arms collapse. With Christa's help, she rolled to the side. "What happened?"

Christa heard a man's voice yelling orders. "Shush!"

She turned her head toward the wrecked plane and saw a dozen men running through the trees, pointing rifles at the fuselage. The man's voice was clear and demanding, even across the clearing, and Christa suddenly remembered Marcia. She started to stand until she heard the man yell, hold your fire! I want prisoners!

Not knowing what to do, but filled with a sense of dread, Christa stayed down, placing a hand on Judy as a signal to do the same. Christa searched for some sign Marcia had gotten out of the plane, but couldn't find her.

Chapter 23

WASHINGTON, D.C:

The President turned off the television, leaned back in his overstuffed chair, and stared at the white acoustical tiled ceiling. It seemed everyone was demanding something from him. His staff and advisors wanted him to make decisions, special interest groups were asking for a larger ration of fuel, and friends were asking for special privileges.

He closed his eyes and opened them at the sound of knocking on the door to his office. "Come in," he said in a voice he hoped hid the weariness he felt. He glanced at the brass-framed clock on the wall above the door and saw it was after seven and realized he had dozed off.

Martin Donner entered and closed the door behind him. "Sorry to disturb you, Sir."

The President noticed Donner's wrinkled suit, the bags under his bloodshot eyes, and the stubble of beard, and wondered if Donner had even left the White House over the past five days. "When was the last time you got some sleep?" Donner smiled at him, but even that had a weary look to it.

"I caught a few hours yesterday."

Bullshit, the President thought, but didn't press it. "What's up?"

"First, I think we should cordon off access to the White House in a five-block radius. Then set up a military command post out front with support troops stationed on the grounds."

The President frowned. "Is it that bad?"

"Not yet, but it will be."

"Continue."

"Set up roadblocks around cities that still have power and try to limit the civil riots that I know will eventually happen."

"The Joint Chiefs will not like wasting our domestic reserves on civilian matters."

"They'll waste more when we have to call them in to enforce Martial Law."

"I know. Okay. I'll tell them. Have you received any word from Alex Cave?"

"The women doing the research are on the way to Alaska. There's still some crude oil there, and that's where the experiments have to continue. All we can do is hope they come up with something."

The President leaned back in his chair. "Get some sleep, Martin." He smiled. "That's an order."

Donner smiled back and stood. "Yes, Sir," he replied and then left the office.

Chapter 24

BOZEMAN, MONTANA:
On the drive back to the college, Alex noticed more cars abandoned along the highway, and a man, woman, and two children walking along the road a short distance ahead. The man turned and held his thumb out for a ride, and Alex slowed as he approached. He noticed the children were mere toddlers, perhaps three and four years old, and the woman was carrying a heavy tote bag. It was still a good five miles to town, and Alex felt sympathy for them, so he pulled alongside and unlocked the passenger door.

The man smiled, opened the door, and leaned down to look inside. "I sure appreciate this, mister. We've been walking for miles, and the kids are pooped."

"I can give you a ride as far as the college, but it's on the outskirts of town."

"That would be great. It sure beats walking."

The woman opened the rear door and helped the children in, while the man sat up front with Alex. When everyone was inside, Alex continued down the highway.

"My name is Joe Dempsey, and that's my wife, Carol. The kids are Jessie and Marie."

"I'm Alex Cave."

There were a few moments of silence before Dempsey spoke. "Things sure are a mess, aren't they? Can't get any gas, can't hardly get any food, and if you can find it, whoever's selling it wants a fortune, I'll tell ya."

"Where are you from?"

"Just over the border in Idaho. Things got nasty, so we headed east. I'm an investment broker, or I should say, I *used* to be an investment broker. There's nothing to invest in anymore."

"Did you have any trouble getting gas along the way?"

"Yeah, yesterday. We couldn't find any stations open, but we came across a man selling gas out of the back of his pickup. What a ripoff, though. He had it in five-gallon cans and wanted fifty dollars per can. It about wiped me out to fill up the tank, but what can you do? I don't know what was mixed in with the gas, but my car didn't run worth a damn from then on and finally quit about ten miles back."

A car was coming in the opposite direction, weaving back and forth across the center line. "Damn fool must be drunk," said Dempsey.

As the oncoming car drew closer, it appeared there was no one behind the wheel, and Alex noticed the car looked familiar. It was an older model blue Cadillac, going very slowly as it continued weaving across the center line. When it was within one hundred feet, Alex could make out the license plate number. "That car is stolen! It belongs to a friend of mine."

The Cadillac drifted farther into his lane as it approached, and Alex had to pull onto the shoulder and slam on the brakes to keep from being hit. He watched it drive past and noticed the small head, barely even with the steering wheel. "Some kid is driving that car. How did. . ." He abruptly stopped when he felt something small and cold against the back of his head and started to turn around to see what it was.

"Don't move a muscle!" The woman snarled in his ear.

Alex couldn't believe this was happening. "What's going on?"

Dempsey leaned forward. "Just give me your wallet and step out of the car."

"Look, you don't have to do this. I'll take you into town, and I promise I won't say anything to the police."

Dempsey chuckled. "Haven't you heard, mister? The police don't have any gas for their cars, either." Dempsey became serious again. "Just do what I say, damn it, or I'll have Carol blow your damn head off!"

"All right, just take it easy." He shoved the shift lever into park and reached into his back pocket for his wallet.

"I've got a family to take care of, mister. You've got to understand that."

Alex brought his wallet out and set eighty-eight dollars on the seat. "That's all I have."

"Just set the money and your phone on the seat and get out!"

Alex did as instructed and stood beside the door as Dempsey slid across the seat while Carol kept the gun aimed out the window at him. Dempsey shifted the car into gear and stomped on the accelerator, leaving Alex in a cloud of dust.

Alex sighed in frustration and began walking, thinking perhaps this was only the beginning and would definitely get worse before it got better. Along the way, he strolled past an abandoned sedan and looked through the broken window, and saw opened suitcases and scattered clothing, but nothing of value.

An hour later, Alex approached the college campus and heard several gunshots. He saw people running across the lawns and quickened his pace until he reached the nearly deserted parking lot, and dove for the ground as someone rose above the hood of a car and pointed a pistol in his direction.

A bullet ricocheted off the asphalt just past his head at the same instant he heard the explosion from the pistol and scrambled to his feet as he looked around for some kind of cover. He made a dash for a black Camaro, twenty feet away, as another bullet chipped the asphalt. He dove onto the broken glass on the ground beside the car, then rolled onto his feet and squatted beside the rear tire.

Several moments passed without another shot fired, but he could hear people screaming in agony, and other voices shouting orders. Windows were being shattered, and two more gunshots echoed from far away.

Alex slowly rose until he could see over the Camaro and the back window lay in shattered pieces across the trunk. People were running down the street in panic as two boys and two girls were climbing into a brown Volkswagen Van. A moment later, he heard the sputter of the engine and watched the van race out of the parking lot.

Alex remained squatted behind the Camaro as he studied the rest of the parking lot, and what few cars remained had shattered windows and flat tires, and he saw three people lying on the ground. When nothing moved, he slowly stood for a better view and saw five more people with red stains on the light-colored shirts lying on the grass near the administration building.

He slowly stepped around the Camaro and approached the closest person, and saw the bloody pool around the body and the dull eyes staring up at nothing. He moved from body to body, occasionally kneeling to feel for a pulse, when the girl closest to the building suddenly rolled over and squirmed backwards on her rump.

Alex stopped and stared into her terror-stricken face. She was about nineteen or twenty, he thought, with soft brown eyes and dark brown hair hanging to her shoulders, and had a small earring pierced through her nose. "It's all right. I'm not going to hurt you." The girl stopped squirming and stared at him, still fearful and apprehensive, so Alex knelt down, but kept his distance. "Are you hurt?"

The girl looked down at herself, as if unsure. She slowly looked up and shook her head no, but didn't speak.

Alex smiled. "That's good. I think it might be a good idea if we went inside the building for protection."

He slowly stood and held out his hand. The girl stared at him for a moment, and then hesitantly reached up, so he slowly stepped closer and helped her stand up.

He released her hand and started walking around the debris scattered over the sidewalk toward the door of the building. He didn't look back, but could tell she was following by the sound of her footsteps on the sidewalk. When they reached the door, he held it open and stepped back to let her through, receiving a quick glance and a timid smile for his efforts.

They listened to the soft echo of their footsteps as they walked down the deserted hallway. As they passed the windows of the admittance office, they saw a woman draped over the counter, and the wall beneath her streaked with a deep red stain. Alex glanced at the girl's face, and she just stared impassively at the sight.

Alex stopped and opened the door to the administrator's office, and recognized the man sprawled in his high back leather chair, his chin resting on his chest above a large red stain on his white shirt.

Alex turned and faced the girl. "What happened here?" The girl just stared past him into the room, transfixed by the horror, which was rapidly becoming all too familiar.

Alex closed the door, and they continued down the hall, stopping occasionally to look into other rooms and didn't find anyone else, alive or dead. Near the end of the hall, Alex noticed the door to the laboratory hanging crooked. "David!"

Alex ran down the hall and grabbed the door frame to slow down. He stopped in the doorway and looked around, and it was as though a tornado had hit the room. Test tubes, flasks, and decanters lay in smashed pieces on the counters and floors. All the portable test equipment was missing, and what hadn't been stolen had been severely damaged.

He saw a tennis shoe protruding past the edge of the counter and ran inside, slipping on fragments of glass. He found David sprawled on the floor, knelt beside him, and grabbed his wrist to feel for a pulse as he frantically searched for a bullet wound. A deep sense of relief washed over him when he couldn't find a wound, and David's pulse was strong and regular. He carefully ran his hands over David's legs and arms, searching for any other injuries, but found none. He gently turned David's head and saw the bruise near the right eye and the swollen knot on the side of his head.

David suddenly moaned, and Alex gently shook his shoulder. "Can you hear me? It's Alex Cave." The young man's eyes slowly opened and squinted up at him. "That's it, pal. You're going to be okay." David's eyes suddenly went wide with fear and darted back and forth around the room as he tried to sit up. "Easy now. It's all right. Nobody's going to hurt you."

David focused on Alex's face and slowly relaxed. "My head hurts," he moaned and lay back down.

"You've got a nasty bump on the head, so just lay still for a moment. Can you tell me what happened?"

David looked as though he was having a hard time concentrating. "I'm not exactly sure. I heard people yelling and a couple of gunshots, so I went to the door and saw people running down the hall. I don't know why they were running like that. Everyone seemed to be crazy, pushing and shoving each other. Some of them were carrying typewriters, computers, and other stuff. I remember someone shoving me back into the room, and then it seemed like a hundred people were coming through the door. They started grabbing things, and I wanted to stop them, but that's all I can remember."

"All right. Just lay here and take it easy."

"No. I'm all right. Just help me stand up."

Alex grabbed his arm, and as they stood, David suddenly went rigid with fear. Alex looked across the counter and saw the girl standing near the door. "It's all right. She's with me. Come on. I need to find a phone."

David nodded and headed toward the door, and looked at the girl, who quickly looked down at the floor and stepped back. David moved past her, trying to collect his thoughts and comprehend the surrounding chaos.

Alex stepped in front of her, and when she looked up into his eyes, he saw the dazed look and knew she needed their help. "Maybe you should come with us. It might be safer." The girl followed him through the doorway into the hall, where David was waiting.

"What's her name?" David asked.

"I don't know. She's still in shock and hasn't said a word since I found her out on the lawn." Alex continued down the hall. "Poor girl must have seen everything that happened in the parking lot."

"What happened?"

"A gunfight and several people were killed right in front of her." Alex explained what he had heard on the news, what Donner had told him, and what happened on the way back from the airport. "I'm just glad our women got out of here safely. I need to find a phone."

David continued down the hallway. "What happened to your cellphone?"

"I was car-jacked on the way here." He stopped at the administrator's office door. "You should stay out here. Director Fernley has been shot."

When Alex opened the door and stepped inside, David couldn't resist the urge to look. He wasn't sure why, but the sight didn't seem to bother him, so he followed Alex into the room.

Alex turned when he heard footsteps behind him, surprised to see David looking around the room nonchalantly. He picked up the phone, heard a dial tone, and dialed the number to retrieve voice messages from his cellphone service. "This is Bob Fisher, from the Federal Aviation Administration office at the airport. Your phone number was on the flight plan for a Cessna, number Sierra November Alpha 3492. I, ah, I wanted to inform you the flight had some mechanical problem and was going to return to the airport, but that was about two hours ago, and we haven't heard from them since. Please call me at this number." Alex pressed the clear button and dialed again.

David heard him and saw the troubled expression on his face. "What's wrong?"

"I'm not positive yet. Hold on a minute," he said as Fisher came on the line. "This is Alex Cave. Have you heard anything from the Cessna?"

"No, I'm sorry, Mister Cave. The last word we received was they were somewhere over Idaho. Are you related to the pilot?"

"No. She's just a good friend. Do you know if they crashed or made an emergency landing somewhere else?"

"No, we don't have any idea what happened. Listen, Mister Cave. I need to get in touch with the pilot's next of kin."

"You must have been tracking them on radar. Where are they?" Alex heard a heavy sigh through the phone.

"Look, Mister Cave. All we know is they were about eighty miles over the Idaho border when they dropped off the radar screen. Now, if you'd give me the number."

"Have you sent out a search team yet?"

"Damn it, Mister Cave! There isn't anything we can do right now. Haven't you heard there's a national crisis going on?"

"I know, but this is very important!"

"They all are. Now if you'd just give me."

"No, you don't understand! That plane was carrying important information, critical to the situation going on right now!"

"Thanks for the help!"

Alex heard a click on the other end and slammed the phone down. He looked up at David, who was staring back with a worried look. "They went down about eighty miles over the border. See if you can find a map."

While Alex searched the room, David saw the muscles at the back of Alex's jaw flexing in anger and frustration. He'd never seen him like this, and the cold, determined look in Alex's eyes scared him a little. He found a world atlas and set it on the desk. "This might work."

Alex looked up and saw the trace of fear in David's eyes and relaxed a little. "It's all so frustrating. We have no transportation, no food, and no weapons. How are we supposed to find the women?" Alex watched David grin and wondered what was so amusing.

David shrugged. "We have food. I've been stashing supplies in some caves I've found. You see, I've always had this idea that I should be prepared for a disaster, but I thought everyone would think I was being paranoid, so I never told anyone."

Alex's frown spread into a grin. "David, my boy, you're all right." He opened the atlas. "Okay. Show me where these caves are."

David pointed at the map. "There are seven of them starting here, about five miles west of town. The last one is here, just west of the Idaho border."

"Good. They're all in the direction we need to go. Are there any weapons in this first one?"

"Yes, as well as food, two sleeping bags, water, and lots of other things I'd need to survive."

"Great. Let's get going. We might get to the first cave before dark."

Alex ripped the pages for Idaho and Montana out of the atlas, and both men walked to the door. When they stepped through, they saw the girl standing in the hall and exchanged troubled looks.

Alex stepped closer to her. "Do you have any family nearby?" She shook her head no. "Where do you live?" The girl turned and pointed toward the girls' dormitory. "Okay. We'll walk you over, and then we have to leave." The girl's eyes became wide with fear and she shook her head no.

Alex sighed and glanced across at David, then back at the girl. "Listen. We have to leave, and we can't take you with us. I'm sorry, but we have a long way to go, and it's dangerous." The look in the girl's eyes reminded him of a lost puppy, but he knew she would slow them down if they took her with them. He stepped away and walked with David down the hall. He looked back as they walked through the door out of the building and felt sorry for the shy girl still standing in the hall.

Chapter 25

BOZEMAN, MONTANA:

After leaving the college, Alex and David walked down the main street of town, and the city of Bozeman seemed deserted. The few people they passed stared at them suspiciously and some dashed inside buildings as they approached, and the few vehicles along the streets had been stripped. The shattered windows and bullet-riddled walls of the buildings gave evidence of the mass hysteria, which seemed to be spreading quickly.

On the horizon, above the buildings, uncontrolled fires cast thick black smoke high into the air. They walked past a bicycle shop, and through the missing front window, saw three bodies on the floor among the empty stands and racks. A police car had crashed into a light pole and the bloodied torso of the officer was still hanging limply out of the door.

Alex felt a deep sense of despair for the people living in a state of panic and fear in a society where the only rule was the law of survival. They continued through the main street of town, passing more shattered windows, burning vehicles, and occasionally, a body.

A dozen young boys stepped out of a tavern advertising six pool tables and stood on the sidewalk. The boys acted nonchalant, but Alex noticed the insolent looks in their eyes. "Let's cross the street," he whispered to David.

When they stepped off the curb, four of the youths left the group and walked on an intercept course, and Alex knew they were due for a confrontation. He stopped and waited for the boys to approach, deciding to let the four of them move as far away from their friends as possible.

The boys stopped a few feet away, their movements bold and assured. "We want your money, man," the oldest and bravest demanded.

None of them could have been over eighteen, and the one doing the talking seemed sure of himself. The others were putting on a good front, but from long experience, Alex sensed a slight trace of fear in their eyes.

They seemed satisfied to let the older boy do the talking, so Alex stared at him. "You have enough problems. You don't want a problem with me."

The boy hesitated. His other victims had given them what they wanted, but this man seemed too eager to fight. "You think you can take us, man?"

Alex shifted his gaze to each of the boys, coldly looking each in the eye, reading a slight trace of trepidation as each of them looked away. A visual picture of the Russian Mafia men he had desecrated in Holland flashed through his mind. Of course, he could take them, but what would be the sense of killing these young boys? He had killed the Mafia men in a fit of savage revenge, but these boys were just scared and trying to survive in a world gone mad, so he focused on the apparent leader. "What's your name?"

"William. Hey, man. I'll ask the questions!"

"You're too late. Someone already beat you to our money. If you want a fight, I'll give you one, but I suggest you just let us go on our way."

William wasn't used to being confronted, and this man seemed sure of himself. He didn't want to lose face in front of his peers, but didn't really want to fight this man either. "If you ain't got any money, you can go, but you'd better not come back! This is our turf. You got that, man?"

Alex knew the dilemma William was in and decided to help him out of the situation. "Yes, I've got it. We'll stay off your turf."

William looked down the street, past Alex and David. "What about her? Is she with you?"

David turned to look, but Alex continued to stare at William, thinking it might be a trick.

"Oh, no!" David mumbled. "It's the girl from the college. She's been following us."

Alex continued to stare at William. "Yes, she's with us. So what's it going to be, William?"

When William pumped out his chest, turned, and led his friends back across the street, Alex and David turned toward the girl standing on the sidewalk a short distance away. He knew she would never make it on her own and waved her over, and she slowly approached and stopped in front of him. "You'd better stay close to us." She nodded gratefully, with a trace of a smile.

The trio continued at a brisk pace and reached the outskirts of town without further incident. At the last telephone booth, Alex tried to call Donner, but couldn't get through.

They walked up the on-ramp and along a highway littered with abandoned cars, trucks, suitcases, and other personal belongings left behind by people too tired to carry more than the bare necessities. He scanned the highway and didn't see anyone, and wondered what had happened to them.

David stopped and pointed at a mountain range across a wide, green valley. "That's where we need to go. The third peak from the right. I've always driven to the base of the mountains, but the road to get there is another five miles. Since we're on foot, there's no reason we can't cut across right here."

They ducked through a barbed wire fence and began their trek across the valley until they reached the dirt road at the foot of the mountain range. "We'll follow this road up a little farther and then cut through the trees." David told him.

Alex, David, and the girl turned to look at the city one more time and saw several large columns of thick black smoke curling into the air above Bozeman. "Damn!" David mumbled. "It looks like the city is on fire. We'd better get going. It's still a long way to the cave."

They crossed a small stream, and the girl stopped and knelt beside it. "Don't drink that!" David yelled. "It's too slow, and probably full of bacteria, and it'll make you sick. There's a good stream a little way up the mountain."

David didn't care to have this girl along in the first place, and her silence only added to his aggravation. "Are you mute or something?" he said coldly. "You haven't said a thing since I met you. I don't even know your name!" he shouted.

Alex grabbed David's shoulder and spun him around. "That's enough! She's been through a very traumatic experience, so just give her some time to recover, all right?"

David nodded okay, looked at the frightened girl, and felt ashamed for yelling at her. "I'm sorry," he said, and the girl nodded.

They continued up the road, occasionally glancing back down at the city as they gained altitude. They stopped next to a fast-moving stream, drank ravenously, and took one more look at the smoke before entering the thick forest. From their vantage point, it appeared the entire city was ablaze.

They continued for another four miles, and then David stopped. "This is it."

Alex looked around, but didn't see an opening. "Where?"

David grinned, ducked between two large bushes, and disappeared. Alex ducked through the bushes and saw a small opening between three stacked boulders and crawled through, emerging into a dark chamber, followed by the girl. The only sound was a quiet, metallic clicking. A moment later, the clicking ceased, and a flame flared to life, illuminating

David's face and the Coleman lantern on the floor in front of him. The lantern hissed for a second as he opened the valve, then it flared into a bright white light.

David stood and set the lantern on a narrow rock shelf, stepped back, and spread his arms as he looked at Alex and the girl. "So, what do you think?"

Alex looked around the chamber, and it was about thirty feet wide, twenty feet deep, and ten feet high. "I'm impressed."

David reached into a plastic bag and brought out several packaged food bars, and passed them out to his guests. The girl wrapped her arms around David's neck and buried her face against his chest, and he felt her body heave with great sobs, so he wrapped his arms around her, pulling her close. "It's all right now. Nothing's going to hurt you."

David felt the girl's sobs subside, and she slowly lifted her head to look up at him, and the terror was gone from her watery red eyes. It took a moment, but she smiled.

"Thank you," she said softly in a velvety smooth voice. "I'm sorry I'm not more helpful."

David found her voice very pleasing and smiled in return. "That's all right. Don't worry about it. What's your name?"

She looked at him. "What?"

"You haven't spoken since we first met, so I don't know your name."

She looked puzzled for a moment. "Sharlett. My name's Sharlett Mason." She looked as if still in a daze. "I know both your names, but I'm not sure where I am. I remember walking across the campus with Mike." Her eyes widened slightly. "Oh, no! Mike was shot!" She frantically looked around the cave. "Where is he?" Tears filled her eyes again, and she looked stricken with grief. "He's dead, isn't he?"

David looked into her eyes. "I'm sorry."

She nodded and tried to compose herself. "Thanks. I guess you'd better tell me what we're doing here."

"How much do you remember?" Alex asked her.

"Just that Mike was shot. And everybody was running."

Alex nodded. "All right." He explained what he saw in the parking lot and how she came to be with them. "We hiked up here this afternoon."

"So what happens now?"

"We're on our way to Idaho to find some friends. I guess you can either come with us or go your own way. Do you have any family in the area?"

She shook her head no. "All my relatives live on the East Coast. I suppose I could take a bus or something."

Alex looked at her for a moment. "Listen, Sharlett. There aren't any buses or trains, and no cars. Only your own two legs for getting around." She didn't reply, and simply stared in bewilderment. "You're welcome to come with us."

When Sharlett asked several questions about what was happening in the world, Alex did his best to explain. She thought these men had been exceptionally nice to her and had probably saved her life. Even though she didn't know them all that well, she felt secure and comfortable with them. "If you really don't mind, I'd like to go with you."

David thought about it for a moment. She was bright and intelligent, and now that she was talking, he enjoyed listening to her voice. She'd already proven she could keep up with them, and they would have plenty of supplies from the caves along the way, so he smiled at her. "I think that would be just fine."

She smiled in return. "I can carry my share, and I won't be a burden."

Alex nodded. "Now that it's settled, let's get packed. We have a long way to go."

"It's too late to continue," said David. "We should wait until the morning to get going." When Alex indicated he agreed, David indicated the floor of the cave. "Might as well get comfortable. At least, as much as possible."

Chapter 26

IDAHO:

As Christa and Judy watched, the soldiers pulled Marcia from the plane and lay her on the ground as one of the men climbed inside. "She's the only one in here, Major Everex," the man shouted from the doorway.

"Get out of the way!" a different voice shouted.

The soldiers stepped away from Marcia and a short, gray-haired man with a white armband knelt beside her. "She'll be all right. Looks like a mild concussion, so you two carry her to the infirmary. And be careful with her!"

Everex looked down at the woman. "You'd better add two more men, doc. She's a big bitch." He looked at his other men. "Search the area. There's too much luggage for one woman."

Christa and Judy exchanged looks. "Can you walk okay?" Christa asked.

"Yeah, let's get out of here."

They crawled for a few yards until the trees hid them. They stood and walked in the opposite direction of the soldiers, and several hundred yards farther, Judy stopped. "Wait a minute. This is crazy. We don't even know where we're going."

"You're saying we should go with the soldiers?"

Judy shrugged. "Why not? The worst that could happen is they give us food, water, and a place to sleep."

Christa shook her head no. "That man said he wanted prisoners, and that doesn't sound very inviting to me."

"What else are we going to do? Face it. We're lost."

Christa looked around and sighed in resignation. "I suppose you're right."

Judy started walking back the way they came, and Christa followed. When they reached the wrecked plane, the soldiers were gone, so they followed their trail.

***

Marcia opened her eyes and stared up at a log ceiling. She turned her head to the right and saw three empty beds, and when she turned to the left, saw a young boy sitting in a chair against the wall, engrossed in a paperback book. "Who are you?" she asked.

The boy looked up at her. "She's come too, Doc," he hollered.

Marcia sat up and looked around and noticed some medical equipment on a shelf above the boy. The door next to him opened, and a gray-haired man wearing a uniform and a stethoscope hanging from his neck strolled in.

"Hello, Miss Story. How are you feeling?"

"Fine, I think. Where am I?"

"At the moment, you're in my infirmary. Do you remember what happened?"

It took her a moment, but he remembered. "The plane wreck."

"That's right. You were unconscious, with a mild concussion, when we found you."

Marcia glanced around nervously. "What about . . .?"

"Go get Miss Story some cold water, Private Woolly," the doctor interrupted and waited until Mark Woolly left the room. "Major Everex searched the area, but luckily, didn't find your friend, so she must be all right."

"There were two women with me. What do you mean by luckily?"

The doctor frowned. "Things have changed around here since Major Everex was promoted. It's not a good place for you or your friends."

Marcia looked at the patch on his uniform. "What does AOS stand for?"

"Army of Survival. Listen, Miss Story. The Major thinks you only had one friend, and he is sending out another search party to find her, so make up a story she wasn't with you or something."

"What about me?"

"Colonel Blackwood and the Major will question you in a little while. After that, I don't know."

Mark returned with a pitcher of water and a glass and poured some for Marcia. "The Colonel stopped me, doc. He said to bring her to his cabin as soon as possible."

"I can delay this for a little while, if you want?"

"No, I don't want to lie here and worry about it. I'd rather get it over with."

"Your bags are under the bed, and there's a bathroom in the next room if you'd like to freshen up first."

Marcia looked down, realized she was wearing a white hospital gown, and smiled. "Thanks." She swung her legs over the edge and stood, and the boy dragged her suitcase out and set it on the bed. "How did you know my name?"

The doctor stepped through the doorway and returned with her purse. "I looked at your driver's license and faculty ID," he said as he handed it to her.

Marcia dug through her suitcase and grabbed what she needed, picked up her purse, and walked into the bathroom. In the mirror, she saw her hair was a mess and her mascara smeared, so she dressed and did what she could to her hair, and once satisfied with her makeup, left the bathroom and found the doctor sitting at his desk. "Guess I'm as ready as I can be."

The doctor looked up and smiled. "Much better." His smile slipped away. "Mark? Take Miss Story to see the Colonel."

Marcia saw the sad look in the doctor's eyes and wondered what was going to be so terrible. Whatever it was, she had no choice, straightened her shoulders and smiled at the doctor. "Thanks for the help, and don't worry. I can take care of myself."

The doctor forced a smile and watched her follow Mark through the door, but his smile vanished. "I hope so."

She and Mark stepped out of the infirmary and headed across the parade ground. "Where are you from, Mark?" Marcia asked in her friendliest manner. She figured the more friends she made in this place, the more she might learn about where she was and what it was all about.

"Seattle, Washington, ma'am."

"That's a long way from here."

"Yes, ma'am."

"What made you come all the way out here?"

"I've always wanted to be in the army, and when things got crazy, my family and I came here with Mister Monroe."

"You came with your parents?"

"Yes, ma'am, and my sister."

"So, what do they do here?"

"Train, mostly. You see, if there's a war or something, we can fight the enemy. Major Everex has stolen enough supplies to last . . ."

"That's enough, Private!" someone yelled harshly.

Marcia looked up at the porch of Blackwood's cabin and saw a tall man with a black patch over his left eye staring down at her. Strangely, she was attracted to him.

"Yes, sir," Mark replied. "This is the woman from the plane wreck, Colonel."

"That will be all, Private."

Mark left without looking at Marcia, who continued to look up at the man on the porch. Blackwood studied Marcia and found her attractive, even with the small bandage visible under her hair. He had seldom met a woman who was as tall as he was and found it stimulating. His demeanor changed, and he smiled graciously. "Please come up on the porch and have a seat, Miss Story."

Marcia thought Blackwood was ruggedly handsome, standing tall and confident in his uniform. Even the black patch over the eye seemed to add to his rugged good looks. She suddenly felt embarrassed, and thought she must look awful with a bandage stuck to her head, and unconsciously reached up and patted her hair.

Marcia walked up the steps, grabbing the handrail in an exaggerated manner, as if she might pass out, hoping to evoke some sympathy. It worked better than she had hoped, and Blackwood quickly descended and took her arm to help.

"Thank you, Colonel," she said, and smiled ingratiatingly. "I'm very sorry about the inconvenience. Your medical staff is very proficient, and I'm immensely in your debt."

Blackwood helped her into a wicker chair. "Think nothing of it. I'm just glad you weren't seriously injured. You could have been killed." Marcia smiled, and Blackwood suddenly laughed. "And I could have been killed, too. Your plane nearly took the roof off my cabin."

Marcia brought her hand up to her mouth in mock astonishment. "Oh, my goodness! I'm so sorry. I had no idea!"

"Yes, well, let's just thank our lucky stars, and don't think anything more about it. You must be thirsty. Can I get you something to drink?"

"Oh, that would be most kind of you."

"Is beer okay?"

"That would be lovely."

"Wonderful. Just make yourself comfortable. I'll be right back."

When Blackwood stepped inside the cabin, Marcia smiled to herself. *At least he's a gentleman.*

Blackwood returned with two beers and glasses and handed one to her. "Tell me what happened and how you came to be flying over my camp."

"Oh, it's this oil problem. I simply had to find somewhere else to live. I'm a college instructor, you see, and when supplies ran short in town, the school was closed. I had no means of support, and no one to teach. What good is a teacher without students? I thought there must be a community somewhere who would need educating their children."

"Yes. Education is a valuable thing."

"Oh, I agree. Anyway, I heard of a community in Alaska looking for teachers, and they would supply living accommodations and meals for my services. My plane was fine when I left Bozeman, but then the engines began acting up. Thank goodness you were here to assist me, Colonel. I'm sure I would have perished if it weren't for you and your people."

Blackwood smiled proudly. "Think nothing of it." He looked thoughtful for a moment and then smiled at her. "We could use a teacher here in the AOS. You can stay right here and teach the children."

"Well, thank you, Colonel, but I've already promised the people in Alaska." Marcia noticed Blackwood's solemn look. "I'm sorry, Colonel."

Blackwood looked up into her eyes with a saddened expression. "I'm sorry, too. You see, we can't allow you to leave."

Marcia was stunned for a moment. "I don't understand, Colonel. Why can't I leave?"

Another voice answered her question. "Because nobody leaves this camp. You either join us or die."

Marcia looked toward the bottom of the steps at John Everex and then turned to Blackwood. "Is that true, Colonel?"

"I'm afraid so. No one on the outside can learn where we are."

"Oh, but I assure you, Colonel. I won't tell a soul. Besides, I don't even know where this place is. Couldn't you blindfold me and take me somewhere?"

Blackwood thought it was a good idea. Before he could reply, Everex answered.

"Not a chance. Now, you have three choices. You can train to be a soldier, become part of the special services, or you can die."

Blackwood couldn't stand the thought of this tall, beautiful woman being a camp prostitute, and shot a menacing look at Everex. "No, John. She's a teacher. She can set up a school for the children."

Everex laughed harshly. "We don't need a damn school here. Hell, I only made it through the tenth grade and look at me. I'm a damn major."

Blackwood slowly stood and stared at Everex. *Yes, and look at what an ignorant, sadistic bastard you are, too.* Having this intelligent, attractive woman with him seemed to spark a sense of honor in him, and Blackwood slowly walked down the steps until he was toe to toe with Everex and looked him squarely in the eyes. "I mean it, Major! The world is changing, and we're like a city here. I want educated soldiers, not a bunch of bumbling morons."

It had been a long time since Everex had seen such a defiant attitude in the Colonel. Something had changed in him because of this woman, and he didn't like it. The Colonel had a point, though. They already had more than enough prostitutes, and the Amazon woman was too old to be a soldier. The camp had grown to over five hundred people, and at least thirty of them were children, too young to do much of anything in the camp. In addition, five babies had been born since he took over as Major. He had to admit the camp was turning into a small city, of sorts, and it would be good to get the little rug rats out of the way.

"All right, Colonel. We'll try it." He looked at Marcia. "We found smaller size clothing in two of the bags, so we know there were two of you in the plane. What happened to the other girl?"

Marcia knew this moment would come and had tried to think of what she'd say. She realized this Major Everex thought Christa's clothes were for a small girl and had an idea. "Those clothes belong to my niece. She was going to come with me." Marcia tried to look as sad as possible. "Oh, it was terrible! Everyone went crazy on campus, and somebody shot her!" Marcia buried her face in her hands and pressed her fingers against her eyes to make them red while she pretended to cry.

"I think that's enough questions for now, Major," said Blackwood.

"For now, Colonel." Everex replied, spun on his heels, and walked across the parade ground.

Blackwood turned to Marcia. "I'm sorry about your niece," he said sincerely.

Marcia looked up. "Thank you, Colonel."

"Well, I guess now you're our teacher. Is that all right with you?"

"He scares me, so I would much rather leave."

Blackwood's smile faded. "I'm sorry. I know Major Everex wouldn't hesitate to shoot you if you tried. Please, just try to make the most of it. We have plenty of food and shelter. Probably more than those people in Alaska. What do you say?"

Marcia knew better than to push the issue and thought it best to stay on Blackwood's good side, and smiled graciously. "All right, Colonel. You have yourself a teacher."

Blackwood's smile spread from ear to ear. "Wonderful."

"What are special services?" she asked.

"It's the, ah, personnel entertainment tents."

"You mean prostitutes?" Blackwood lowered his head. "Then I'm glad I'm a teacher. Well, Colonel. Show me where I'll be staying and where I can set up our school."

Blackwood's joy returned. "I'll have one of my men set you up in a private tent and make arrangements for the use of the main building as a classroom."

Marcia took a sip of beer from her glass to hide her sense of relief. Now she knew Christa and Judy would be somewhere nearby, and perhaps they would help her escape.

Chapter 27

COOK INLET, ALASKA:

Blustery gray clouds filled the sky as Bull stood on the bridge of the oil tanker, watching the last fifty-caliber machine gun being assembled by quiet, competent men in green, camouflaged clothing. Behind him stood Navy Commander Dale Anderson, an old combat vet now commanding the Navy's elite SEAL team. Anderson wore the same camouflaged clothing, and his short-cropped gray hair was nearly hidden beneath the matching ball cap. Captain Parks was standing inside the bridge, barking orders to the sailors who would steer the tanker down to Washington.

Bull stepped to the railing and looked down at the Black Hawk combat helicopter parked on the tanker's main deck and two more fifty-caliber machine guns stationed and manned around the helicopter then turned and looked at Anderson. "I'm impressed, but from what I've seen, I don't think you have to worry about external forces attacking this tanker."

Anderson grinned agreeably. "Yes, I've read the report. My job is to protect this tanker any way I see fit. With the oil shortage, the Russians or Chinese might try an assault."

"You mean the fanatics with the little tubes of crystals?"

Anderson looked at him quizzically. "I wasn't informed about little tubes. Only that this ship could be attacked, and this supply of crude oil had to reach Washington. What are these tubes of crystals?"

"I don't know all the details. Just there are thousands of them, and they do something to the oil."

"Hmm, interesting. Well, that's just like the military. They only tell me what I need to know. Are you sure you don't want to come with us?"

Bull shook his head no. "I'm just a civilian, so I'll let you take the responsibility."

"Fair enough."

"Good luck."

Bull climbed down the ladder to the main deck and walked across the gangway to the dock. The feisty little loading supervisor, Bruce Sullivan, was waiting for him. "So, how's it going?"

Bruce leaned in close to Bull's ear. "It's done. Ready when you are."

"All right, I'll get started as soon as the ship leaves the harbor."

Bull and Bruce watched the crane remove the gangplank and the civilians on the dock toss off the mooring lines. Two tugboats blew long blasts from their horns and pushed the tanker away from the dock, and then gray smoke blossomed from the tanker's stacks as she headed out of the harbor.

Bruce looked up at Bull's troubled expression. "Do you think you'll get in trouble for this, Bull?"

Bull strolled next to Bruce along the pier. "Not a chance. They have no idea how much crude oil is supposed to be in the tanker. If they make it to Washington, fine. If not, at least I'll have a supply for Christa when she arrives."

At the end of the pier, Bruce said goodbye as Bull climbed into a black All-Alaska SUV and drove away from the pumping station. He stopped at the front of two unmarked flatbed trucks, each with a canvas covering the ten fifty-five gallon drums of crude oil stacked on their beds. He grabbed a portable radio, climbed out of his vehicle, and walked to the driver's side of the first truck. "All set?"

The driver smiled while his passenger held up a twelve-gauge shotgun for Bull to see. "Just like driving a stagecoach across the frontier, Bull."

Bull grinned at the driver and raised the radio close to his mouth. "Are you ready, Kirk?" he asked of the man who was driving another SUV at the rear of the convoy.

"Ready when you are, Bull."

"All right, let's move out."

Bull climbed into his vehicle and led his convoy onto the highway. Once they were up to speed, he dialed a number on his cellphone. A moment later, Herb Bell answered from the station in Valdez. "Any word from Christa?"

"No, Bull, but Director Donner called and asked the same question. He said it's urgent for you to call him. Do you have his number?"

"Yeah. We're on our way and should be there sometime tomorrow afternoon. I'll call if we have a problem."

"Right, Bull. We'll be ready."

Bull dialed Donner's number, but the secretary told him Mister Donner was in a meeting. Bull gave her the number for his cellphone and informed her he'd be waiting for a return call. After he hung up, he settled back in his seat for the long drive. Now all he could do was wait for the call.

***

ARCO TANKER, SENTRY:

Captain Parks felt a shiver run down his spine as he watched what looked like a crescent moon moving across the horizon toward his ship. As it drew near, the strange object resembled a massive hockey puck with a mirror surface, but in the blink of an eye, it vanished. He quickly glanced through all the widows, but could not find it, and looked over at Commander Anderson. "Did you see it?"

"What did you see?"

"I'm not sure. Something shiny was shooting across the water. I thought it was coming in our direction, but it disappeared."

"We've just lost radio reception, Captain," said the operator.

Anderson stood and walked out the door onto the starboard lookout station to one of his men. "See anything out there, Dagan?"

"Just the moon a few seconds ago, but . . ."

When Dagan looked up, Anderson saw the astonishment in his eyes and did the same. Above him, the lights from the tanker were moving across the sky and he ducked his head through the doorway onto the bridge. "There's some kind of aircraft directly above us! It's too late to get the helicopter in the air, so sound the alarm!"

Anderson leaned over the railing and hollered to his men stationed below. "Twelve o'clock high! Fire at will!"

The night air was ripped open by the exploding gunfire, and men ducked for cover as bullets ricocheted off the mirror surface directly above them. Anderson and Dagan ducked behind the rail to escape the onslaught of flying pieces of metal. His men quickly realized what had happened and stopped firing, so Anderson stood to look down at them. "Hold your fire. Let's see what it does next."

"Over here!" a voice hollered from the main deck below.

Anderson watched one of his men running across the deck toward a dark figure leaning over one of the inspection hatches. "Shoot him!"

As his man stopped and fired, Anderson watched the dark figure topple into the open hatch. "*Damn it!*" he swore in frustration. "Check it out!"

Just as the man reached the hatch, eerie neon blue light burst from the opening and his man vanished. The light appeared to envelop the entire deck, and Anderson stood helpless to save his men as they disappeared. An instant later, he and Dagan were gone, too.

Parks heard a moan from his left and turned towards the helmsman. At least he thought it was the helmsman, but he couldn't tell for sure because of the dense blue light surrounding the man. He shot a look at the radio operator, also enveloped in the light. For a few seconds, Parks had the feeling he was floating, then all his senses seemed to shut off, and he felt nothing at all as his body vanished in the blue light.

Chapter 28

A0S CAMP:

Harold realized they had been in camp for a week now, and it just kept getting worse. He sat at a table in the men's barracks and stared out the window. *This is just a nightmare. Any minute now, I'm going to wake up, and I'll be lying in my own bed next to Cally.*

"I have to go to work, Dad," Mark said, and put his hand on his father's shoulder.

Harold looked up. "How's your mom holding up? She hasn't spoken to me since they shot Chuck Berry."

Mark shrugged. "Fine, I guess. She seems tired, though. It's a lot of work, cooking for the soldiers."

Harold thought about when Everex ordered Cally to be a prostitute, he'd nearly fainted. When she had looked at him with a stunned expression, expecting him to do something courageous, he'd felt like the biggest coward in the world. *Chuck may have been overweight and led a pampered life, but he had guts and stood up for his wife. All I did was cower down.* If it hadn't been for Mark asking Major Everex to let his mom be a cook, Cally would have gone into special services. *I am the biggest coward in the world.*

From the melancholy look in his father's eyes, Mark knew what he was thinking. "You couldn't have done anything, Dad. You would have been shot, like Mister Berry. I'd rather you be alive."

Harold managed a dry, sarcastic laugh. "A live coward."

Mark couldn't think of anything to say. "I'll see you later."

When Mark left the room, Harold looked at his watch. He still had an hour before he had to report for his fourth day of training. *I do seem to be getting stronger.* Today, his unit would be practicing on the rifle range, and he looked forward to his first attempt at shooting a rifle.

He was staring out the window and caught a movement near Monroe's trailer, and then watched two unfamiliar women step into the clearing and stop. They were looking around as if lost, so he stood and ran out the door, and then took a shortcut through the forest to the RV sites.

***

Christa and Judy had lost the trail and wandered through the woods for hours before hearing truck engines. Following the continuous, low-pitched rumble, they had walked through the rows of big trucks and semi-trailers until they emerged from the trees into what they thought was an RV campground and stopped to look around.

There were rows of recreational vehicles and trailers, most with tables and chairs in front of them, and some even had artificial grass carpet on the ground. At first, they felt elated at finding a civilized setting in an insane world, but they didn't see any people lounging around, and their elation evaporated. A short, bald man with a large nose ran from the trees, scowling at them.

"What do you want?" Harold demanded.

Judy noticed the little man kept looking around, paranoid about something. "Can you tell us where we are?"

Harold looked Judy in the eyes. "Hell."

Judy glanced at Christa and then looked at him curiously. "What?"

"This place is as near to hell as you can get without dying. Where did you come from?"

"Our plan was to reach the highway. We tried a shortcut, but we got lost."

Harold looked around nervously. He realized these two women didn't know about this place yet, or what would happen to them if they stayed here, and he had to warn them. "Come inside! Quick!"

Judy and Christa exchanged looks and followed the seemingly harmless, but tense, man into the trailer.

When the door was closed, Harold indicated the living area. "Better have a seat, and I'll tell you about this place. You don't want to stay here."

Christa and Judy sat on the couch and listened to Harold describe what the AOS camp was all about. When he finished, they exchanged nervous glances, and Christa decided to confide in him. "A friend of ours was brought here by the soldiers, and it's important we find her and get out of here."

"They brought a tall woman out of the woods late this morning. She was on a stretcher, and my son said she was in a wrecked airplane. Is that her?"

"Yes. Is she all right?" Christa implored, feeling guilty for not being quicker at helping Marcia.

"Yes. My son was assigned to watch her in the infirmary and said she's a nice woman. He took her to Colonel Blackwood's cabin, and he heard she was going to start a school here."

Christa sighed with relief. "Do you know where she is?"

"Yes, but I wouldn't go there right now. They'd catch you, and you don't want that."

"But we have to speak to her! It's very important!"

Harold considered the situation and knew he'd get in trouble if they caught him, and God only knew what they'd do to him. In his mind, he could see Chuck Berry being shot, but at least he'd been a whole man. Again, Harold felt ashamed. He looked at his watch, and he still had thirty-two minutes. *Show some courage, you coward!* "Listen. I'll take you to her tent, but if they catch you, don't tell them what I'm doing, okay?" Christa and Judy nodded their assent, and Harold sighed in resignation as he stood up. "Come on."

He led them back into the trees and around the perimeter of the camp and stopped when they could see a row of cabins through the trees, and then led them farther until they were behind several tents at the end of the cabins. "She's staying in the last tent. I'll go first and see if there are any guards. When I signal, run around front and get inside, fast. Understand?"

"Yes," Christa answered.

Harold took a deep breath and exhaled long and slow to stop the fierce pounding in his heart. He stepped out of the trees and dashed between the tents, then stopped, looking in both directions. He didn't see anyone, so he stepped out into the clearing and with a last look around, waved to the women. As he watched them run from the trees, he heard a door slam and spun toward the sound.

"What are you doing?" A serious-looking man yelled.

Harold strained to keep from wetting his pants as he stared at one of Major Everex's elite guards. *I'm going to die!* His mind went blank as the guard approached, staring at him sternly.

"I asked you a question, mister!"

Harold felt himself shaking, and couldn't stop as he stared up at the guard glaring down at him. "I, uh."

Christa and Judy heard a man shout just as they ran from the cover of the trees. Their feet slid in the dirt as they tried to stop, and Christa lost her balance, falling on her rump. She saw a soldier suddenly appear in the gap between the tents and stop in front of Harold, and at the same moment, she felt Judy's arms slip under her shoulders, pulling her up.

Harold glanced past the guard, saw Christa fall, and felt his bowels losing control. *I'm dead!* His heart wanted to explode from his chest, and it felt like he had an apple lodged in his throat. *I have to turn them in! That's the only thing that can save me! He looked up at the guard.* "I saw two women." *You're a Coward!* He looked away from the guard, and the women were gone.

"And?" the guard demanded.

Harold tried to think. "From the special services tent," Harold said meekly. "And I, ah."

The guard suddenly grinned. The special services tent was at the opposite end of the cabins. "You wanted to get a little?" When Harold looked down and nodded he did, the guard continued to grin. "Have fun, little man," he said, and walked away.

Harold felt as though his legs had turned to rubber and he had to fight to keep standing. It took a moment before he quit shaking, and he took several deep breaths before looking back at the trees. After a quick look around, he waved to the women as they reappeared. While they cautiously approached the tents, he held his breath as he turned and looked in both directions. He heard the flap on the tent rustle and turned to look as it dropped closed, then released his breath, and on wobbly legs, hurried away.

***

Her heart was pounding as Christa followed Judy into the tent, and when the flap closed behind her, she abruptly stopped. She heard her heartbeat in her ears as she tried to listen for threatening voices and studied her surroundings. The air inside smelled oily, as her eyes adjusted to the meager light entering through screened openings on both sides. After a few moments, her heart settled down, and she sat on one of the two cots in the sparsely furnished tent. Judy sat across from her, and for several minutes, neither spoke for fear of being discovered.

Judy leaned close to Christa's ear. "I hope this is the right tent."

Christa looked around again, and there was no place to hide. They sat in silence for what seemed like an hour, and both flinched when they heard voices outside the tent. The flap suddenly opened, and a tall silhouette was outlined in the opening, and they held their breath as the opening closed behind it.

"Thank goodness you're okay," Marcia whispered.

Christa leapt off the cot and threw her arms around Marcia's neck, hugging her fiercely, and then looked up. "Are you all right?"

Marcia smiled. "Yes, for now." She looked over at Judy, still sitting on the cot. "How about you? How's your head wound?"

"A little sore, but I'm fine. So what's going on in this place? Are you a prisoner? Can we leave?"

Judy and Christa sat across from Marcia as she told them about Colonel Blackwood and the AOS camp. "The Colonel's a gentleman, and very handsome, and I think he finds me attractive," she said and smiled. Her smile faded. "It's Major Everex I'm worried about. I've never been afraid of any man until now. Even his eyes are cold and menacing. He's psychotic and loathes women, treating them brutally, and wouldn't hesitate to kill anyone who gets in his way."

Judy got up off the cot. "I say we get the hell out of here!"

Marcia shook her head no. "If I disappear, the Major would hunt us down, and I'm sure he wouldn't hesitate to kill us."

"We have to do something!" Judy insisted. "I'm not joining this army, and I sure as hell am not going to be a prostitute!"

Marcia knew she was right and looked at Christa. "I told them I was alone in the plane. They found your clothes, but I told them they were my niece's, and she was killed. Do you have the disks?"

"Yes, and the ampoule."

"Then you both have to leave," Marcia insisted. Christa started to protest, but Marcia held up her hand. "You have got to get them to Alaska. That's more important." She saw the hurt look in Christa's eyes and smiled reassuringly. "I'll be fine. The Colonel likes me."

Christa stared at her, thinking about the other man Marcia had mentioned, and another thought occurred to her. "Maybe if you talked to the Colonel and told him about the crystal and enzymes, he'd let us have a car and some extra gas?"

Marcia thought about it for a moment. "Colonel Blackwood might go for the idea, but Major Everex wouldn't. From what I've seen, Everex is in power right now, so I'd have to wait until I was alone with the Colonel. I'm not sure when it will be, and you can't stay in this tent." That sparked another thought. "How did you know this was my tent?"

Christa told her about Harold Woolly. "He was terrified."

"If he lives in a trailer, he might hide you for a while. At least until I have time to talk to the Colonel."

"Ha!" Judy laughed sarcastically. "The poor guy probably pissed his pants when the guard caught him sneaking around."

"But he didn't turn us in," Christa added. "We could ask him. He helped once, so he might do it again."

"And if he says no?" Judy asked. "I don't think so. The little guy might turn us in just to save his own butt, and I don't want to chance it. I say we get the hell out of here."

Christa thought about the matter for a moment. "If he says no, we leave on foot. If he threatens to turn us in, we tie him up."

"Okay," said Judy. "But we might have to kill him. It's more important to get the disks to Alaska. What's one life compared to the madness that's going on right now?"

Christa shuddered at the thought, but knew Judy had a valid point. She saw the determined look in her eyes and knew Judy would do it, too. "Let's see what happens."

Judy thought about it for moment. "Would these soldiers let you go to Harold's trailer?"

"I don't see why not?"

"If we're not there, you'll know it didn't work."

Marcia stood. "I'll see if it's safe to leave." She lifted the flap and looked around outside but didn't see anyone, and waved them out. "Good luck," she whispered as they darted past and disappeared into the trees.

***

After working all morning and afternoon in the big kitchen, Cally was bone weary as she trudged across the parade ground. She thought she'd died and gone to hell when Everex had told her if she didn't pull her load, she'd be put in the special services tents. After four days of hard work, she was thinking, irrationally, it might be easier to just lie on her back and let the men do what they wanted. She wondered what Harold would think and decided she didn't care. He was a spineless wimp!

She heard a familiar giggle and looked up. Pamela and a young soldier with a pimply face were sitting on a log, and she shook her head in amazement her children actually enjoyed this place. Pamela was living in the young girl's dormitory, attached to the main building, and loved training to be a soldier, so she hardly ever came to the trailer, and Mark had moved into the barracks with his friend Brian.

She continued through the camp, past the people living in tent city, as everyone called it, and past most of the trailers and RVs. As she passed the big Roadmaster motorhome, she heard the door shut and looked that way, and Joyce was standing outside, staring at her.

That poor woman, Cally thought, and walked over to her. She noticed Joyce looked haggard, with dark circles under her eyes. She wasn't wearing makeup, and her hair was in disarray. She had tried to comfort Joyce after Berry had been shot, but that afternoon, Major Everex came and took her to the special services tent, and she had seen little of Joyce since. Some soldiers had told Mark Joyce had put up a fight at first, but Everex had hit her a few times, and then raped her. The soldiers told Mark they all wanted the model and lined up for their turn.

Joyce ignored her and started to walk past as Cally reached out to touch her arm. "Don't you dare touch me!" she snarled in her high-pitched voice, and jerked away.

"Wait a minute. What's wrong?"

"Your husband didn't get shot! You didn't have to become a whore!"

Cally could only stare at her. Joyce was right, so what could she say? Joyce spun around and stomped away, and Cally stared after her for a moment, and then continued to the fifth wheel trailer. She opened the door, stepped inside, and froze in place when she saw two women sitting on the couch. She'd never seen them before and started to demand to know what they were doing in her trailer, but she was just too exhausted, and thought. they must be friends of Jerry Monroe.

Jerry had moved into the officer's barracks, but liked to get away occasionally, and he sometimes brought a friend or two back to the trailer. Cally turned and walked up the few steps to the bed and crawled on top, and a few moments later, she was sound asleep.

Christa and Judy started to get up when the woman entered, but when she turned and went up the steps, they stayed seated and looked at each other quizzically. They had looked through the cupboards, but couldn't find any food, and both were getting ravenously hungry. The hours dragged by, and most of the time, they sat in silence.

Judy stood and paced the floor nervously. "You know, without food or water, we won't last long trying to walk out of here. We don't even have a compass or a map, so we could wander for days."

The door suddenly opened and Harold stepped into the trailer, turned toward the living room, and stopped with his mouth hanging open. "What are you doing here?"

Judy put her finger to her lips. "Shush!" she whispered, and pointed behind him.

Harold spun around and saw Cally on the bed, turned back, and hurried into the living room, pulling the corrugated partition closed behind him. "You have to leave! You can't stay here or I'll get in trouble!"

Christa stood and walked to him. "It will only be for a couple of days. Please?" Christa explained to him about their mission and its importance to the entire world.

Harold shook his head adamantly. "No! You don't understand. If my son stops by and finds you here, we'll all be in trouble!"

"Your son?" Judy asked.

"Yes! He loves this place, and Major Everex is his idol. He'd tell him about you the minute he found out!" He shook his head no. "You have to leave."

Christa looked at Judy. "Let's go."

"We can't," Judy said sternly, and moved her face a few inches in front of Harold's. "We're staying, and you're going to bring us food. If you don't, or if you turn us in, we'll tell this Everex person you offered to hide us. I'm sure we can think up all kinds of things to say, like your son was in on the deal. You get my drift?"

Harold stared up at her, dumbfounded. *I should never have helped them in the first place. I was nice to them, now they're blackmailing me!* He looked away while he thought about it. *If Mark is kicked out of this sick army, he'd be devastated! I can't do that to him!* He could see Joyce's motorhome through the window and thought about how quick Everex had shot Chuck. If these women turned him in, the same would happen to him, and they might even shoot Mark for treason! He sighed in resignation and nodded agreement.

Judy continued to look down at him. "We also need a map, compass, canteens of water, extra food, and sleeping bags."

"I can't get all that! They keep it locked up!"

"Try. We need . . ."

"If you can," Christa interrupted, and looked at Judy. "If he gets caught, we do, too."

"At least get us something to eat," Judy told him. "We're starved."

When Harold nodded yes and left the trailer, Judy smirked at Christa. "See? No problem."

Chapter 29

THIRTY-FIVE MILES EAST OF ANCHORAGE, ALASKA:

So far, so good, Bull thought as he led his convoy east on State Route 1, toward Valdez. He had expected trouble from the locals as he passed through Anchorage, but his only obstacle had been a group of fifteen men, women, and children blocking the road. The men were armed, and when Bull stopped, they demanded one of the trucks and his SUV.

Bull grinned to himself as he remembered the stunned expression on their faces when he had smiled, waved his hand out the window, and fourteen shotguns and rifles suddenly appeared from the windows of the trucks in the convoy. He had called Herb four different times and Christa still hadn't arrived, and an ominous feeling crept over him as he kept his convoy moving east. The cellphone rang, and he answered. "Yeah?"

"Martin Donner here, Mister Peterson. What can I do for you?"

"I haven't been able to reach Alex or Christa. Have you heard from them?"

There was a pause before Donner replied. "They should have arrived by now."

"I know. My man in Valdez said they aren't there yet."

"I thought that's where you were."

Bull grinned. Nobody knew what he was up to, but his grin quickly faded with his worry for Christa. "I'll be there later. If you hear anything, call me day or night and I'll do the same." Donner agreed, and Bull hung up. "Shit!" he mumbled, as his sense of dread deepened.

***

WASHINGTON, D.C.:

Donner entered the President's office and sat in front of the desk. "The tanker left Cook Inlet, sir, but they haven't been heard from for a while."

The President studied Donner for a moment and could tell he still had not gotten any sleep, but knew it would be a wasted effort to push the issue. "Have you had any luck tracking down Menno Simons?"

Donner shook his head no. "Out west someplace, but it's hard to do anything without gas stations, and some of our people have been attacked by civilians."

"I received a call from Russian President Matvelick this morning. One of their oil storage facilities was infiltrated somehow, and they lost all the reserves in that area."

"I wish there was something I could do about it, Sir."

The President looked out the window at the dozens of soldiers stationed around the Capital. He saw the command tents had been set up next to the building, and the tanks and assault vehicles were stationed along the perimeter. He saw the rioting in the western cities on the news broadcasts, and was frustrated he could not stop it. The civilized world, as he knew it, was going to hell. "Any word from Alex and the Avery woman?"

"The air station at Whidbey said no one arrived. I've tried raising Alex on his cellphone, but he doesn't answer."

"If you want to go, you can use my helicopter."

Donner shrugged. "Where would I go? This is where I belong."

"I appreciate the help, Martin."

"We'll get through this, Sir. I know we will."

The President smiled. "I'm glad to see somebody is still optimistic. I hope you're right."

Chapter 30

IDAHO:

In order to follow what Alex thought was the flight path of Judy's plane, Alex, Sharlett, and David had left the nearest road and hiked along a game trail through the dense forest. Sharlett had managed to keep up, but this was the third day of relentless walking, and David could see she was fatigued and insisted they stop.

Alex studied the map. "If they flew in a direct route, they should be somewhere in this area."

"This is useless!" David growled in frustration. "If they strayed off course by even a mile, we may never find them. We could spend several days, weeks, even months trying to find them! We should just head for Washington."

"No!" Alex shouted. "We've got to find them! Christa and Marcia may be the only hope of ending this nightmare."

"They're probably dead. The plane crashed, and they're just rotting corpses."

Alex grabbed David's vest and slammed him against a tree, glaring at him. "They're not dead! I'm the one who sent them, damn it! They're my responsibility, and I'm going to find them!"

David's heart leapt into his throat, beating a thousand times a second. The look in Alex's eyes nearly made him wet his pants.

Sharlett was sitting on a fallen tree and leapt up to separate the two men. "Stop it, both of you!"

Alex stared into David's frightened eyes. *What am I doing?* He gently released him. "I'm sorry." He turned away.

David tried to catch his breath. *I pushed him too far*. He watched Alex walk away and stop with his back to him, and took a couple of deep breaths before walking over. "I could be wrong." When Alex didn't respond, he turned and moved to the nearest tree, squatted, and leaned his back against it.

Sharlett suddenly took a few steps to the left of the trail. "Do you hear it?"

Alex turned and looked at her. "Hear what?"

"I'm not sure, but it sounds like a running engine."

Alex listened, but heard nothing. They were seven miles from the nearest road, so there was no possibility she had heard an engine. "It's just the wind."

David looked up at her. *She is still a little crazy.* "We're too far from the roads."

"No! I'm sure I hear something running!" She slowly turned and faced into the wind, hands cupped around her ears. "That way!" she told them

David picked up the map and held the compass against it, then looked up at Alex. "It's a little south of a straight route. It might be worth checking out."

Sharlett saw the skeptical look in Alex's eyes. "I'm not hearing things! I hear a machine sound."

David looked at Alex and shrugged. "What have we got to lose?"

Alex looked at Sharlett and David's pleading stares. "All right."

They adjusted their backpacks and followed Sharlett in the direction she had determined was the source of the noise. Ten minutes later, the trio stopped abruptly when they emerged from the trees into a small meadow.

Alex ran across the clearing to the wrecked plane, looked through the open doorway, and smiled at his companions as they stopped beside him. "They're alive!" He saw David look at the doorway. "No, they're not in there, it's empty, but it means they got out. They must be in the area."

David walked around the broken branches and trees. "Over here!" he shouted. When Alex and Sharlett were beside him, he pointed at the ground. "There were a lot of people here and the tracks lead that way."

When Alex jogged in the direction of the footprints, David caught up and grabbed his shoulder to stop him. "Wait!"

Alex stopped and looked back at him. "We can't wait!"

"No, it's the foot prints! They're combat boots!"

"There must be a base nearby."

"No. They're not all the same. They're old Army surplus."

"How do you know?"

"I had a friend in the reserves. The tread pattern is an old style."

"So, what are you getting at?"

"You've heard about the Neo-Nazis, and they were based here in Idaho."

Alex's heart felt like it had dropped into his shoes. "Okay, but it still means they were taken to a camp and we have to find it. We just have to be careful."

David glanced over at Sharlett and back to Alex. "They probably have guards in the woods. No offense, but I'm a lot quieter than either of you, so I'll go on ahead to check it out. Give me a five-minute lead and then follow. I'll leave markers, but don't run. Keep as quiet as possible."

When David disappeared, Alex kept glancing at his watch until five minutes had passed, then he and Sharlett headed in his direction, following the broken branches and small mounds of rocks David had left to mark his path. Fifteen minutes later, they caught up, and David was squatting next to a huge pine tree. When they stopped, they could hear engines running.

David stood and looked at Alex. "There are dozens of big trucks and trailers stashed in the trees, about three hundred yards ahead, but a guard walked past a few minutes ago."

"Military vehicles?"

"No. Food trucks, like Safeway and Thriftway. Also, tankers with gas and diesel."

"They must be the trucks hijacked from the interstate highways. We should wait until dark, and then you and I can take a look around."

Sharlett grabbed David's arm. "What about me? I'm not staying here alone!"

David gently touched her hand. "It might be dangerous."

"I don't care! I'm not staying here by myself!"

"Freeze!"

The trio spun around and saw three men in camouflaged clothing, pointing rifles at them. Alex estimated his odds of shooting the three soldiers. If he had been by himself, no problem, but the chance of Sharlett or David getting shot were too great. "Damn!" he swore under his breath.

Chapter 31

AOS CAMP:

When Cally awoke, Harold introduced the women to her and explained what was going on. At first, she had thrown a fit, but when Christa told her about Marcia and their plans to drive to Alaska, Cally agreed to let them stay if she and their children could go with them, but she didn't include Harold.

Harold felt crushed, but didn't blame her after the way he'd been such a coward. However, she insisted he come with her to find their children so he could help her convince them to leave with them. When they left the trailer, he knew it would be dangerous telling Mark about their plan, and he could only hope Cally might listen to reason before they found their son.

Christa and Judy were nearly caught when Jerry Monroe stopped by to check on the Woollys. They hid in the cramped bathroom, listening to him knock on the trailer door, but he had left without coming in.

Now Judy was kneeling on the couch, keeping watch through the front window. "Marcia's coming!"

Christa peeped through the window, and Marcia seemed to be in a hurry, looking troubled. She went to the door to let her in and saw the frown creasing her brow. "What's going on?"

"I just saw the guards bring Alex, David, and a young woman into the camp at gunpoint."

Judy leapt off the couch. "How did they find us?"

"I don't know. The guards locked them in jail until Major Everex and the Colonel get back."

Judy grabbed the doorknob. "We'll have to leave!"

Christa grabbed her arm. "No! We have to get them out of jail!"

Judy yanked her arm away. "You don't understand. If Alex and David tell them they are looking for the three women from the plane, they'll tear this place apart to find us."

Marcia stared at Christa. "She's right. I'll get word to them not to mention you. I'll be back as soon as I can."

"What about the Colonel? Did you talk to him about us?"

"I haven't had a chance." With a reassuring smile, she left the trailer.

***

AOS JAILHOUSE:

Alex had told David and Sharlett not to say anything until they learned more about the camp. After they were placed in the cell, he asked the guard at the desk where they were and what was going on, but the man just sneered at him and said he would learn soon enough.

Alex stared through the rusty bars of the window at the green pine trees and noticed movement in the woods. A tall woman suddenly stepped out, and he smiled when he recognized Marcia.

When she saw Alex, Marcia looked around nervously before hurrying to the jailhouse window while putting a finger to her lips.

Alex glanced over his shoulder and the guard was sitting with his feet on the desk, engrossed in a paperback novel, so he turned to Marcia and whispered. "Are the girls all right?"

"Yes, they're hiding. Don't mention us or the plane!" She suddenly looked away. "A car is coming!" She hurried back into the trees.

Alex stepped away from the window and sat on the cot next to David. "The girls are here."

"Break it up!" the guard snarled, staring at them.

Alex heard a car stop outside the building and saw the guard suddenly sit up and put the book away. A moment later, the door opened and a stocky man stepped inside, followed by a tall man with a black patch over one eye.

When the short man approached the cell, Alex saw the look of a cold-blooded killer in his eyes. The man's muscles appeared to be trying to rip through his shirt, and he knew an interrogation wouldn't be pleasant. He also knew David could never take the punishment and would give in to the man's interrogation. The only way to save David and the women was to make himself the target of the man's torture and did his best to look intimidated and meek as he scurried back from the bars like a frightened little animal.

Everex studied the prisoners, and the young boy looked him straight in the eye, but the other man looked as if he would shit his pants if he said boo. "What were you doing to our trucks?" he growled.

Before David could answer or turn to him for help, Alex spoke, raising the pitch of his voice. "We don't mean you any harm. Please don't hurt me! We weren't doing anything! Honest, mister, I'll tell you anything, but please don't hurt me!"

David looked at Alex in stunned disbelief. *What is he doing?* He had never considered Alex a coward, but now, seeing him like this, he wondered how he could have been so wrong. He felt disgusted to see that Alex was such a cowering wimp. *Well, I'm not a coward.* He turned back to the man at the bars and thrust his chin out as he stared him in the eyes. "I'm not telling you anything!"

Everex stared at the boy and smirked. *He had guts. It might take a while to break him, but he'd give in eventually.* His men had told him they were hiding by their supply trucks and thought they were there to sabotage them. If it was true, he needed to know who had sent them.

Everex looked at the sniveling man pressed against the wall. "Answer me!" he shouted, and watched the man cover his face with his hands and squat in the corner. He loathed a coward and thought about just shooting him. *No. I'll kill him after he answers some questions.* He turned to the guard. "Bring that scared little bastard to the showers." He turned to look up at Blackwood and grinned. "Now the fun begins. Care to watch?"

A cold chill ran up Blackwood's spine. "Uh, no. I have to check on some things." He turned and walked out through the doorway.

Everex stepped outside and watched Blackwood walk up the road. When he started to get into his jeep, one of his elite guards walked up to him. "What's going on?"

"That amazon woman went to the Woolly's trailer a little while ago."

Everex thought about it for a moment. Something about the teacher had bothered him from the start, and he didn't trust her. He also didn't like the influence she had on Blackwood. She gave him courage, and that was bad. "Follow the Woolly woman to the trailer when she leaves and have someone keep an eye on the amazon. There's something going on, and I want to know what it is."

***

Alex allowed the guard to shove him into a large room with rows of gray metal lockers and benches and he smelled sweaty clothes and mentholated muscle rubbing ointments as they continued to the end of the room. Through the opening into the showers, he recognized the muscular man from the jail, sitting on a wooden chair with his back against the white-tiled wall.

The guard removed the handcuffs and shoved Alex through the opening, nearly causing him to slip. He kept his balance, but didn't look

Everex in the eyes. "Please, mister!" he moaned as he squatted on another wooden chair. "I'll tell you anything, just don't hurt me!"

Everex stared disgustedly at the man. "What's your name, besides chicken shit?"

"Alex. We got lost and heard your trucks."

Everex leapt from the chair, wrapped both hands around Alex's throat, and shoved him out of the chair and slide him against the wall. "Don't give me that crap!"

Alex was on his butt and could barely speak with hands around his throat. "Honest, mister. I'm telling you the truth."

When Everex kept one hand around Alex's throat while he lowered his other arm, Alex knew what was coming and tightened his stomach muscles, but the blow had the force of a sledgehammer and drove the air from his lungs. He collapsed sideways onto the floor, sucking in several deep breaths.

Everex reached down and grabbed Alex by the belt and shirt, then lifted him with the ease of a man lifting a small child and slammed him down in the chair. A bolt of intense pain erupted through Alex's skull as his head smacked against the tile wall. It took a few seconds to regain his senses, and he fought hard to control his raging desire to beat the man to a pulp. *If I fight back, the guard will undoubtedly help his tormentor, and I'll be no good to my friends if I'm dead.*

"What were you doing to the tankers?" Everex hissed.

"We got lost in the woods." He caught the movement just in time to roll his head with the punch as Everex backhanded him across the face, but it still stung, and the coppery taste of blood filled his mouth.

Everex grabbed Alex by the throat. "This is your last chance!"

Alex realized the being lost story wasn't going to work and tried to think of a believable excuse without mentioning the women. He realized the man was extremely paranoid and must be worried about being discovered, so decided to give him an enemy.

Alex watched Everex raise his hand for another blow and threw his arms up to ward it off. "All right! All right!" He waited while Everex held his arm up, fist poised in the air. "We were ordered to steal one of the fuel trucks!" he shouted, and watched Everex lower his arm.

"Okay, who sent you?"

"Menno. Menno Simons."

Everex stared at him. "Who in hell is Menno Simons?"

"He's our leader."

Everex remembered hearing about Menno from his father. They were some kind of back to nature fanatics. "What does he know about us?"

Alex thought quickly. "He knows you've got supplies, and he sent us to find out how big an army you have."

"Why?"

"His army is running out of food and gas, and he wants to take your supplies."

Everex stared at Alex. *Another army*? "How many soldiers does he have?"

"Seven hundred, maybe more."

Everex let go of Alex's throat. *Shit! Seven hundred? Could I hold off that many? Probably not. At least not here.* He paced across the floor, his boots making a clicking noise on the tiled floor, and then he stopped and faced Alex. "Where are they now?"

"About fifty miles south of here, waiting for us to report back."

Only fifty miles? Shit! That's too damn close. I'll have to stop them before they get here. A surprise attack! Yes, hit them first! He turned and left the shower room. "Throw him back in jail," he hollered at the guard as he strode past.

Alex stood as the guard approached, but realized he had made a mistake. He had let his meek facade slip, and the guard must have seen it.

The guard noticed the insolent look and drew his pistol, pointing it at the prisoner. "Turn around and get down on your knees, hands behind your back!"

Alex did as instructed and heard the clicking of boots as the guard approached. He tried to think of a way to overpower the man, but knew there was no way while he was on his knees. He felt the handcuffs tighten around his wrists and then heard the guard stepping back.

"Get up."

Alex stood and faced the guard, who was still pointing the pistol, and he knew his chance of escape had passed. He resigned himself to wait for another opportunity, and when the guard waved the pistol toward the door, he strolled out of the shower and back to the jail.

***

Once locked in the cell with his handcuffs removed, he sat on the cot and saw David glaring at him.

"You told them, didn't you?" David asked with a note of disgust.

Alex winked at David before glancing at the guards, who were watching intently. "They were going to hurt me. I didn't want them to hurt me!"

David looked at him and saw the small spot of blood at the corner of Alex's mouth. He saw the guards watching them and decided not to ask any more questions. He sat on the cot and watched one guard leave while the other returned to reading his book. *What the devil is Alex up to?*

***

Everex burst through the door into Blackwood's cabin. "There's another army out there!" he yelled. "Some fanatic named Menno Simons is bringing troops here to steal our supplies!"

Blackwood frowned for a moment as he stared at Everex and then grinned. "So? Our army is well trained, and we have plenty of ammunition."

"Our army ain't shit, Colonel! We have about one hundred combat soldiers, and the rest are just a bunch of scared men and women forced to learn how to shoot and do what we tell them to do. This Menno person has seven hundred troops, and we wouldn't stand a chance if they attack us."

Seven hundred soldiers? My God! Everex is right. They'd be overrun in no time. "Maybe we could make a deal. Offer to let them join us and share our supplies."

"No! We have enough supplies to keep us going for maybe a year. Seven hundred more mouths would wipe us out in a week! No. We have to attack them first, before they get here. I want you to take most of our troops and hit them with a surprise attack."

Blackwood looked aghast. "Me?"

"You're the big hero combat veteran."

"That was a long time ago."

Everex drew his nickel-plated Colt 45 automatic pistol and pointed it at Blackwood's chest. "Then I don't need you anymore!"

Blackwood's jaw hung slack as his eyes darted between the gun and the look in Everex's eyes and knew he would pull the trigger. "Wait! I mean, it's just that I'll need time to get organized. Lay out a battle plan. I can't just charge in like the Calvary!"

Everex slowly put the colt back in his holster. "I figure it will take the rest of the day to get ready to move out, so that's all the time you have, Colonel. If you're not prepared by then, you'll have to figure it out as you go. My men will be your first officers, and I'll have them get started with the organizing. We'll modify some truck trailers as troop carriers and use a motor home for a command center."

"All right. I'd better get started."

Blackwood stood and pretended to be going through the maps. When he heard the cabin door slam shut, he looked over his shoulder, and then collapsed into the chair. "Oh, dear God!" he moaned. *I'm no war hero. Shit! I was a Major for only a week before they sent me out with a squad of men.*

His thoughts went back to that fatal day. When the shooting started, he had panicked when his men started shouting at him for orders. While his men were being butchered, he'd hidden in a hole. The rest of his time was spent in the POW camp. Sure, he'd received a purple heart for his eye, but he'd lost it while being rescued, when he had tripped getting into the helicopter and shoved his face into a rifle barrel. Now Everex wanted him to lead a bunch of civilians against trained soldiers? He shuddered and buried his face in his hands. "This can't be happening."

***

As Everex hurried across the parade ground, a soldier ran over to him. "That Woolly woman left the kitchen with stolen food and I followed her to their trailer."

I did her a favor. Why would she steal food? "Find Davis and two of my guards. Meet me in tent city as fast as you can."

***

Judy stared out the window from the living room of the trailer, and as she watched Cally approach, she thought she saw a movement in the trees. She rubbed her eyes and stared at the area, but nothing changed. *I must be tired.* She stood when the door opened.

Cally climb in, pulled several zip-lock bags out of her blouse, and set them on the table. "The guards seem to me nervous about something. I can't risk being caught, so make it last."

Christa was asleep on the couch, so Judy shook her shoulder. "The food's here."

Christa followed Judy into the kitchen and noticed Cally looked terrible. Her eyes were sunken, surrounded by dark brown circles. "We really appreciate this."

"Harold convinced me to not tell our children about our plan until we're ready to leave. Just hurry and get us out of here," she said over her shoulder as she walked to the bedroom.

Judy and Christa sat at the table and opened the bags of food. I appeared to be stew and tasted wonderful. Judy was in mid-bite when she realized the camouflaged clothing the soldiers wore would look like a bush moving. She jumped up from the table and grabbed Christa's arm, dragging her out the door as she explained what she suspected. Her first thought was the woods, but Christa had suggested Joyce's motorhome, because the forest would probably be the first place the soldiers would search for them.

***

Everex stood between two tents while he waited for his men to arrive. He peaked around the corner of the tent and saw Marcia walking toward him, and she appeared nervous and kept glancing back over her shoulder. He wondered what she was up to as he quickly stepped back into the trees. She walked by, and he watched her enter the Woolly's trailer.

Everex stepped out and walked up the road to intercept his men before they entered the RV area. "Work your way through the woods to the last trailer. When I signal, move in."

Everex ducked back into the trees, made his way around the meadow, and stopped when he was across from the trailer door. He watched his men get into position, and then he stepped into the clearing and signaled for them to follow.

***

Marcia knocked lightly on the trailer door, but no one answered. She tried the handle, and the door opened, so she stepped inside and closed it behind her. She was looking at Cally on the bed when the door was suddenly yanked open behind her. She spun around, and her eyes went wide with fear as she stared down at the pistol and the cold, dark eyes of Major Everex standing at the bottom of the steps.

Everex waved the pistol at the woman. "Out!"

Marcia held her head up, climbed down the steps, and saw three more soldiers pointing rifles at her. All she could do was cover for her friends.

Everex stared up at the big woman. "Who else is in there?"

"Just Misses Woolly, but she's asleep. I just stopped by to talk to her."

"Just shut up," Everex snapped, and leapt into the trailer. He saw the woman on the bed, but ignored her and dashed into the living room. It was empty, but there was a blanket and pillow on the couch. When he turned back to the kitchen and saw the open zip-lock bags on the table, he stomped across the floor to the bedroom and yanked roughly on Cally's leg, dragging her off the bed. "Get up, bitch!"

Cally thumped onto the floor and stared up into his eyes. It took her a second to come fully awake and realized with sickening dread she was in deep trouble.

Everex yanked her to her feet and shoved her toward the door. "Get Out!"

Cally stumbled down the steps and saw Marcia staring at her. When she saw the armed soldiers, she believed she was going to die.

Everex grabbed Cally's arm and spun her around. "Where are the others?"

At that moment, her first thought was she was going to become a whore after all, and smiled to herself. *Well, it beats sweating over a hot stove all day.*

Everex couldn't believe the woman was smiling, and his rage doubled, so he shoved the pistol against Cally's forehead. "What's so damn funny?"

Cally saw the savagery in Everex's eyes and knew she would be dead in a second. She tried to step back, but his fingers dug painfully into her arm. "I don't know," she moaned. His grip tightened and tears blurred her eyes.

"Who was in the trailer with you?"

"I don't know. I was asleep."

Marcia couldn't stand to see Cally in such pain. "I'll tell you everything, just let her go!"

Everex glared at Marcia. "Start talking!"

Marcia looked at Cally, and when Everex shoved her away, she told him about Christa, Judy, and the plane wreck. "We were just trying to get out of Bozeman."

She's lied from the beginning, Everex thought, *and she's probably lying now.* "Menno sent you to spy on us, didn't he?"

Marcia blinked in surprise. "I don't know what you're talking about."

She is a good actor, too, Everex thought. *Well, he'd get it out of her soon enough.* "Lock them up. Search the camp and the woods and find these other women. They're spies."

***

Christa and Judy watched through the window as Marcia and Cally were escorted up the road at gunpoint, then Judy leaned back from the window. "That was close."

"Yes, and now Marcia's cover is blown. We have to get them out of that jail."

"I know, but we can't leave yet. I imagine this place will be crawling with soldiers in a moment."

As if on cue, two dozen soldiers ran past the RV camp and spread out into the trees. Judy and Christa exchanged looks and stepped away from the window.

***

Alex was lying on his cot and didn't bother to look up when the jailhouse door opened, but what he heard next made him leap to his feet.

"Marcia?" David asked without thinking.

Alex watched the guards exchange looks and knew they would tell Everex. When he looked at David, the boy averted his eyes as if in apology. None of them spoke as Marcia and Cally were shoved into the other cell with Sharlett. He watched the guards whisper to each other, and when one left the building, he looked at Marcia, his eyes asking about Christa and Judy. He sighed with relief when Marcia shook her head they were not caught.

Cally stood at the cell door, looking at the guard. "Hey! I was blackmailed. I don't even know these people."

The guard stared at Cally. "You can tell Major Everex when he gets here. Just sit down and shut up!"

***

Everex burst through the door of Blackwood's cabin. "Your amazon lady is a spy, and the Woollys have been hiding two more spies! Shit! The whole damn camp could be full of spies!"

Blackwood felt a sinking feeling in his heart. "I think you're wrong."

"Who gives a shit what you think? Right now, get moving and stop this Menno bastard." Everex looked at the desk, which appeared just as it had when he left. "Have you worked out your plan?"

Blackwood hadn't expected Everex to be back this soon and hadn't done a thing, but knew he'd better say something. He stood and held up a map of Idaho. "Damn right. I've got it all laid out in my head."

Everex looked at Blackwood suspiciously. "Good. You'll be leaving at sunset."

"What about Miss Story?"

"She's in jail with the others." Everex heard a knock on the open door and turned to the soldier who had escorted the women to jail. "What?"

"The two men know the amazon woman."

Everex spun back to Blackwood, a leering grin stretched across his face as he watched Blackwood's jaw drop open. "You know what happens to spies, Colonel. Only now, there's no Geneva Convention, just *my* rules. Now the fun begins."

Chapter 32

AOS CAMP:

Mark Woolly walked beside Joyce as they passed through tent city and stopped when they saw the guard next to Monroe's trailer. Joyce waited while he walked over and recognized the guard as one of Everex's men. "What's going on?"

"Your mom's been arrested for hiding spies."

Mark was dumbfounded. "What? Spies? She wouldn't do that!"

The guard shrugged. "That's what I was told."

"Where's my mom?"

"In jail, for the moment. You know the Major."

Mark understood the guard's meaning and knew the major was probably going to kill her. He slowly shuffled away, lost in thought, and continued past Joyce without seeing her.

"Hey Joyce!" the guard hollered. "How about one for the road when I get relieved?"

Joyce showed him her middle finger and then walked to the door of her motor home. As she grabbed the handle, a sudden urge to pea was nearly overwhelming.

Christa and Judy saw Joyce approaching and scrambled into the tiny bathroom. They heard the door open and close, and a moment later, the bathroom door opened. Judy saw Joyce's surprised look and thought she might scream out a warning, but she just stared at them.

"I have to go really bad."

Christa and Judy exchanged puzzled looks, stepped out of the bathroom, and waited while Joyce hurried inside and closed the door.

Joyce came out and stared at the two women. "What's going on around here?" Neither of them answered. "Look, I've seen you through the window of the Woolly's trailer and I know you've been hiding, but I don't care. I won't turn you in to these assholes, if that's what you're worried about."

The woman sounded sincere, Christa thought. She looked at Judy for confirmation, who simply shrugged, so she explained everything to Joyce and waited for a response.

Joyce sat down at the kitchen table. "Everex is sick in the head and will kill your friends. If you want to save them, you'll have to do it soon. Most of the soldiers are leaving tonight, so that might be a good time for a rescue."

Christa could see the bitterness in Joyce's eyes. "Will you help us?"

"Everex shot my husband and made me become a prostitute, so I'd love to kill him and some of the bastards who have been using me. What do you want me to do?"

"First, we need to get word to our friends in the jail, and then we'll need some kind of diversion while we get them out."

Joyce smirked at them. "The diversion's not a problem, and it might be tricky getting word to them in the jail, but I think I know of a way."

***

While he walked through tent city, Mark realized if his mother was hiding spies, his father had to know about it as well. *No. My dad wouldn't do that to me. He knows how much I love it here.* He quickened his pace and looked at his watch, and 5:00 PM meant Pam was probably at the dormitory.

He hurried through the parade ground and noticed the way everyone moved with a sense of urgency, and he could hear the growl of diesel engines. Someone yelled his name, and he turned to the sound, and saw Brian Everex running across the parade ground, so he stopped and waited for his friend.

Brian could not stop grinning as he stopped in front of Mark. "Did you hear we're leaving tonight to attack another army?" He didn't wait for a reply. "My brother said I can go with them. What about you? Are you going with us?"

At any other time, he would have loved to go, but right now, his parents were more important. "Maybe. I have something I have to do first."

Brian looked at him curiously. He found it strange Mark wasn't as excited as *he* was, but shrugged it off. "Okay. I'll see you later."

Mark watched Brian run off, and realized if the Major was leaving tonight, he wouldn't want to leave his parents in jail while he was gone. Mark knew he'd have to hurry and find Pam and somehow warn his dad. He had no idea how to get his mom out of jail and hoped Pam could think of something.

***

Mark entered the long corridor of the girl's dormitory and it smelled of perfume and sweaty clothes. Women carrying backpacks rushed past him, and one of them smiled and winked at him as he hurried to Pam's room. "Mom's been arrested!"

Pam leapt up from the bed. "What are you talking about?"

"The Major had Mom arrested for hiding some spies. I think they'll arrest Dad when he gets back, even though he didn't have anything to do with it."

Now Pam looked puzzled. "What do you mean by spies?"

"I don't know all the details. I just know the Major is probably going to kill them before he leaves tonight, so we have to hurry."

Pam grabbed a jacket off the back of a chair. "Tell me what happened."

Mark walked at a brisk pace along the corridor while he told her what he knew. "The thing is, Everex won't even give Dad a chance to clear himself."

They hurried out of the barracks and headed toward the jailhouse. "Okay," said Pam as they approached the back of the dining hall. "You go find Dad and I'll go to the jail and talk to Mom to find out if it's true about the spies."

Mark ran toward the road that led to the big meadow where his dad was training. He just hoped he was still there.

***

The three women exchanged frightened looks when they heard a knock on the motorhome door. Joyce stood, peeked out the window and recognized Sergeant Major Davis. He was the sadistic bastard who treated her so brutally in the special services tent. She opened the door and looked down at him. "What do you want?"

"You look like shit."

"That's your fault, so leave me alone."

"Get out. We're taking your motorhome."

Joyce held back the panic she suddenly felt. "What? You can't just take it."

"I can do whatever I want!" he snarled, and started to grab her arm.

"All right!" she said bitterly as she stepped back. "Just let me pack a few things. Tell me where you want it, and I'll drive it over."

The guard looked at her suspiciously for a moment. "Park it in front of my cabin. The rest of the guards and I are going to use it while we're traveling."

"I want it back when you're through."

Davis grinned. "Sure thing, if there's anything left of it." He laughed sarcastically and walked away.

Joyce closed the door and looked at Christa and Judy. "Did you hear that?" Both women nodded solemnly, and Joyce grinned at them. "Don't worry. I'll let you out as we pass tent city, so no one will notice."

Joyce walked around the end of the bed and knelt down, opened a drawer underneath, and brought out a large black suitcase. She opened it and reached inside, and held up two small blocks of tan-colored clay wrapped in cellophane and smiled. "Plastic explosives." She saw the stunned expressions on Christa and Judy. "My husband sold this stuff, and he always kept samples around in case he met a prospective customer."

Judy grabbed one of the blocks. "Do you know how to use it?"

"Yes. He liked to use this stuff instead of firecrackers on the Fourth of July, and taught me how to set up the demonstrations while he talked to customers. There's nothing to it, really." She dropped the explosives onto the bed and held up an electronic device. "All you need is a timer and detonator."

"So, what do you plan to do?" Christa asked.

Joyce grinned. "Get even."

***

Mark's heart beat fiercely as he forced himself to keep running along the road. He'd forgotten it was nearly four miles to the meadow, and stopped when he saw movement through the trees. While he tried to catch his breath, a truck suddenly came around the bend and he waited for it to come closer. Three more trucks followed, and the last truck slowed to a crawl when it came by.

"Jump in back, Mark," someone hollered.

Mark looked up and recognized a sergeant in the passenger seat. "I'm looking for my dad," he hollered as he trotted beside the truck.

"He's in back. We were told to put him under arrest, but I don't know why."

"Can I ride with him?"

"I don't see why not? Jump in."

Mark waited until the truck had nearly passed before jumping onto the bumper. Two sets of hands helped him over the tailgate, and when he looked up, he saw his father sitting between two men with rifles. He walked back, knelt in front of him, and saw the frightened look in his eyes.

"They arrested me, Mark!" Harold said in a quivering voice. He suspected the women had been caught and wondered if his son knew about it. The imploring look in Mark's eyes told him he had. "I didn't have a choice, son." When he saw the hurt look in his son's eyes, his heart dropped into his stomach. He knew he was going to be shot, but the look from his son made him feel as though he already had a bullet in his heart. He stared at his hands and saw them shaking.

Chapter 33

AOS CAMP:

Joyce slowed the motorhome and Christa and Judy jumped out, taking the suitcase of samples with them as they ran between the tents into the woods. Joyce had told them where to hide, and she would join them as soon as she could.

Joyce parked in front of Sergeant Major Davis' cabin and walked through the motor home to the side door. When she opened it, Davis and four men were standing in front of her. "I need a place to stay," she told him. "Let me use your cabin while you're gone."

Davis grinned sadistically. "Okay, Joyce, but if you move in, you stay here with me when I get back."

Joyce knew she wouldn't be there, even if he returned, and smiled at the thought, knowing Davis would misinterpret it. She grabbed a suitcase before stepping out of the motor home.

Davis waited until the other men were in the motor home and then indicated for Joyce to go into his cabin. He followed her as far as the door and stopped, and when she started unpacking her suitcases, he smiled leeringly, knowing he now had what all the other men in camp wanted. "If I wasn't so busy, I'd get a quick one before I leave," he said to her.

Joyce turned to him and smiled. "I think there will be plenty of time for that when you get back, don't you?"

Davis smirked at her. "Save it all for me, Joyce. I'll arrange it with the Major."

Joyce grinned. This was working out better than she had hoped. "Sure thing, honey. I'll see you off." She followed him out to the motorhome.

Davis saw the other men watching from the windows and grinned up at them. "Guess who's out of service, guys?" he said and grabbed Joyce around the waist, pulling her close. He gave her an overly zealous kiss and then climbed into the motorhome.

When the door slammed shut, Joyce spit nastily, wiped her hand across her mouth, and then grabbed a short piece of string hanging out of a side compartment door. She yanked it out, and with string in hand, smiled and walked into the cabin.

***

The truck stopped in front of the jail, and Mark followed his dad and the two soldiers into the building, and watched them shove his father into a cell with two other men he didn't recognize. He also saw his mother in the next cell with Marcia and a nice-looking girl. His parents exchanged stares, and then turned toward him, and he saw a pleading look in their eyes. He glared at them for a moment, spun around, and stomped out of the jail.

Mark was filled with so much rage he paid no attention to all the people rushing around him. He found Pam sitting on a log bench outside the dormitory and sat next to her.

"Did you find Dad?"

"Yeah. He's in jail." He stomped his feet and leapt off the bench. "How could they do this to us?" He screamed and stared at his sister.

Pam thought the camp was all right, and was glad she'd found a boy who really liked her, but she knew this army meant everything to Mark. "It wasn't their fault."

Mark looked away. "I hope they get shot!"

"Sit down and listen to me," she asked, but he continued to pace in front of her. "I said sit!"

Mark stopped and stared at her. She looked just like his mom did when she was scolding him, so did as instructed, a scowl frozen on his face.

"They didn't have a choice." Pam continued. "The spies were blackmailing them and threatened to make up stories to get you into trouble if Mom and Dad didn't cooperate. That's why they did it." She watched his scowl melt away in surprise.

"They did it for me?" Mark asked. Pam nodded, and Mark thought his heart would rip apart. *I didn't know they loved me that much. If I try to help them, I'll be kicked out of the army. I love being a soldier! I have a uniform and everything! But I can't let Everex shoot my Mom and Dad!* He buried his head in his hands. *What should I do?*

Pam saw her brother's anguish and knew he was torn between two loves, and decided to make the decision for him. "We're going to get Mom and Dad out of jail," she said firmly.

Mark looked up at her, his eyes still full of anguish. "If I help you, they'll kick me out of the army."

Pam laughed harshly. "So what? This isn't a real army. It's just a bunch of sick-headed people holding a bunch of scared people hostage. You saw what they did to Mister Berry. Do you think a sane person would have done that?"

He knew she was right. As much as he admired Major Everex, he seemed awfully mean to everyone. "So, what do we do now? Everex will probably shoot them before he leaves."

"I found out Colonel Blackwood is going to lead the army, and Everex is staying here in case the Colonel fails."

"How will we get them out of jail?"

"I don't know yet, but whatever we do, we'll have to wait until the Colonel leaves with most of the soldiers. Let's go to my room and try to think of a plan."

***

Joyce met up with Christa and Judy at the secret location and told them about getting into the cabin. "I think the army is ready to leave. When they've gone, come to the cabin. I'll be waiting."

Christa gave Joyce a hug. "Thanks. We really appreciate this."

"Anything to get out of this madhouse."

***

It was after 8:00 PM when Monroe parked his truck in front of Blackwood's cabin. He and the Colonel had become friends, of a sort, and he had offered to use his truck as the lead vehicle and act as the Colonel's driver. He was surprised by Blackwood's reaction and gratitude and realized the Colonel was scared to death about all of this.

He climbed out of the truck and climbed up the steps. The door was open, and he saw Blackwood scurrying around inside, his arms full of papers and rolled maps. "Can I give you a hand, George?"

Blackwood turned and smiled nervously. "Thank God you're here, Jerry. I can't decide what I'm going to need."

Jerry took the maps out of Blackwood's arms. "Let's see. I don't think we'll need all these. Put your gear in the truck while I sort these out."

Blackwood smiled gratefully. When he stepped out of the cabin, Everex was waiting for him.

Everex noticed Blackwood's nervous expression. "I hope you're ready, because the rest of the convoy is waiting."

I don't think I'll ever be ready for this, Blackwood moaned inwardly. He saw the wary look in Everex's eyes and tried to think of something appropriate to say, and then Monroe stepped around the truck.

"I've loaded everything you ordered, sir," he said, for Blackwood's sake. "We're ready to move out."

Blackwood gathered his courage and stood tall in front of Everex. "Take good care of my camp, Major," he said with forced bravado. "I expect everything to be in order when I return victorious." He turned and climbed into the passenger side of the truck and released a deep sigh. *If I return.*

Everex moved to the passenger window to look at Blackwood. "If you're not victorious, you'd better not return."

Everex turned and strode across the parade ground and down a trail that led to the end of the convoy. At the end of the line of troop carriers were two fuel trucks, followed by the big Roadmaster motorhome Davis and the rest of his elite guards had taken from the whore. He hated to send all his personal guards with the convoy, but he didn't trust the Colonel's leadership. He preemptively gave his guards orders to shoot the Colonel if he decided to back out of the attack or tried something stupid.

Everex waited until the last taillight disappeared, then climbed back up the trail as his thoughts turned to the spies in jail. *I think I'll have a little fun with the amazon woman before I shoot her and her friends.* As he walked across the parade ground, a young soldier ran up to him, panting fiercely. "What's wrong?"

"Some soldiers have deserted!" he managed to say between breaths.

Everex knew he only had a dozen soldiers left in camp and couldn't afford to lose a single person. "Sound the assembly bugle. I want everyone here on the double!"

When the boy ran off, he stared across the far end of the parade ground at the jail. The bugle notes played through the speakers, and he continued across the parade ground and stood on Blackwood's porch as the first soldiers ran to assemble before him.

***

Christa and Judy listened to the growl of the convoy trucks fade away and ran from the woods to the cabin Joyce had indicated, with Judy carrying the suitcase of samples. Although Joyce had said the plastic explosives couldn't go off without being detonated, Judy was still nervous about being so close to the suitcase. As she followed Christa through the door, she gently set it down just inside and hurried to the far wall of the room, collapsing into a cushioned chair as she stared up at Joyce.

Christa smelled dirty socks and sweat in the room and wrinkled her nose in disgust. "I suggest we try to come up with a plan."

The three of them exchanged looks when they heard a recorded bugle echo through the camp. Joyce indicated for Christa and Judy to sit tight and stepped out of the cabin. She watched several soldiers run past and knew they were going to the parade ground at the other end of the cabins, and stepped back inside and closed the door. "Everyone's assembling. I don't know why, but this might be our only chance to help your friends."

"What should we do?" Christa asked.

"I showed you how to set the timers on the explosives. Now's a good time to set them up as a diversion."

"Out on the main road, I think." Judy told her. "When the soldiers run in that direction, it will give us a chance to blow a hole in the wall of the jail."

Joyce shook her head no. "The road is fine for the diversion, but we can't use this stuff on the jailhouse. We'd kill everyone inside. When you get back, I'll try to get the guard to come outside, and you can hit him over the head or something."

Judy stood. "Okay. Let's do it." She walked nervously to the suitcase, but stopped short and looked at Joyce. "Maybe you'd better show us one more time."

Joyce smiled, opened the suitcase, and showed them what to do. "When you're ready, set the timers for thirty minutes."

* * *

Mark and Pam heard the bugle call and followed the rest of the soldiers. They stood to the right side of the crowd in front of Blackwood's cabin and saw Everex as a silhouette in front of the porch light.

Everex stared down at the small crowd. Nearly all of them were people he'd forced into training, and most of them were never issued a rifle or pistol, and he tried to decide which people he could trust. He decided to let them come forward on their own. "Listen up!" he shouted. "I need volunteers to watch for deserters. I'll issue a rifle and give a promotion to anyone who wants to stand guard. We need everyone here to protect our supplies from the fanatics if the Colonel fails, but if even one person leaves, it increases your chances of getting killed."

Pam poked her elbow lightly into Mark's ribs. "Raise your hand."

"I thought we were going to rescue Mom and Dad?"

"We'll have a better chance if we have guns."

Mark agreed and raised his hand. *Maybe I'll get a pistol.*

Everex saw several hands rise from the crowd and recognized Mark and Pam in front and to his left. He was surprised, since their parents were in jail. "Follow me to the munitions issue building," he told everyone, and descended the steps.

***

In front of the munitions building, Everex took Mark and Pam aside. "What are you two up to?"

"We're soldiers, Sir," Mark answered and stood at attention. "This is our army, and we have to protect what's ours! Right, Sir?"

Everex looked at him skeptically. "What about your parents?"

"They got what they deserved," Pam told him. "A little time in jail will straighten them out."

Everex grinned, but not for them. They didn't know he was going to shoot the prisoners personally. "Very well. Check out your rifles."

"I'd like a pistol, Sir," Mark told him, but Everex didn't reply. "You said if I proved myself, I could wear a pistol."

Everex remembered when Mark first came into Blackwood's cabin. *Why not? A pistol was the only thing the boy really wanted. Maybe this would assure his devotion to him.* "Very well, Sergeant Woolly."

Mark felt a stirring of pride. Did he hear right? A promotion? He smiled at Everex and saluted smartly. "Thank you, Sir!"

When Everex walked away, Pam looked at her smiling brother. "What are you doing?"

Mark looked down at her, still grinning. "Did you hear that? I've been promoted!"

"What about Mom and Dad?"

Mark's grin faded. "Well, they could have turned the spies in right away. I think Major Everex would have believed me instead of the spies."

Pam was surprised by Mark's change of heart. "So, you're going to let them be shot?"

Mark stared at the ground, slightly ashamed. "I just can't be a traitor. The Major needs me."

"Does that mean you'd shoot me if I try to save them?"

Mark glanced at her, then back at the ground. "I, uh. Well, no, I won't try to stop you." He looked into Pam's eyes. "But if you get caught, you have to tell the Major I didn't know anything about it, okay?"

Pam felt a deep disgust for her brother. "Fine," she said curtly, and stepped in line to get a rifle.

Chapter 34

AOS CAMP:

It was 12:30 A.M. when Christa and Judy emerged from the woods, ran inside the cabin, and found Joyce pacing nervously. Judy closed the door behind them and grinned at her. "We did it!"

"I was beginning to think you got caught. How long before the first explosion?"

Christa looked at her watch. "Twenty minutes."

Joyce took a deep breath. "All right, take these. They're the best I can do for a weapon." She handed each of them a pink tube sock with a baseball-sized rock inside. "Follow me to the jail and act like you belong here."

They stepped outside and walked boldly past the rest of the cabins. A few soldiers hurried past them, but didn't stop, and when they reached the jail, Christa and Judy stood on either side of the door as Joyce entered.

When Joyce opened the door and stepped inside, the elderly guard suddenly jumped out of his chair behind the desk and pointed a pistol at her. She hesitated a second before stepping up to him. "So, how's it going, Randy?"

Randy smiled nervously and set the pistol on the desk. "Oh, hi, Joyce. I'm getting a little twitchy in my old age. What are you doing here?"

"Everyone else has something to do, and I'm bored. I just wanted to stop by to ask the prisoners what's happening in the real world." She heard a muffled explosion, but it was too far away to be their diversion.

"What the hell was that?" Randy asked, as if he thought Joyce would know. A moment later, they heard another muffled explosion, then a third. "It's them!" Randy moaned. "They're attacking the Colonel!"

Joyce tried to look frightened, which wasn't hard. "Oh, my! What should we do?"

Randy looked at the prisoners, who were staring at him. He didn't know what was going on outside the jail, but knew he couldn't leave his post. "I'd better call in for orders."

When Christa and Judy heard the explosions, Christa looked at her watch. "It's too soon!"

They both flinched as a female soldier ran past them, then Judy grabbed Christa's arm. "We have to get inside!"

Randy picked up the phone to call central control and his finger was pushing the second digit when the door suddenly burst open and two women rushed in. Joyce was as startled as Randy was, but she threw herself across the desk, covering the pistol with her body.

Randy looked up at the two women and the taller one was moving toward him, and he saw the hostile look in her eyes. He needed the pistol and looked down at Joyce on the desk, then realized he was still holding the telephone receiver and raised it over his head, intent on bashing Joyce's head in. He saw a pink blur of motion and felt a searing pain in his right hand as it was smashed aside; the receiver flying out of his grip.

He turned his head to see what had happened to his hand and saw the short woman at the end of the desk with a long, pink object extended from her raised right hand. As if in slow motion, he watched the pink object move toward him and he wanted to duck out of its way, but felt frozen in place. His eyes crossed as the pink weapon smashed against his forehead, and then everything went black.

Christa heard a sickening thud and watched the man stagger back a step before toppling backward onto the floor. She stared down at the limp body and suddenly felt sick to her stomach. *I've killed him!*

Joyce rolled off the desk and moved to Randy's side, kneeling as she grabbed his wrist. When she felt a pulse, she nodded up at Christa.

Only then did Christa notice Alex standing on the other side of the bars, and the men and women around him. She wanted to hold him, but couldn't because of the bars.

"The keys are in the desk," Alex told her.

As Christa stepped over the old man's body to open the drawer, Judy stepped up to Alex behind the bars. "We came as soon as we could, and we don't have much time."

***

Pam was sitting on the far side of the parade ground when she heard the muffled explosions. She saw people running around, most looking scared and not knowing what to do, and realized this might be her only opportunity to rescue her parents. She leapt off the bench and ran toward the jailhouse.

***

Everex jumped out of his chair when he heard the first faint explosion, then ran to the door and stepped out onto the porch, searching for the source. He recognized the Woolly girl among the other people running across the parade ground, but was distracted by two more explosions. In the far distance, he saw a bright orange light reflecting off the clouds and knew the battle had begun. As he turned to enter the cabin, he saw the Woolly girl standing against the wall of the jail, and when he realized what she was up to, he was torn between calling central control for the bugles and stopping the escape of the prisoners.

***

Christa first unlocked the cell door for the men, then the one that held the women. As she turned, she saw Judy wrap her arms around Alex and hug him tightly. She fought to hold back her tears and walked back to the desk where Joyce was sitting, holding the pistol in her lap.

Harold started to approach Cally, desperately wanting to hold her and ask forgiveness, but she folded her arms and turned away. He felt sick at heart and stopped.

Alex looked over Judy's shoulder and saw the anguish in Christa's eyes just before she turned away. He gently pushed Judy aside and was about to walk over to Christa when the door suddenly burst open and a young girl rushed through, her rifle swinging back and forth at everyone. He saw the frightened look on his friend's faces and saw the Woolly woman and her husband smile.

"Pamela!" Cally shouted, and rushed to her daughter.

Pam wasn't sure what to make of the situation and wondered why everyone was out of the cells. She recognized Joyce and her parents, but had no idea who the others were. She kept the rifle pointed at the strangers as her mom tried to hug her. "Are you all right?" she asked, trying to keep an eye on everyone. She saw her father smile and lowered the rifle. "What's going on?"

"We're being rescued," Cally told her.

Alex was trying to sort out what was happening when a deafening gun blast suddenly filled the room. He watched the young girl stagger forward and topple to the floor; the rifle sliding away under the bars of the cell. Everex stepped through the doorway with a large caliber pistol leading his way.

Cally rushed to her daughter and knelt down. "Pam!" she screamed, and threw her body over her daughter as protection.

Harold stared open-mouthed at his precious little girl lying on the floor and flinched when he heard the bark of Everex's voice. *Do something, you coward!* His inner voice yelled.

"Get away from her, bitch!" Everex yelled. "Everyone back in the cell!" He looked at the others and recognized Joyce, and a brutal smile spread across his face.

Joyce saw the leering smile and couldn't control the rage swelling inside her. She swung the pistol up at Everex and squeezed the trigger, but nothing happened.

Everex saw the pistol in Joyce's hand and instinctively brought his own gun up, fired, and watched Joyce fly backward and hit the wall before collapsing to the floor. He saw the Woolly woman turn to face him, her eyes filled with hate, and when she stood up, he aimed the pistol at her, grinned sadistically, and started to squeeze the trigger.

Harold felt a savage rage course through his every vein and turned to Everex, releasing a barbaric animal scream as he rushed him. Blinded with hate, he didn't notice the gun swinging up at him.

Everex heard the scream and turned his head to find the source. He brought the pistol around to fire just as a loud explosion shook the camp. He flinched, squeezed the trigger, and saw Harold suddenly spin around like a top before tumbling to the floor.

Another explosion rocked the camp, and Everex knew it was close and thought he was being attacked! He decided to shoot all the prisoners before trying to organize a defense.

He caught a movement to his right and saw the Woolly woman holding her fingers out at him like claws as she rushed forward and swung his pistol around.

Alex saw Joyce's pistol lying on the floor and dove for it. He grabbed and released the safety as he rolled to his feet and aimed it at Everex. He heard two different sounding explosions fill the room; one loud, the other slightly muffled, and stared at Everex and the large bloody hole where his chest had been. He watched Everex topple forward against the Woolly woman and both collapsed to the floor with a dull thud, and then swung the pistol at the doorway as a young boy stepped into the room.

"Mom!" Mark screamed and dropped the pistol as he grabbed Everex by the shirt and rolled him off Cally, then saw the blood all over her chest and stomach. "Mom!" he screamed in fear.

Harold tried to push himself up from the floor, but his left arm didn't want to work. His eyes focused on Cally and the blood that covered her chest. "No!" he shrieked, and crawled toward her. "Cally!" he moaned as he got up on his knees next to his son.

Cally blinked a few times while she caught her breath and saw Mark and Harold kneeling above her. "I'm all right," she gasped, and saw the stunned relief on the faces of her son and husband. "Pam!" she yelled, and struggled to sit up.

Mark leapt to his feet and rushed to his sister, lying face down on the floor. He saw the small hole in the outside edge of her back and rolled her over, and the cloth on the right side of her shredded shirt was a bloody mess.

Alex ran over next to Mark and knelt near the girl's head as he sized up the damage. He felt her neck and found a strong pulse, then ripped the shirt away and saw the torn flesh along the outside of her ribcage and the cracked white bone of an exposed rib. "She'll be all right," he told everyone. "It looks like the bullet glanced off a rib." He looked into Mark's eyes. "Run and get a doctor." Mark jumped up and disappeared out the door.

Sharlett hurried over to Harold, knelt beside him, and saw the cloth on his left shoulder was torn away, along with some flesh. The wound was oozing blood, but apparently, the bullet had missed an artery or vein, so she ripped part of Harold's shirt away and tied it around the wound. "You'll be fine," she assured him.

Alex looked around at the frightened faces of his friends, then down at the dead woman named Joyce. Everything had happened so fast they were stunned and motionless, all staring at the bloody people on the floor. "Close the door, Judy," he ordered. "Okay, tell me what's happening out there."

Harold looked into Cally's eyes, she into his. "I thought you were dead."

Cally remembered hearing Harold's savage scream and watching him rush the man with the gun. *He was trying to save our lives,* she suddenly realized, and for the first time in her life, felt proud of her husband. Tears rushed into her eyes, and she reached out and hugged him fiercely. "Oh, I do love you, Harold."

Christa and Judy explained what they had done as Marcia, David, Sharlett, and Alex listened.

The door suddenly burst open and Mark rushed in, the gray-haired doctor right behind him. The doctor glanced down at the open eyes of Major Everex, saw the blown open chest, and knew the man was dead. He knelt next to Pam and studied her wound for a moment, then moved over to Harold and gently untied the piece of cloth on his shoulder.

Sharlett watched the doctor checking the wound. "It's a clean hole. The bullet passed through without hitting a vain or artery."

"You look too young to be a doctor."

"I'm a second-year medical student."

"I'm going to need your help."

"I'll do what I can."

The doctor stood and glanced around the room at the others, and from the look in Alex's eyes, figured he was in charge. "We'll need a stretcher for the girl. I don't think the rib punctured the lung, but we need to be careful. We'll take these two to my infirmary, and we'd better hurry. There's going to be a lot more wounded when the battle is over."

"There won't be any battle," Alex told him. "I made up the story for that asshole." He indicated Everex.

The doctor looked puzzled for a second, but understood. "You'd better tell the rest of the people out there before they shoot each other by accident. They're all pretty scared right now."

Alex looked at Mark. "I heard an assembly bugle a while ago. Do you know how to turn it on?"

"I think so. They play it from central control."

"Turn it on and meet me on the parade ground." Mark left the building.

"I know where the infirmary is," Marcia told him. "David and I will bring back a stretcher."

"Good," said Alex. "The rest of you stay here and help the doctor, and I'll meet you at the infirmary later." He picked up the pistol, tucked it into his belt, and left the jail.

***

No one paid any attention to him as Alex walked to the center of the parade ground and waited. A bugle blared from the speakers, and a moment later, Mark ran up beside him as people assembled, all staring at the porch in front of Blackwood's cabin.

"You need to stand up there." Mark told him. "That's where the Colonel and Major Everex stand when they talk to everyone."

"Okay. Come up there with me."

They walked up the steps and looked down at the people gathering below. It was apparent no one knew what was going on, and all they could do was wait until some stepped forward to take command.

One man approached and stood at the bottom of the steps and stared up at the stranger on the porch. "Who are you?"

Alex looked at the man and saw the challenge in his eyes. He was slightly taller than he was, and in good physical shape from what he could tell under the uniform. "Major Everex is dead, and I'm taking over," he said firmly, locking stares with the man.

The man stared into Alex's eyes and saw an air of authority, with a glint of cunning, that told him to back off. The man looked away toward the crowd of people, then back up at Alex. "My name is Luke Ardle, the senior camp instructor. I was in charge of training, and I guess I'm the next senior officer in charge."

Alex looked over at Mark, who nodded affirmation, and reached out for Luke's hand. "Alex Cave. Why don't you come up here while I tell everyone what's going on?"

Luke climbed up the steps and then turned to look at the ten people with rifles assembled in front of the cabin. "That's about it, I think," he told Alex. "The rest went with the Colonel."

Luke stepped up to the railing. "Listen up!" he bellowed in a raised voice. As the muffled conversations faded, he stepped back out of the way.

Alex saw he had their attention. "Major Everex is dead, and we will not be attacked by another army. I want everyone to calm down before someone gets hurt."

A young man stepped forward. "Oh, yeah?" he said with a haughty attitude, standing with his arms folded across his chest and a glare in his eyes. "Who put you in charge? You're just a civilian!"

Alex stared down at the young man without replying for a few seconds. Telling them he was a teacher wouldn't impress them, he realized. "I work for the Director of National Security." Alex watched the young man suddenly lose a bit of his assurance and step back into the crowd. "I'm not here to take over. Mister Ardle will do that. Right now, I need for all of you to relax and do what he tells you."

Alex turned to Luke. "I'd appreciate it if you found something to keep them occupied. Mark and I need to get to the infirmary and check on our friends and family."

"Okay. I'll join you in a moment. I have a lot of questions."

Alex walked down the steps, with Mark close behind him. "I guess you know the way." Mark smiled up at him in response, so he indicated his appreciation.

Chapter 35

IDAHO. ROUTE 22 NORTH:

Jerry Monroe looked at the odometer on the dashboard, and they were fifteen miles from camp when the steering wheel suddenly jerked in his hand as the concussion from an explosion violently shook the truck. He heard the roaring boom and stomped on the brake, spinning the steering wheel around to pull onto the shoulder of the road. A troop carrier skidded to a stop on his left side, and he glanced at Blackwood, who stared at him wide-eyed; his mouth hanging open.

Blackwood closed his mouth. "They're attacking us!"

Monroe thought the same thing. "Out of the truck!" he hollered as he threw open his door and leapt out, and ran to the passenger side as Blackwood tumbled out the door. He grabbed him by the arm and helped him stand, then pulled him out into the field.

Both men stared at the flames of what was left of the motorhome, its shell ripped apart, lying on both sides of the road. A few seconds later, a fuel truck behind it exploded with a concussion that knocked them both off their feet. A massive ball of yellow-orange fire soared into the air, and flaming fuel rained down on the troop carriers.

Monroe and Blackwood rolled over and stared at the carnage, and the stench of burning rubber filled the air as horrified screams filled the night, and watched soldiers entombed in flames stagger from the trucks and roll on the ground. The second fuel truck erupted like a volcano, hurling the last troop carrier off the road like a toy and sending it rolling across the field.

Fire was consuming huge areas of dry grass in an expanding circle on both sides of the road, and Monroe saw the flames moving their way. He yanked Blackwood to his feet, and they ran to the front of the pickup and squatted down with the soldiers from the troop carrier.

After a few minutes, the flames died off, and Monroe realized he didn't hear any gunfire, and slowly stood and looked around. The light from the remaining flames illuminated the fields for several hundred feet in all directions, and he didn't see any signs they were being attacked.

One of the soldiers crawled over to Blackwood. "What should we do, Sir?"

Blackwood stood, looked around for a moment, and came to the same conclusion as Monroe, then turned to the soldiers. "Help the most seriously wounded into the remaining vehicles and take them back to camp. Move it, people!"

Blackwood turned to Monroe. "What do you suppose happened?"

"From what I can see, I think it started in the motorhome. Maybe there was a gas leak."

Blackwood stared at the wreckage as they walked through the disaster area. The stench of burnt flesh permeated the air, and pitiful moans of pain came from all directions. They stopped and stared down at the wide-open eyes looking up from a charred face, and Monroe turned to throw up. Blackwood felt his stomach churn and bile rise in his throat, but he'd seen worse in the P.O.W. camp, and managed to maintain control.

They continued along the road, and debris from the explosions littered the ground in all directions for as far as they could see. Around them, dozens of able soldiers were making their way through the bodies on the ground in the light of the burning fuel, finding the living among the dead, and carrying them to the drivable trucks. The air reeked of oily smoke and burnt flesh, and screams of agony echoed across the valley.

Monroe looked at Blackwood. "What now, Colonel?"

Blackwood stared at the wreckage. "I'll call the camp and tell them what happened. Once the wounded are taken care of, I'll have the trucks come back and pick up the dead, and we'll give them a proper burial at the camp."

"I don't remember seeing a cellphone in the truck, and I didn't grab one. Did you?"

Blackwood tried to remember. "I'm not sure."

"What about the attack on this other army?"

Blackwood laughed bitterly. "We couldn't attack a convalescent center with what's left here. We'll wait for them to come after us and do our best to repel them."

"Let's help with the wounded."

Blackwood solemnly nodded and led Monroe back along the road to his truck. Four wounded soldiers had crawled into the truck bed, and Blackwood gave each one a reassuring pat on their shoulder.

***

The sun was rising over the eastern horizon and creeping through the window of the infirmary, and Sharlett felt its warmth on her face. She looked over at Mark, who had not left the recovery room since he arrived with his sister and parents.

Alex stood outside the building with his friends, while Marcia, Judy, and Christa told him and David what had happened after the plane crashed on the way to Washington. He told them about the trek he, David, and Sharlett had made to find them, and then looked at Christa. "Do you still have the computer disks, the crystal, and the vial?"

"Yes. They're in the cabin that Joyce . . ." Her voice trailed off for a moment as she thought about the poor woman who had helped them through so much.

Alex saw the sorrow in her eyes. "Okay. I guess our next step is to continue what we started to do. They must have a cellphone around here, so I'll try to get through to Director Donner and see if he can send some help."

They watched a truck drive up in front of the infirmary, and then the driver jumped out. "Get the doctor!" The young woman yelled. "I've got a truckload of wounded people out here!"

Alex spun around to the door and yanked it open, and then hollered into the room before running to the back of the truck. When he threw open the canvas curtain, a burnt odor escaped from inside and he turned and saw his friends standing behind him. "Grab the stretchers and let's help these people," he told them. "Sharlett, run and find some soldiers to help."

"I've got medical training. I should stay here."

"I'll go," Judy told him, and ran toward the parade ground while Christa, Judy, and Marcia ran back into the building to get the stretchers.

The doctor ran out of the infirmary and looked into the back of the truck. "Good grief!" He turned to the driver. "What happened?"

"Everything started blowing up, and more trucks will be coming in a few minutes."

"How many more wounded?"

"A lot."

Alex wondered how there could be wounded when there shouldn't have been an attack and turned to the driver. "Was there a battle?"

"No, the Colonel said it started with a gas leak in the motorhome. It exploded and set the fuel trucks on fire, and they blew up."

"All right. Thanks." When the driver walked away, he wondered if it could just be a coincidence. Without a forensic investigation, he knew he would never know for sure.

Sharlett jumped into the truck and helped the ones who could stand to get out of the back. When the last of the walking wounded was on the ground, she jumped out and looked at the doctor. "What do you want me to do?"

The infirmary was already full, so he looked up at the brightening sky and saw it was clear of clouds, and then looked at Sharlett. "Start triage out here. We'll take care of the critically wounded first, and the rest will have to stay out here to be treated."

"All right. I'll make them as comfortable as I can." She moved from person to person, doing what she could for them.

Christa and Marcia helped David bring the stretchers out just as Judy came back with Luke and five soldiers. Luke took over, ordering his people into the truck to load the rest of the wounded onto the stretchers. Once the truck was empty, the driver climbed into the cab and drove back to the disaster area. A few minutes later, another truck arrived with more wounded, and the ground outside the infirmary became crowded with patients.

Alex took Luke aside for a moment. "Is there a cellphone around here?"

"In Blackwood's cabin, on the desk. He forgot to take it with him."

***

BLACKWOOD'S CABIN:

Alex sat on the edge of the desk, grabbed the phone, and entered Donner's private number. A moment later, he answered. "It's me."

"Alex! Thank God you're all right!" He listened while Alex explained what had happened and what was going on. "I see. I have more bad news. We were notified that the tanker in route from Cook Inlet was attacked, so none of the crude oil made it the west coast. Your friend from All Alaska has been calling, and he's just as worried as we've been. Here's his number."

"All right, I'll call him." Alex hung up and was about to call Bull when he noticed Christa standing in the doorway. "What's going on?"

She had followed him to the cabin and had been watching him the whole time he was on the phone, desperately wishing he would hold her for a few moments when he was through. She walked into the cabin and stood in front of him. "Would you mind giving me a hug? I promise not to get in the way of you and Judy."

Alex stood and wrapped his arms around her. "There's nothing between us."

Christa eased back a little and stared at his chest. "You don't have to lie to me. I heard you that night back at your house."

"Judy was blackmailing me. She wasn't going to fly you to Washington if I didn't sleep with her. Please believe me."

Christa stared up into his eyes and saw his sincerity. Tears suddenly clouded her vision, and she smiled and pulled him close.

Alex felt her kiss him on the neck and started to turn his head so he could place his lips against hers, but a picture of Sevi's mangled body lying dead on a stretcher flashed into his mind. He didn't want to hurt her, but he just wasn't ready for a relationship, and gently eased her away. He saw the puzzled look in her eyes and felt a deep anguish ripping at his heart, his frustration burning in his soul. He tried to think of a way to explain to her just how he felt, but couldn't find the right words to ease her pain. Instead, he just stood there, helpless to ease her suffering.

Christa stared up at him and saw the sadness in his eyes. She pushed him away and turned her back to him, not wanting him to see the painful look she knew she couldn't hide. "I'm sorry," she said as she fought to keep her voice steady, and then rushed out the door.

Alex dropped heavily into the chair at the desk, staring at the parade ground through the open doorway. He heaved a deep sigh and then dialed the number for Bull.

"Yeah," Bull answered in his unmistakable voice.

"It's Alex."

"Thank God! Where the hell have you been? What's going on? When will the women get here? You've had me really worried!"

Alex filled him in on the women's plane crash and the A.O.S. camp. "Martin told me about the attack on the last tanker. Even if we could get up there to Valdez, there isn't much we could do."

Bull didn't hide the smugness he felt. "I still have some crude oil. I didn't trust the military, so I stole a few hundred gallons."

"That's great! I'll try to arrange for transportation to get it down to Nevada. They have everything we need."

"No way, pal. I'm not letting this stuff out of my sight. Especially to the military."

Alex knew where Bull was coming from. The military had bungled every attempt they tried. "All right. Give me some time to think of another way, and I'll call you back as soon as we come up with something."

"Fair enough. I'll be waiting."

Alex turned the phone off and sat thinking. He had an idea and called Donner back. "Where is the nearest military base with helicopters?"

Chapter 36

STATE ROUTE 22 SOUTH, IDAHO:

I lost sixty-three good people, Blackwood thought, as he and Monroe drove into the camp. Monroe stopped to let him out in front of his cabin, and Blackwood strode up the steps to the door. When he entered, he abruptly stopped when he saw a black-haired stranger sitting at his desk and talking on the phone. "Who the hell are you, and what are you doing in my quarters?"

When the stranger held his hand up for silence and kept talking, Blackwood couldn't hold back the rage he had kept buried since the explosions. His face flushed with anger and he drew his pistol, adjusting the sights on the stranger's forehead. A tall woman suddenly stepped in front of the gun, and Blackwood looked into her eyes. "Get out of my way, Marcia!"

When she saw the look in Blackwood's eyes, Marcia was scared, but stood firm. "Just wait a moment, George!" she pleaded.

Blackwood looked past her and glared at the stranger, who was now holding his hand over the mouthpiece of the phone. "What's going on here?"

Alex recognized Blackwood by the black eye patch. "Sorry to be here without your permission, Colonel, but you were gone. I'll explain everything in a moment, but first I'd like you to talk to someone. It's the Director of National Security."

Blackwood looked at Alex skeptically, thinking the man was joking, but from the look in his eyes, he decided that wasn't the case. He stepped around Marcia and took the phone, keeping the gun aimed at the stranger. "This is Colonel Blackwood. Who am I talking to?"

Marcia and Alex watched the stern expression slip off the Colonel's face as he recognized the voice on the other end of the phone. They listened to his side of the conversation and saw Blackwood smile and stand a little taller.

"Yes, Sir. Thank you, Sir. That was a long time ago." Marcia and Alex saw the Colonel look up at the plaque on the wall that held his Purple Heart.

"Yes, Sir. I'll do my best. Yes, Sir. You can count on me." Blackwood handed the phone back to Alex and stepped over to Marcia, a smile forming on his lips as he gently held her hand.

Alex listened to Donner for a few moments and then hung up. When he saw Marcia and the Colonel smiling at each other, he cleared his throat to get their attention. "My name is Alex Cave," he said, and extended his hand.

Blackwood took it. "The Director asked me to help you, Mister Cave, and I'll do my best. But first, I have to prepare to defend my camp. There's an army on its way here." He stopped when he saw Alex grin. "You think this is funny?"

"No, Sir, but there isn't any army coming this way. I made the story up to keep your Major from killing us." He saw the cold look in Blackwood's eyes.

"Sixty-three of my soldiers are dead because of your story, mister!"

"I'm sorry, Colonel, and I assure you I had nothing to do with the explosions that killed your people. I would never have told that to the Major if I thought people would get killed."

Blackwood saw the sincerity in Alex's eyes as he thought about it. If it hadn't been for whatever Everex's guards had been doing to blow up the motorhome, no one would have died. Everex was the culprit, he realized. Now, without his guards to protect him, Blackwood knew he could have the bastard locked up. "Okay. There's something I need to take care of, then you can tell me what this is all about."

Blackwood walked out onto the porch and looked around. He spotted his training officer and an attractive blond woman walking across the parade ground. "Mister Ardle. Come here for a moment."

Judy had become infatuated with Luke from the moment she saw him standing on Blackwood's porch and had asked him to help. Now she was with him nearly all the time and paid little attention to Alex.

Luke stopped at the bottom of the steps. "Yes, Sir?"

"Get some men and arrest Major Everex. Put him in jail until I decide what to do with him."

"That won't be necessary, sir. He's dead."

Alex saw Blackwood's baffled expression turn into a grin and wondered what he was thinking. At least he didn't still hold him accountable for the deaths of his people.

Blackwood felt as though the weight of the world had been lifted from his shoulders, and wondered if the nightmares would finally end. He decided to see for himself, and only then would he really be free of the demon. "Where's the body? Have you buried him yet?"

"No, Sir. He's with the other bodies, up past the trees."

"Take me to him." Blackwood turned to Marcia and Alex. "You'll have to excuse me for a moment. There's something I have to do."

As Blackwood left with Luke, Judy walked up the steps and smiled at Alex and Marcia. "Isn't he handsome?" she said with genuine delight and stared after Luke.

"He seems like a fine man," Marcia assured her.

Alex felt a sense of relief. "I'm happy for you, Judy."

***

Luke led Blackwood up the road to the garbage dump, where they heard the low growl of a small track hoe at work through the trees. "Since you weren't around, Colonel, I took it upon myself to start burying the dead."

Blackwood was stunned. "In the garbage dump? That's not a proper way for my people to be buried!"

"Not in the dump, Sir. Farther up the trail, there's a small meadow. That's where they're digging the graves. It's pretty up there, Sir. You can see for yourself it has a nice view."

Blackwood followed Luke for another half mile, and as they entered the meadow, Blackwood stopped and looked around. *Luke was right*, he thought as he studied the magnificent view of the surrounding mountains. He had never taken the time to come up here and didn't know it existed. His reverie was dulled by the sight of a row of bodies placed along the edge of the trees, and a few men waiting to place them in the graves being dug by the track hoe.

Blackwood followed Luke along the row of dead soldiers, lying face up on the grass, most of them still wearing bloody bandages from when the doctor had tried to save their lives. The pungent odor of charred flesh and clothing hung in the still air, but Blackwood no longer felt nauseous at the smell. He recognized Joyce Berry among them and stopped. "What happened to her?"

"Everex shot her in the jailhouse. She was helping Alex and his friends escape."

Blackwood indicated for Luke to continue to Everex's body. At the end of the row, he recognized the face from his nightmares. He was set apart from the others, his glazed eyes still open and bloody red flesh ripped open in the chest. "Is this some kind of tribute?" he asked, a harsh edge in his voice.

Luke shook his head no. "No, sir. I didn't think it was proper to put him with these decent folks."

Blackwood's demeanor changed. "Good thinking." He knelt beside the body. "Who shot him?" he asked as he studied the missing section of Everex's chest.

"Private Woolly, sir."

"Give Woolly a promotion to sergeant." He stood and looked at the bucket of the track hoe digging narrow trenches. "Bury everyone but Everex in the meadow. He doesn't deserve to remain here with them. I want him buried in the dump with the rest of the garbage."

Luke thought the idea was a little morbid, but didn't say so. "Yes, Sir." He followed Blackwood back along the row of bodies and paused long enough to give orders to the waiting men before following him down the trail.

"Luke, I'd like you to be my new second in command. You seem levelheaded, and I've seen the way the soldiers look up to you. What do you say? Want the job?"

Luke thought about it for a moment. The idea wasn't so bad, but he and Judy had been making plans to leave. "I'll have to discuss it with someone first, Colonel."

"The blonde woman?"

"Yes, sir. You see, we really care about each other. I've never met a woman like her before, and I'd hate to lose her."

Blackwood thought about the new woman in his life and understood what Luke was getting at. He suddenly realized Marcia would probably want to leave, too. "All right. I think we both need to talk things out with the others members of this camp."

***

Alex, Marcia, and Judy sat on the porch as Blackwood and Luke approached and ascended the steps. Blackwood slid a chair up next to Marcia and sat, and Luke leaned back on the handrail next to Judy's chair.

Blackwood turned to look at Alex. "Okay, Mister Cave. Tell me what this is all about."

Alex explained everything he knew, with Marcia adding details about what they had discovered about the enzymes and the crystal. "That's why it's so important we get to Nevada. It's a secret base at Groom Lake."

"I've heard of it. A top-secret research facility. So, what would you like me to do?"

"Use your army and supplies to get us there."

"Why not have the director send a helicopter? It would be a lot faster."

"There just isn't any place for them to refuel."

Blackwood smiled. "Well, I just happen to have a tanker full of jet fuel that was taken by mistake. I was planning to use it for heating this winter. You can have it, but on one condition."

Alex sat up, more optimistic about his mission. "I'm listening."

"I might be in trouble with the law. You see, we hijacked the interstate for supplies, but Everex took it upon himself to kill the truckers, and I know I'll get blamed for it."

"Everex did a lot of nasty things on his own," Luke spoke up on Blackwood's behalf. "I'll testify if need be."

Alex had no idea if his mission would solve the oil crisis, but he had to try. "I'm sure a prosecutor will take that into consideration, but I don't have the authority to make any promises. I can tell them about your assistance in this crisis, but that's the best I can offer."

Blackwood looked at Marcia for confirmation and saw her smile. It was all he needed to know.

"He's a man of his word, George."

Blackwood looked across at Alex. "Take all the fuel you need."

Alex left the others on the porch as he went inside to contact Donner and Bull. When he finished, he walked back outside. "The helicopter will stop and pick up Bull and the oil before heading here to refuel for the trip to Nevada. It should arrive in about four hours."

Blackwood noticed Jerry Monroe walking across the parade ground and waved him over. When Monroe stopped at the bottom of the steps, Blackwood stood from his chair. "I'm going to be arrested soon, and I'll accept my punishment, but I'm hoping you might take over for me. It may be awhile before these people can go back to a regular life, and I want them to feel safe here until that happens."

Monroe was surprised by the offer and looked Blackwood in the eyes. "If I do this, there are going to be some major changes. Anyone who wants to leave may do so and no more special services."

Blackwood nodded vigorously. "Of course. That was Everex's doing, not mine."

Monroe held out his hand to Blackwood. "Then we have a deal."

Chapter 37

GROOM LAKE, NEVADA:

Alex and Christa were cordial to each other on the flight to Nevada, but there was a constant strain between them. David and Bull were in the seats between them, but all conversations were drowned out by the high pitch whine from the engines of the gigantic Sea Stallion helicopter.

Alex felt a soft thud as the aircraft touched down in front of a hangar. The rotors slowed to a stop and engines shut down, then the tail ramp opened. He stood and walked out of the helicopter, and it seemed deathly quiet on the tarmac as he waited for his friends. He looked along the rows of hangars facing the taxiway, wondering what kinds of secrets were stashed at the top-secret facility.

Bull stood and followed David down the ramp to the group. "Well, we made it. What are we supposed to do next?"

Christa could tell her big friend was eager to get started. "You can just relax for a while. Now it's up to us scientists to figure things out."

The side door from the hangar opened, and two men walked out. One, a small, gray-haired man in civilian clothes, the other in an Air Force uniform, who introduced them to the group. "I'm Colonel Sterns, the base commander, and this is Doctor Henry Heinz, the civilian Director of the base."

Christa stepped forward and handed the crystal to Henry. "I found this in the empty oil tanker."

When Henry held the crystal in his open palm, tears clouded his vision for a moment. "I have been looking for this since 1949," he told them with a slight German accent.

Christa took an instant liking to the director. "And why is that, Doctor Heinz?"

He smiled. "Please, call me Henry. It is best if I show you and Mister Cave. Come with me."

Sterns indicated for David and Bull to follow him instead of Henry. "I'll take you to the barracks, and you can clean up and get something to eat."

David grabbed Alex's arm. "Wait. I want to go with you."

Alex saw the pleading look in David's eyes. "I'm sorry, but this is a top secret facility, and you don't have clearance."

"What about Christa? Does she have the right clearance?"

"Yes, she does. I'll work on getting you access when I'm through."

"All right. Just don't take too long. My curiosity is driving me crazy."

Bull looked at Alex. "I don't like leaving this oil here with no guards."

"It'll be safe. We'll meet up with you later."

Bull nodded reluctantly as he and David followed Sterns past the hangar to a separate building. He glanced back once before they entered, hoping Alex was correct about the oil being safe in the helicopter.

Henry waited for the others to be out of hearing distance. "In 1948, we found something very interesting out in the desert," he told them as they strolled between the hangars to the main road connecting the rows of buildings. "We have been studying it ever since, but we were forced to stop three years ago when the spacecraft was nearly out of power. There was nothing more we could do, until now."

Henry stopped at a small door in the back of a different hangar, and Alex studied the exterior. There were no windows in the building, and the big sliding doors were chained shut. He also noticed the number 5 was stenciled in black letters above the smaller door.

Henry entered his code and opened the door, turned to his guests, and saw them looking up at the number. "This is the actual infamous hangar." He stepped through the doorway.

Alex and Christa followed Henry into the dark interior and stopped when he began flipping switches. Rows of light-emitting diodes bloomed into a bright white light overhead, and Alex and Christa's jaws opened slightly at what they saw. A forty-foot diameter, twenty-four-foot high hockey puck-shaped object with a mirrored surface was sitting in the center of the hangar.

***

TWO HUNDRED MILES WEST OF GROOM LAKE:

Sagebrush and sand stretched away in all directions as Menno drove Elizabeth along an abandoned dirt road in the Nevada desert. The sun was setting behind the low mountains on the horizon when he pressed a small button in the dashboard, and directly ahead, a horizontal line of light appeared across the road, growing taller by the second as a gigantic door opened in the desert floor.

The vehicle entered the opening and descended at an angle, following the paved driveway under the desert. The door above them closed, and the overhead lights illuminated the square concrete tunnel, one hundred feet underground.

The vehicle stopped in front of a steel door in the cement wall, and Menno helped his mother out of the car. He opened the metal door, and they stepped into a two hundred foot square by one hundred foot high room. In the center was a forty-foot diameter, by twenty-four-foot high hockey puck-shaped object with a mirrored finish.

A man who looked as though he were in deep deliberation approached them, and his facial features were nearly identical to Menno's, except for the hair, which was light brown. "Hello, Reverend. Miss. Simons."

Menno smiled, hoping to evoke the same from the man, but Lewis Norton's expression didn't change. "Always so serious, Lewis. How many crystals have we collected?"

"Four hundred and eleven thousand, three hundred and seventy-nine. Come. I'll show you."

Lewis led them across the chamber to a ten foot square metal hatch in the floor. He pressed a button on the wall, the hatch opened, and dazzling white light radiated from the inside.

Menno leaned over the opening, and it was like looking at a pile of sparkling diamonds. He leaned back and placed his hand on Lewis's shoulder. "Our destiny awaits us, but first, I want to show Elizabeth the inside of our ship."

They walked across the chamber to the craft, and Menno placed his hand on its mirrored surface. An eight-foot by eight-foot section near the bottom shimmered for a moment, and then suddenly became transparent, exposing the airlock doors in to a large room inside the alien spacecraft.

Menno stepped inside, and Lewis and his mother followed him into the craft, then up the stairs to the control room. In the center, four chairs were facing a control console. The most fascinating aspect of the room was the transparent ceiling and sides of the ship, through which they could see the massive room outside.

Menno sat in one of the chairs and stared up at Lewis, who stood in front of him with his hands clasped behind his back. "It is time I told you and Elizabeth how I came into possession of this craft. You are my younger brother, and our real parents were space travelers." Menno studied Lewis for some sort of surprised response, but true to his nature, his brother remained impassive and waited for further explanation.

Menno chuckled. "Have you ever wondered why I sought you out, Lewis? Or why did operating this craft came so easily to you?"

"I assumed it was because of my exceptional intelligence," Lewis said stone-faced, without a trace of seeming egotistical.

Menno laughed at his response. "Yes, I guess you could say that was part of it."

Elizabeth stared wide-eyed and open-mouthed at Menno. "Why didn't you tell me any of this before?"

"Our race was the original inhabitants of this planet, 180 million years ago. One of their experiments went horribly wrong and started a chain of events that caused a super volcanic eruption, and a thick layer of ash blocked the radiation from the sun and they were forced to evacuate this world. They sent one ship back with four devices capable of cleaning the atmosphere, but it was never heard from again."

Lewis's eyebrow went up. "Did our race evolve on this planet?"

"No, they evolved on another world in this galaxy, and now they live on one similar to this one. Many years ago, they began receiving primitive radio signals, and once they deciphered the language, they realized a similar race of humans once again lived on this planet. Two ships came back to this world to learn about the new inhabitants. Four scientists were in this one, and we were in the other one with our parents. They didn't realize they were passing over a section of desert directly above a nuclear test site during the detonation. They were caught in the explosion and lost control, and both ships were damaged in the crash. They managed to repair this one, but it is only capable of near Earth orbit, and could never return to our home world."

Elizabeth brought her hand up over her mouth in surprise. "It's all true? I remember there were several reports in the newspapers about people claiming to see unidentified flying objects. Their claims were dismissed by the government."

"Yes. The military found the other spaceship and took it to Groom Lake."

"How did we end up being raised by these humans?"

"While making the repairs, the scientists became infected by microorganisms for which they had no natural immunity, and since you and I were infants, we became immune to the disease. They decided to let the people of this planet raise us and thought it best not to burden one human with two infants, so they left me on your front porch, Mother, and Lewis was taken to another home, in another town."

"Why are you telling us now?" Lewis asked.

"My main intent was to eliminate the fossil fuel used by the machines that have been polluting the atmosphere. I was going to share the crystals with these people, but now I'm not so sure I should. I haven't liked the way they are always fighting each other, and if I let them have access to the crystals, they will start fighting over them the way they fought over the crude oil. Only this time, the power of these crystals could annihilate entire civilizations."

Elizabeth brought out her inhaler and took two deep puffs. "Why can't we choose who we give them to? We can select one country to be in complete control of how to best use the crystals for the betterment of the entire world."

"And who would you choose?"

"*This* country, of course. We stand for freedom all over the world."

"Not as long as we have just one leader. Even the most noble of men can be corrupted by the lust for power over their enemies."

"He's right," Lewis added. "Perhaps we should wait and see which nation becomes the most compassionate toward their fellow beings."

"So, what do we do in the meantime?" Elizabeth asked.

Menno smiled and held her hand. "Would you like to go for a ride?"

Elizabeth nervously looked around the inside of the spaceship for a moment. "I'm a little frightened by all this, but I think I'd like that."

Lewis sat in one of the chairs and his fingers pressed different colored touch pads on his console. The lighting in the chamber blinked out, the flat ceiling slid open, and Lewis engaged the artificial gravity.

Chapter 38

HANGAR 5:

"So it's all true?" Christa asked in amazement as Henry led her and Alex across the floor of the hangar. "All the rumors I've heard? I just didn't believe them."

A large section of the exterior of the ship had been torn away, exposing unrecognizable pale blue machinery. Above it, the mirrored surface was intact.

"This is the only spacecraft we have found, and as you can see, it is badly damaged. I seriously doubt it is capable of flight."

Henry moved around to the other side of the craft and stepped through the eight-foot by eight-foot airlock doors into the ship. Christa and Alex were fascinated as they followed Henry up the metal steps along the curved wall and stepped onto the second floor.

"This is the control room." Henry explained as he stopped at the control console in front of the four chairs. He touched a colored pad and a small drawer slid out, and they saw four circular shaped depressions in the surface. Henry's hand shook as he held the crystal above one of the depressions and saw it was the same size.

"When we first entered this ship, there were small remnants of these crystals in each of the depressions. At first, we did not know what they were, but over the years of tests, they kept getting smaller, and we realized they were the power source. There is only one small fragment left. Just enough to power the lights and the door we entered. We decided to end our experiments lest we deplete it and end a way to get back inside."

With a sense of reverence, Henry slowly placed the new crystal into an empty depression and it immediately radiated soft neon-blue light. The ceiling and sides shimmered for a few seconds before becoming transparent, allowing the interior to be illuminated by the lights overhead, and they saw the walls and floor of the hangar around the ship.

Christa looked around the room, and then her eyes settled on Henry. "This is incredible!"

Henry could not stop smiling. "Let us go see if you can create more of these power crystals." He led them down the steps and out of the hangar, locking the door behind them.

***

The test area for the experiment was located three hundred yards east of the farthest structure. It comprised a one hundred square foot concrete pad, with a two foot high cement wall around its perimeter, and a fifty-five gallon drum of crude oil in the center.

An underground bunker with thick glassed view-ports was located three hundred feet away, and Alex and his friends stood outside, watching four scientists position a robotic arm over the oil drum. Christa pointed up at the stars, glimmering like jewels in an ink black sky. "Look how bright the moon is tonight."

Alex looked up and had an immediate sense of Déjà vu. He saw Colonel Sterns standing with two security guards and walked over to join them.

Christa watched Alex talk to the three men for a few seconds, and then he pointed up at the moon. A moment later, one of the security guards leapt into a jeep, kicking up a cloud of dust as the vehicle sped away.

Alex jogged back to the group and looked at Henry. "That isn't a moon. It's another spacecraft, like the one in the hangar. We're going to follow it in the helicopter."

"Are you sure? How do you know? How can you follow it if it returns to outer space?"

"I'm betting it won't."

"What is your reasoning?"

"Just a hunch."

Henry raised an eyebrow. "You would waste irreplaceable jet fuel on a hunch? Colonel Sterns would never approve it."

"He just did."

Alex jogged back to Sterns, and they climbed into the remaining jeep and drove off.

When the scientists finished setting up the experiment, everyone took shelter in the bunker to watch what would happen. The robotic arm dumped a small portion of rainbow powder into the drum of crude oil, and everyone held their breath, then a brilliant beam of neon blue light shot up from the barrel and destroyed the extended robotic arm. It only lasted mere seconds before the light stopped, and then two rainbow crystals spilled over the side of the fifty-five gallon drum onto the ground. Inside the room, everyone applauded as they congratulated one another for their success. Now Henry could send two men out in silver fire retardant suits to inspect the situation and determine if it was safe to approach.

***

While he waited for the helicopter to warm up, Alex called Donner and explained what he suspected about the false moon. He also asked if one of the spy satellites could be tasked with looking down at that area of the United States. It would need to be ready to photograph several hundred square miles of an area he would designate when he knew the approximate destination of the alien ship.

"You're talking about thousands of dollars to divert a satellite on a hunch."

"We have to find out where this spaceship is hiding if we want to stop Menno from depleting the world's oil supply."

"All right, I'll see what I can do."

"Thanks."

Alex hung up and saw Sterns standing in the doorway, staring at him. "Ready when you are."

"All right. Let's go."

Chapter 39

NEVADA DESERT:

Inside the spacecraft, Elizabeth strolled around the perimeter of the control room, staring out the side at the view in rapt fascination. "Menno, come look at the rainbow."

Menno stood and walked around to see what she was talking about, and recognized the process of changing the crude oil to crystals. "I don't believe it!"

Lewis moved over to join them. "It appears the scientists at Area 51 will have the crystals they need to power the other spaceship."

Menno's mind raced with thoughts of the possible repercussions. Even though it was severely damaged, the other ship could track its counterpart, even underground. If they discover the supply of crystals, the United States would be the dominate country on the planet. "It doesn't appear they've detected us. We need to get back underground."

***

The helicopter was parked on top of a hill with the engines at idle, about two hundred miles east of Area 51, with Alex outside, staring through binoculars, focused on the false crescent moon moving across the desert. "It's coming down fast. Be ready."

Sterns looked through an electronic range finder and pressed the execute button. The craft dropped rapidly for several seconds, then disappeared when it fell below the reflection from the real moon rising over the horizon.

Alex lowered his binoculars, now useless, without a target to focus on. "I've lost it!"

Sterns wrote on a pad in his lap, and then looked over at Alex. "If it came straight down, I've got an approximate range and a direction." He turned to the copilot. "Did anything show up on your radar?"

"Negative, Sir."

"Okay. Punch in two six four degrees. Range, one eight seven miles."

The co-pilot typed on his keypad, and a red dot appeared on his view screen map. "Got it."

Alex climbed inside with Sterns. "Let's go."

The jet engines whined to a high pitch as the rotors speed increased, and then the helicopter leapt from the ground. The pilot swung them around on a southern heading, leveling out at one hundred feet above the desert.

Fifteen minutes later, they were hovering over the area indicated on the map. Using night-vision goggles, Alex and Sterns stared down at the empty desert below through the open doors on the left and right sides of the helicopter.

"Anything?" Sterns said into his headset.

"No, Sir. I don't see any sign of the ship. We're just wasting fuel."

"All right. I know, but it's out here somewhere. It couldn't have just disappeared."

Alex turned and stared out the window. *I wouldn't bet on it.*

***

As they approached the underground facility, Lewis saw a flash of light reflected off something on the top of a hill. "It appears we may have been discovered. We cannot enter without them pinpointing our location."

Menno released a deep sigh. "I showed the world what it would be like to go back to the old ways, where living was simple and the air was clean. I think it's time to shut them down. Permanently."

Chapter 40

HANGAR 5:

Christa felt useless as she watched two scientists performing experiments in the control room of the spaceship. The man, who was introduced to her as Doctor Polanski, had red hair and a matching beard. The woman, Doctor Fielder, had gray hair and sad looking eyes. The two scientists were kneeling in front of an open section of the wall, studying a maze of fiber optic cables glowing with a pale blue light, while Henry was entering information into his laptop computer.

With nothing to do but watch, she sat in one of the four chairs in the center of the room, and on the small control console in front of her, fifteen touchpads radiated soft colored lights. She tried to decipher the tiny characters on the buttons, but they looked like some type of hieroglyphic. Henry had explained that none of his people knew enough about what the symbols represented to take the chance of pushing them, and had warned that since the ship was damaged, the result could be devastating.

Christa shifted her thoughts to Alex, and still found it difficult to be near him without feeling a strong desire to hold his hand, or wishing he would take her in his arms and kiss her passionately. She was startled when he was suddenly standing in front of her and leapt out of the chair, accidentally brushing her arm across the control panel.

The floor shook, and she stumbled, instinctively grabbing him for support. They both tumbled to the floor, with Christa lying across his chest, and Alex watched the roof of the hangar rushing toward him. "Oh, crap!"

Brilliant sparks cascaded across the transparent ceiling as the overhead light were crushed, and then the hangar roof parted with the sound of screeching metal as the shredded pieces slid down the sides of the craft. The horrible squeal abruptly ceased, and above them was a black velvet panorama filled with sparkling dots.

***

Bull and Sterns were standing outside the hangar when the quiet of the night was shattered by the sound of screeching metal. They stared up in numbed fascination as the alien craft rose out of the hangar, then exchanged worried looks and ran into the structure. Three men and two women were standing near the door, staring up at the hole in the ceiling, and Bull stopped in front of a woman. "What happened?"

"We have no idea. It just suddenly started moving."

A thought suddenly rushed through his mind, and Bull looked around the interior of the hangar. "Where are Alex Cave and Christa Avery?"

She pointed up at the hole in the roof. "In the ship."

A sickening sense of dread swept through him, and Bull dashed outside, desperately searching the sky, but the spaceship was nowhere in sight.

***

Christa rolled off Alex and stood, then looked around the control room. Someone grabbed her arm and spun her around, and she stared into the savage eyes of Polanski.

"You did this!" he wailed like a frightened child. "I saw you! I saw you push the buttons!"

Alex leapt to his feet, ready to shove Polanski away, and then saw the tears running down his cheeks and gently grabbed his arm and tugged him away from Christa. "It was an accident, and I need your help if we're going to get back down."

Doctor Fielder did not notice the confrontation as she studied the readings on her monitoring equipment. "I'm detecting a massive power spike in the engine compartment."

Henry walked up to Christa, looking more excited than angry. "Look!"

Christa stared at the twenty-four inch holographic screen above the touch pads. Similar symbols to those on the control console were scrolling across a white background, but they didn't mean anything to the scientists.

Henry sat in the chair in front of the console. "Tell me what happened."

"I'm sorry. I guess I accidentally slid my arm across the console, and then suddenly we were moving."

"Do you know which buttons you pushed?"

Christa looked down at the touch pads and tried to visualize what had happened. "I think it was these first two buttons on the bottom row."

"We have spent years trying to decipher these symbols, and from what we have learned, that makes sense. We thought these two indicated propulsion and direction."

Christa moved up beside him to study the console. "Well, Henry, I think it's time to push a few more buttons. It appears we are still ascending."

Henry studied a series of alien numbers expanding across the screen. "Yes. I think these indicate our elevation." He held his finger poised above the console for a moment. "This one, I believe." He touched one of the buttons and the numbers at the top stopped expanding. He smiled in satisfaction as he felt the pressure in his seat slacken for a second, like being in an elevator and coming to a stop. "If everyone will take a seat or hang on to something, I will try to bring us down."

Alex pointed over Henry's shoulder at the moon's reflection off the second ship, hovering over the base. "There may not be time to go back. We have company."

***

Lewis stared at the sister ship rising out of the hangar. "They have learned more than we assumed."

Menno stared at the copy of his ship and the damaged area facing in their direction. "Perhaps, but I doubt they know the full potential of this spacecraft. They're no match for us, and that damaged section is vulnerable." He lightly tapped the buttons on his console and felt the speed and direction of his ship change as he steered it towards the other spacecraft. "Let's be rid of them. Target the damaged area."

***

Christa spun around to see what Alex was staring at and saw a spaceship matching theirs. "They're coming this way, Henry. I suggest you start pressing some buttons."

"Hang on! I have no idea how this ship will react."

Polanski leapt into one of the seats as Alex shoved Christa into another. Fielder locked stares with him for the fourth chair, and he indicated for her to take it. There was enough room to stand between each pair of seats, and he moved into the area between Christa and Henry, grabbing the backs of their chairs. "We'd better get moving!"

Henry pressed a button, and the stars moved in a circle around them, gradually gaining speed as the ship began spinning like a top. Henry felt a moment of panic, and then concentrated on the other symbols, desperately trying to determine their meanings.

***

Elizabeth stared across the void as the damaged spaceship spun, her hands tightening on the armrests of her chair as she looked over at Menno. "What are they doing?"

Menno's brows bunched together in bewilderment. "I'm not sure."

Lewis looked over at his brother. "I cannot get a lock on the damaged area. I will fire a random pattern. Perhaps we will get lucky."

Menno whipped his head around in surprise. "Did you just say *lucky*?"

"I think that is our best option." He tapped a series of buttons on his console.

***

Alex had to turn in a circle to watch the other craft. When a narrow streak of brilliant blue light shot out from the other spaceship, everyone was driven sideways from the impact. Polanski tried to brace himself, but the blast drove him out of his chair and his hand slid across the console, then spears of blue light shot out from their ship.

***

Menno stared at the short streaks of blue light shooting from the spinning ship, like a Pulsar, sending bursts of colored light out across the universe, but none of them were coming anywhere near his ship. "They're out of control. They don't know what they're doing."

***

"I'm getting dizzy!" Christa moaned.

"Don't look up," Alex told her. "Stare at your hands and concentrate on them, not on what's going on around us."

Henry was torn with indecision. "I just don't know which one to push!"

Alex didn't know which button did what, but knew they had to do something. In desperation, he reached across Henry and pressed two buttons, and although the stars were still spinning, they shot past the other craft.

***

"Look!" Elizabeth screamed, her heart beating hard in her chest as she watched the spinning ship rush toward her.

Menno watched in stunned surprise as the other ship approached with incredible speed, the flashes of blue light still shooting out in a circular pattern like a beacon. Before he could react, he saw Elizabeth suddenly tumble forward out of her chair, clutching at her chest. He leapt up and knelt down beside her, her expression reflecting her agony. "Mother!"

"My . . . heart!" she gasped.

In helpless frustration, Menno watched her body go limp and her head tilt to one side. "Mother!" he moaned and shook her, though he knew it was useless.

Lewis knelt beside Elizabeth and placed his hand on her neck, searching for a pulse. He looked into Menno's pleading eyes and shook his head no. "I'm sorry," he said softly. As he watched, he saw the look in Menno's eyes transform from hopeful fear to savage rage.

Menno stood and stared out into space, catching a fleeting glimpse of the other spaceship as it raced away. "After them!" he growled at Lewis through clenched teeth, his hands opening and closing into fists at his sides.

Lewis stood and looked at the other craft, its streaks of blue light fading as it rushed away across the desert. "They are using a great amount of energy by firing so often, and they will deplete the crystals in a short time. I think we should destroy the military base first . . ." Lewis ceased to argue when Menno spun around to face him, clutching the gold cross hanging from his neck. He quickly sat down in Menno's chair, pressed three buttons on the console, and the desert raced past beneath his ship.

Menno stood staring forward as they slowly gained on the other craft, still spinning and sending out flashes of blue light. "Begin firing!"

Lewis knew he would need a lucky shot to hit the damaged area, but did as instructed. He sent bursts of blue light out at thirty-second intervals to conserve the energy in the crystals.

Menno watched as the streaks of light bounced off the mirrored surface of the other ship, still moving away. "Move closer!"

Lewis increased their speed, and they were quickly gaining on the other craft. He noticed the streaks of light from the other ship were not traveling as far into space and knew the ship was losing energy. It was only a matter of minutes before their crystals would be depleted.

***

Alex clung desperately to the backs of the two chairs to keep his balance as the blows from the blue light increased in magnitude, causing their ship to lurch forward with increasing severity. Every time he tried to look for the other craft, the spinning stars would cause him to become nauseous.

***

The shots coming from his ship suddenly ceased, and Menno spun to face his brother, seething with rage and still clutching his gold cross. "Continue to fire!" he screamed.

"Can you not see that the spinning is slowing down and their speed is falling off?" Lewis replied testily, as they rapidly closed the distance between the ships, now only two hundred feet away.

"I said fire!" Menno screamed.

Lewis pressed a button and sent out a single pulse of blue light.

***

The next blow was overwhelming, and Alex was thrown from between the chairs. He accidentally pushed his hand down on the console before crashing into one of the cabinets, sending an eruption of blue sparks cascading into the control room. Polanski and Fielder were hurled viciously from their chairs and slammed into the wall, and Christa and Henry were driven into their seats as the ship came to an abrupt stop.

***

Menno's jaw dropped in stunned shock as the ships suddenly sped up toward each other at an unfathomable rate. The effect of the collision was like two silver hockey pucks slamming together with such severity, Menno shot through the air and smashed into the wall, and Lewis was hurled shoulder first into the cabinet in front of him. The damage on Alex's ship tore into Menno's, tearing a massive gash through the side and locking them together. The two spinning ships plummeted toward the ground and the impact drove Alex to the floor and bounced Christa and Henry out of their seats.

***

Bull watched the collision and stared helplessly as the ships dropped below the horizon, and the reflection disappeared. He spun around to stare at Sterns. "Where'd they go?"

"I don't know, but it doesn't matter now. I'm sure everyone's dead."

Bull grabbed the front of Sterns' shirt, an angry scowl on his face. "The hell, you say! I won't just write them off until I see the bodies." He glanced at his watch, turned, and strode purposely across the tarmac.

"Where are you going?" Sterns hollered after him.

Bull stopped and turned to face him, his eyes blazing with determination. "To get the helicopter pilot. I'm going out there to find out for sure. Are you coming or not?"

Sterns thought it hopeless and a waste of fuel, but jogged to catch up with him. "They could be anywhere!"

Bull did not reply as he continued across the tarmac, with terns nearly jogging to keep up with him.

***

In the ship from Area 51, what was left of the ceiling was solid again, and the glow from the lights was dimming as the power in the crystal was depleted. Alex sat up and stared at the motionless bodies on the floor, then crawled over to Christa and rolled her onto her back. She opened her eyes and tried to sit up, but he gently held her down. He watched a drop of blood splatter against her blouse and felt the thick red liquid running down from his forehead into his eye. He wiped it away and stared at her. "Are you hurt?"

Christa looked at him, shook her head no, and slowly sat up. "I'm all right. Just a few sore spots."

Henry sat up and looked around the interior of their ship, amazed it was still intact. He did a quick assessment of his own body, and other than a slightly sprained wrist, he seemed to be in one piece and not in any pain.

Alex saw Henry's surprised expression. "How you doing, Doc?" He waited for a reply, but Henry just pointed to something behind him. He turned to see what it was, and saw the interior of Menno's ship through the shredded hole that had once locked them together, and the low mound of dirt between the two spacecraft.

Henry pushed himself up onto his hands and knees and then slowly stood and studied the interior of both ships. "To be honest, I am surprised any of us are still alive."

Alex stood and helped Christa stand up, then made his way across the debris and knelt next to the bodies of Polanski and Fielder to feel for a pulse. He turned to look at Henry and Christa and slowly shook his head no.

They turned to look when they heard the soft moan coming from the interior of the other spaceship, and the three of them made their way through the debris into the other craft. The light was brighter than in their ship, making it easier to see.

Henry was the first one to see the bodies of a woman and a blond man on the floor. When the man tried to roll over, he quickly knelt beside him to help.

Menno felt two hands grab his shoulder to help him roll over, and then he looked up at the stranger and could see the concern in his eyes. Everything had happened so fast he could not remember why he was on the floor. "What are you doing on my ship?"

Henry ignored the question. "How badly are you injured? Can you sit up?"

Menno allowed the man to pull him up into a sitting position, but grimaced at the pain in the right side of his abdomen. He looked around the interior and realized what had happened, then looked down and recognized Elizabeth, and remembered she was already dead.

His head snapped around frantically as he searched for his brother. When he saw Lewis's body, he tried to get up, but a wave of dizziness forced him to stay seated. He looked up and gave the stranger an imploring stare as he pointed to the body of his brother. "See if he's still alive!"

Henry stood and made his way to the stranger on the floor, then knelt down and touched the side of the neck to check for a pulse. The man suddenly bolted upright, panic in his eyes. "Just take it easy for a minute. How bad are your injuries?"

Lewis did a quick assessment of his body before he looked up at the stranger. "My contusions appear to be superficial, but my left ulna is fractured, rendering the arm useless. Please help me stand up so I may assess our situation."

Henry found it difficult to understand how this man could maintain such a cool composure after everything that had happened. "Of course," he said as he grabbed Lewis's right arm and helped him to his feet.

Lewis quickly made his way through the debris and knelt beside his brother. "To what degree are your injuries?"

Menno looked at his brother and lightly shook his head, a smirk forming on his lips. "I think my right leg is broken. At least, that's where I feel the most pain." He looked up at a dark-haired man and a short woman. "Were you the one flying my other ship?" The man and woman indicated their companion, and he looked at Henry.

Henry held his palms out, pleading for understanding. "I had no idea what I was doing. It was an accident."

Alex looked down at Menno. "So you're the one who started all this? I'm Alex Cave, and this is Christa Avery. Why are you tearing apart our infrastructure?"

Menno stared at them for a moment. "I wanted to make a point. Your crude fossil fuel burning machines will destroy this world. My kind tried to save this planet once before, and I was trying to save it once again."

"I don't understand what you mean by your kind."

Menno looked over at his brother, and then up at Alex. "This was one of our planets millions of years ago, but we were forced to leave by a cataclysmic event. An accident, if you will. That's all I have to say."

***

Bull was furious when Sterns refused to allow the use of the helicopter, justifying his argument with the lack of fuel. "Can you at least send an airplane out to look for them?"

"Yes, but not while it's still dark." He looked at his watch. "The sun will be up in twenty minutes, so try to be patient."

Chapter 41

CRASH SITE. SEVENTY MILES SOUTH EAST OF AREA 51:

Everyone took refuge from the cold desert air inside Menno's ship, which had the least amount of damage. Henry was excited to learn more about the spacecraft and kept pressing Menno for answers, but the man remained silent.

Menno folded his arms across his chest as he leaned back in a chair, trying to hide the pain in his abdomen. The constant badgering for information by Henry was getting on his nerves, and he wished he had the strength to shut the man up.

Lewis could see the anger building in his brother's expression, and the instant he saw Menno reach for his cross, he stood, gently took Henry by the arm, and led him outside the wreckage. "I would prefer you did not press my brother further. His temper is extremely short, so I will try to answer your questions."

"I have heard you can make this ship invisible. How is that possible?"

"All matter oscillates at its own frequency. The exterior of the ship is composed of various elements, two of which do not exist on this planet, and we cause them to resonate at frequencies which cannot be seen by the human eye or the type of radar used by the military."

"What about converting the oil? How do you make the powder?"

"It is a complex process, too difficult to explain without a common frame of reference."

They heard an aircraft approaching from the west and saw the sunlight reflecting off a single-engine aircraft coming their way, so Henry turned and ran back into the ship. "There is a plane coming. We need something to make a signal. Matches, flashlights, anything at all." He spun around when he heard a voice behind him and looked at Lewis standing just outside the opening.

"That will not be necessary, Doctor Heinz. The aircraft is coming directly toward us. Now we must wait."

***

Bull paced back and forth across the grey-tiled floor while he listened to Sterns and the voice of the pilot searching for the spaceship.

"I'm flying over two of them right now," the pilot was explaining. "It's a mess down there, and the wreckage looks like two silver hockey pucks. What are they?"

"Never mind about that. What about casualties? Do you see any bodies near the wreckage?"

"I see a man standing outside. Wait a minute. A red-haired woman and two more men just walked out of the wreckage. They're waving, so they must be all right. Here are the coordinates."

Sterns jotted down the information, then turned and handed the note to Bull. "Take it to the helicopter pilot and tell them you're cleared. I'll call and have two medical technicians ride with you. Just remember, we don't have a lot of fuel left, so try to get in and out as soon as possible."

Bull's only concern was Christa and Alex, and from the description given by the pilot, they were still alive. "Thanks, Colonel. I'll call you after we set down."

***

Once the pilot waved his wings in acknowledgment, the aircraft turned and headed in the direction of the base, and the group returned to the interior of Menno's ship to await a rescue helicopter. Menno had remained impassive about their rescue until Alex sat in front of him. "What's going to happen next, Mister Cave? Are you going to arrest me?"

"It's not up to me. I'm just a college teacher."

"I have broken no laws."

"How about theft and murder? You took a lot of crude oil and people died in the process."

"Those charges will never hold up in court. I wasn't the one murdering those people. Those things were done by others. In fact, I doubt this will ever go to court. The government will never tell the public about aliens and spaceships."

"You're right. They won't make this public, but they *will* make up some excuse to hold you in custody."

Menno grinned sarcastically. "They want my new type of energy. I'm sure I can work something out for my freedom."

Alex heard the deep thumping sound of an approaching helicopter, and everyone except Menno walked outside to watch. The aircraft set down in a cloud of dust, and they saw Bull jump out the side door as they approached.

Bull threw his arms around Christa and hugged her fiercely, then saw Alex smiling at him. "Damn, I'm glad to see you two. When you busted through the roof of the hangar, I thought I'd never see you alive again." He let go of Christa and gave Alex a manly hug before he noticed the blood in his friend's hair. "Are you okay?"

"Just a minor cut. Menno is inside with a broken leg." He noticed two people climb out of the helicopter and grab a stretcher before walking over.

Bull turned to the approaching medics. "You're needed inside." He noticed the stranger standing next to Henry. "Who's that guy?"

"That's Menno's brother, Lewis Norton. They're aliens."

Bull's mouth opened for a moment in surprise. "No shit?"

"It's a long story, my friend. Let's get out of here."

The medics walked past them with Menno on the stretcher, and the rest followed them to the helicopter, but one of the medics stopped Alex before he climbed inside. "He has internal injuries. I can't tell how badly right now, but he should be taken to a hospital as soon as we get back to the base. He needs surgery, and we're not set up for it."

They both climbed in, and the helicopter took off and headed for the base. Christa noticed the concern in Alex's eyes as he sat next to her. "What's wrong?"

"Menno has internal injuries. If he doesn't make it, we won't have any way of learning how to use the crystals for our own benefit."

"Won't his brother know the same things he does?"

"I don't know. I haven't had a chance to talk to him. I want to apologize for getting you involved in all this, Christa. I'm just glad you're all right."

***

The helicopter pilot had radioed ahead, and once they set down in front of the main building at the base, the plane that had searched for them was waiting to take Menno to the hospital in Las Vegas. Lewis wanted to go with his brother, but Alex had the feeling it would be best if he stayed behind. He still needed answers and hoped Lewis would cooperate.

Once the airplane had departed with Menno, the group walked into the main building and Alex went straight to the office to use the telephone. He informed Donner of what had happened, his plans to keep Lewis there for questioning, and hoped he would cooperate in helping them understand how to use the crystals. "One more thing. They were not born on this planet."

Donner was silent for a moment while he took in the enormity of the situation. "Are you positive?"

"Yes. I'll call you back once I have more information."

"All right. I'll let the president know what's going on. Call me when you can."

Alex strolled into the lounge and saw Lewis sitting next to Henry on the couch, and Christa and Bull standing off to one side.

Christa waited until Alex joined them. "Lewis said the powder Menno gave his followers won't work anymore. He said they would become inert after three days. It turns out Menno never intended to convert all the crude oil at one time. He just wanted to make a point."

"That's good news." He noticed Henry grinning and sat next to him. "What's going on?"

"Yes. Lewis is going to help us."

Alex looked at Lewis. "I was hoping you would. A lot of people are interested in your accomplishment."

"Henry will accompany me to our underground facility, and I will explain how the crystals work."

Alex remembered something Menno had mentioned. "Your brother said you tried to save this planet once before. What did he mean by that?"

Lewis told him about colonizing the Earth 180 million years ago, and the result of one of their failed experiments. "Once the volcanic activity had ceased, one of our ships was sent here to distribute four devices at predetermined locations around the planet. They would remove the toxic molecules from the atmosphere so our people could return. We knew the ship had arrived on this world, but we lost contact. That's why our parents were sent here in the late 1940's. To find out what happened."

"Why didn't your brother talk to us about this new form of energy? Didn't he realize the damage he would cause to life and property by suddenly stopping fuel production?"

"My brother is not a patient person, and I warned him he was being irrational. I would have preferred gradual introduction of the conversion process. The people of this planet are currently too dependent on fossil fuel."

Everyone turned when the door opened, and Sterns had a concerned expression when he walked into the room and looked down at Lewis. "I've just received word your brother died on the way to the hospital. I'm sorry for your loss." He looked at Alex. "Could you step outside for a moment?"

Alex stood and followed Sterns into the hallway. "What's going on?"

"Director Donner just called. The Secretary of Defense wants Mister Norton arrested and held in confinement."

"We need his help, Colonel. We need to get him back to the underground facility. Can you help us?" Sterns remained silent for a moment and Alex could see the indecision in his expression.

"I could lose my commission over this, but take the jeep and I'll cover for you as long as I can. For now, my people are the only ones who know about the facility, and I'll do my best to keep them from talking."

"Thank you." Alex hurried back into the room. "You need to leave right now, Mister Norton." They all turned and looked up at him.

"What's going on?" Christa asked.

Alex told them about Stern's orders. "They want to arrest you, and I need time to contact the right people and stop it from happening, so you need to leave right now. You have transportation waiting outside."

Christa and Henry both talked at the same time, each making an argument about why they should go with Lewis. "I understand, but what I'm doing is illegal. Both of you could be arrested for helping me with this."

"I do not care," Henry said adamantly. "This is too important."

"I'm going, too." Christa insisted.

Alex knew it was urgent they leave right away, so did not argue with them. "Then you'd better get moving." Henry and Lewis rushed past him, but Christa waited. "I thought you were going with them?"

"I am, but I wanted to talk to you in private first. I'm sorry I tried to force myself on you, Alex. Could we at least be friends?"

"I'd like to be more than friends, but I just need a little time. You see, since my wife was murdered, I've had a difficult time getting close to anyone new. I'm really sorry, but I don't want the same thing to happen to you."

"The cold war is over and you're not an agent anymore. You're just a professor, remember?"

He did not feel like a teacher, not with everything that had happened lately. "Maybe you're right, but this is not over yet."

"I can wait. Just do what you need to do, and I'll be waiting." She reached up and put her arms around his neck and gently pulled him down and kissed him on the cheek. "You'll know where to find me."

Alex hugged her tightly for a moment, then released her and smiled. "I'll walk you outside."

***

FOUR DAYS LATER. WASHINGTON, D.C.:
Alex entered Donner's office and set a manila envelope on the desk before sitting down across from him. "As it turns out, Menno knew most of the powder he gave his people would never be used. It seems it only works when it's fresh. Bull had his people start up the refineries, and the first ships are already on their way south."

"That's the best news I've had all day. The President convinced the Secretary of Defense that we need Lewis's cooperation, so he's backed off. Lewis will remain in his facility for now, but under constant supervision. Blackwood is being held in custody until his trial, and he'll probably receive the death penalty for his atrocities. You did a great job with this situation, Alex. Thank you."

Alex indicated the envelope on the desk. "Lewis told me a story about some other devices that his people were going to use to clean the atmosphere on our planet. It's all in the report. Their spaceship made it here, but they lost contact, and the way I understand it, the devices are cylinders that when activated correctly, will draw certain harmful elements from the atmosphere."

"What do you mean by activated correctly?"

"I don't know all the details, but imagine if we had something like those cylinders right now, we could stop this global warming before it's too late."

"Does Lewis know how to build them?"

"I'm afraid not. For now, it looks like it's up to us to solve our own problems."

Donner saw Alex smile slyly. "I've seen that look before. What are you thinking?"

Alex continued to smile as he stood and tapped his finger on the envelope. "I wonder where that spaceship crashed."

The End.

I hope you enjoyed Dead Energy, and I would appreciate it if you will take a moment to write a brief review.

Thank you.

James.

The next exciting Alex Cave adventure.

COLD ENERGY
Part one.

Chapter 1

ALASKA. A TINY ISLAND IN THE ALEUTIAN CHAIN:
Geophysics instructor Alex Cave entered the opening in the rock face of the volcano and saw the light from his flashlight reflecting off a mirror surface. He followed the mirror deeper into the volcano until he reached the airlock doors of the alien spacecraft and then stepped into a large circular room. His light reflected off a six-foot diameter sphere with a mirror surface before he aimed the flashlight at the floor, exposing the powdered remains of a human-shaped body in a one-piece silver suit. As he picked up the shiny fabric, the powder flowed through the material onto the floor. "Tough luck for the first time traveler."

He set it aside while removing all his clothes, then stepped into the suit. "I hope this works." He cautiously placed his palms against the mirror surface of the sphere, felt an electrical shock, and vanished.

***

SEVEN DAYS EARLIER.

PACIFIC OCEAN SIXTY, MILES WEST OF VANCOUVER, BRITISH COLUMBIA.
On board the sophisticated research ship *Mystic*, billionaire Mike Tanner was ready to try his new high-powered ultrasound unit, hoping to find methane hydride in extremely deep water. He pressed the button, and the unit activated.

***

SEATTLE FEDERAL BUILDING. FEMA REGIONAL OFFICE:

"Listen up everybody," Director Charles Simson hollered across the control room. "We've just received a report there has been a major seismic event on Vancouver Island. It hit Victoria the hardest, but the United States' San Juan Islands also felt some seismic activity. Call your contacts and find out the extent of the damage so we can get the emergency response teams moving. Make it happen, people."

The USGS, (United States Geological Survey), supervisor from the sixth floor, Sharon Aniston, stepped out of the elevator and hurried across the room into Simon's office. "Charlie, it didn't register as a major earthquake."

Simson stared up at her. "What do you mean?"

"We don't know what it was. All we know is the ground suddenly rose beneath Victoria and only affected that specific area."

"Is that even possible?"

"Logically? Not a chance. We don't have a clue how to explain what happened."

"Do you think it's a prelude to a major earthquake in the Pacific Northwest?"

"I don't want to speculate because we just don't have enough information. I'll tell you one thing, Charlie. If whatever caused the destruction in Victoria happens here, in Seattle, there won't be anything left standing. There's a helicopter on its way to pick me up on the roof. I'll look at the damage and try to figure out where it started, and I'll call you when I have more information."

Simson stood from behind his desk. "I need to see the San Juan Islands to get a better idea of what I'm dealing with, so I'm going with you."

"It's only a two-person helicopter, but I'll let you know what I find out."

Simson sat back down. "Okay. Thanks, Sharon."

***

Sharon left the elevator and climbed the stairs to the roof access door, then stopped to look at the digital thermostat mounted on the wall. The outside ambient temperature was close to eighty-nine degrees Fahrenheit, when it should be in the upper seventies, but global warming was changing the weather patterns across the planet, and no one country had enough influence to stop the major contributors to the problem.

She stepped out onto the roof, hurried across to the two-person Bell helicopter, and climbed in next to the pilot, Steve Bolton. A few moments later, they were flying north over the Puget Sound. The damage to the San Juan Islands appeared to be minimal, so she asked Steve to drop lower for a closer view of the damage to Victoria.

She stared down through the smoke and saw the devastation was far worse than she had imagined. The beautiful castle was now a pile of shattered marble, and large sections of the majestic hotels had collapsed into mounds of concrete and shattered glass. The mooring docks had been tossed around the harbor like rubber bands, and beautiful yachts lay smashed into tangled heaps of sunken wood, fiberglass, and sail masts. Dozens of emergency workers and dogs were searching through the rubble for survivors, and bodies were stacked in long rows on what remained of the streets. For registering as a minor tremor, the damage was horrific.

"I've seen enough, Steve. Take me back to the Federal Building."

She leaned back in her seat and stared out the front window as the helicopter turned south, back to Seattle.

***

Steve set the helicopter down on the roof of the Federal Building, and Sharon climbed out and hurried across to the door to get out of the heat. She entered the building and went down the stairs to wait for the elevator, and when the doors opened, her geophysics expert, Patrick Chandler, was waiting inside.

She entered and looked at the thin stack of papers in his hand. "I hope you've figured out where this started, Patrick."

Patrick shook his head no. "This was unlike any seismic disturbance we've dealt with before, and we have no idea where the epicenter was. What did it look like from the air?"

"The damage in Victoria is extensive and very precise, as if planned to hit only that specific city. I need to find out if the CIA knows of any terrorist activity in the area."

"You can't be serious, Sharon. It was a seismic disturbance, not a bomb."

Sharon sighed in exasperation and leaned back against the wall. "You're probably right. I'm just frustrated and searching for answers."

The doors opened, so they stepped into the hallway of the USGS Command Center, where they collected and analyzed all the seismic data for the western region of North America. Using sophisticated software, her team was trying to pinpoint the origin of the event.

A young woman ran up and handed Sharon a sheet of paper, so they stopped walking while she read the information. She finished and gave it to Patrick. "This day just keeps getting worse by the hour. The tsunami warning detectors in the northern Bering Sea activated at the same time as the seismic event in Victoria." She looked at the young woman. "We need to find out if there was any seismic activity in that area. Put it up on screen number three, please."

Sharon turned and moved across the room to study the information displayed on one of the large video screens. The image changed, showing no seismic activity in the Bering Sea.

Patrick had stopped while he read the report, and then caught up to her. "This is very bad, Sharon. If this is happening along the entire northwest coast, it means there is some major tectonic activity along the Pacific Rim. I'm just surprised we haven't noticed an increase in volcanic activity."

"Did you call Wesley Patterson about this? He must be monitoring the activity here in the Pacific Northwest."

"Three times, but he didn't answer."

"After the Mount Saint Helens incident, can you blame him?"

Patrick looked down at the floor for a moment as he remembered what had happened. He had ignored Patterson's warning about an imminent eruption, and many lives were lost. He stared up at the monitor. "I guess not. Even so, he must have noticed what happened."

They stopped in front of a large display showing all the seismic detectors in Western North America, and the only flashing red dot was in Victoria. The tsunami sensors in the Bering Sea showed a ten-foot surge radiating south toward the Pacific Ocean, with nearly no surge past the Aleutian Islands.

"That's a bit of luck," stated Patrick. "It seems the islands broke up the surge before it reached the Pacific."

Sharon folded her arms across her chest and continued to stare at the screen. "I don't think luck plays any part in all this. If it wasn't an earthquake that created the surge, what did?"

"I know. None of this makes any sense."

***

MONTANA STATE COLLAGE, BOZMAN:
Alex Cave sat on the edge of his old wooden desk, looking at his

second year geology students while they headed toward the door. He heaved a deep sigh at the thought of having to teach the same old material to his *first*-year students. The subject was becoming so routine, he could do it in his sleep. Ever since the Dead Energy operation, he yearned for the adrenalin rush of being on the hunt again.

David Conway waited until the last student walked out of the room before strolling over to Alex. He noticed the nearly healed scar just above his left eyebrow. "What did you do last weekend to get so banged up?"

Alex grinned. The physics student was like the little brother he never had. "Just a field trip, David. You never can tell when a few rocks might fall when you go underground."

"Speaking of a fall, Greta Bernstein, the English Literature teacher, seems to be really interested in you. She keeps asking me if you're gay, since you never accept her offer to go out on a date." He noticed the look in Alex's eyes change to one of deep sorrow, and realized Alex was still mourning the death of his wife in Holland not too long ago.

"I'm sorry, Alex. Hey, listen. I thought you might find this interesting. I logged into one of NASA's northern imaging satellites and it was taking pictures over the Arctic Ocean when a small section of ice suddenly changed color from white to clear."

"That's interesting. Could it just be a refraction of the light through the ice?"

"It's possible, but that's not what it looked like to me. It took several seconds before the satellite moved out of range, but even when the angle changed, the ice was still transparent."

"Have you contacted anyone who was watching at the same time?"

"I've been trying, but so far, no one has responded to my request."

"Let me know what you find out."

"I will."

Chapter 2

C.H.A.R.S., (CANADIAN HIGH ARCTIC RESEARCH STATION), CAMBRIDGE BAY, NUNAVUT:

Sonja Hanspevin studied the computer map of the Polar Ice Sheet north of Canada. One of the GPS units on was flashing a warning the elevation had just increased by two hundred meters in only three minutes. "This cannot be right," she whispered.

She grabbed her phone and entered the number for her District Manager, Peter Hendrix. "Hallo, Peter. We are getting a warning from GPS unit 635. I want to fly out to look for myself, but I need your approval for the helicopter."

"Tom is scheduled to pick up the Regional Director at the airport in three hours. Can it wait until he returns?"

"I would rather not. We could have a serious problem."

"What kind of problem?"

"The elevation of the ice sheet has gained two hundred meters in only a few minutes. Peter?"

"I'm still here. That's impossible. It has to be a malfunction."

"There is only one way to find out. If it *is* a malfunction, I will exchange the unit and be back in time for Tom to pick up the Director, but we need to be sure."

"Okay. I'll call Tom and tell him you're coming."

"Thank you, Peter."

***

Thirty minutes later, Sonja and the helicopter pilot, an American named Tom Hatfield, thought they were seeing an illusion. Directly ahead, a vertical wall of transparent ice had risen two hundred feet out of the Arctic Ocean.

Tom whistled softly. "Now that's different."

Sonja was speechless as they closed the distance to the ice wall. "Take us higher, Tom."

When Tom increased their altitude, she saw the transparent block of ice was ten miles wide, and extended three hundred miles south into the Beaufort and East Siberian seas. "This is not logically possible, Tom. We should find the GPS unit and retrieve the data. That will help us determine how this could happen."

Tom gave her a nod and entered the new coordinates into the navigation system. "If all this happened as quickly as you say, I would imagine it made a powerful wave."

The surface of the newly formed ice block was as transparent as the sides, and Sonja's heart broke at the sight of dozens of white pilot whales frozen in the surface. "I do not understand what could have caused the water to freeze that quickly."

Tom set the helicopter down fifty feet from the GPS receiver and brought the engine's speed down to idle. Sonja opened the side door and noticed the air felt extremely cold. When she stepped out, the rubber sole of her shoe touched the ice and immediately stuck to the surface. She struggled to pull it free, and when it tore loose, chunks of the gray rubber sole remained stuck to the ice, so she slid back inside onto the seat.

"The ice is extremely cold, and I do not think we should stay here. We will have to come back with different equipment."

"That works for me."

Tom shoved the throttle forward and pulled up on the collective, but the helicopter runners were frozen to the ice in a vice-like grip. He shoved the throttle to full power, but when he pulled up on the collective, the runners remained frozen to the ice and vibration threatened to tear the helicopter apart.

He let go of the collective and pulled back on the throttle until the engine was idling. "We're stuck here until the ice melts."

"Can I do something to help?"

"If we can't break free with the rotors, there's nothing we can do."

"Call for another helicopter to pick us up."

"Are you kidding? No one else can land to get us, because they would get stuck, too. Until something changes radically, we're trapped out here."

Sonja wrung her hands together on her lap while she tried to think of a way out of their situation. "Call the research station and tell them what happened. We have many intelligent people working at the facility, and perhaps someone will think of a way to help us."

Tom entered the research facility's frequency into the radio. "Chars research station, this is chars helicopter one. Come in, please?"

No one responded, so he tried again, but after several minutes without a response, he changed frequencies. "This is the Chars research helicopter calling anyone on the emergency radio frequency. Please, respond." When no one answered, he looked over at Sonja. "Something must be interfering with the radio signal."

"Do you have any survival equipment?"

"Not much. Spare water, a small supply of power bars, first aid equipment, and signal flares."

"If we do not return to the station, they will send a search and rescue unit to find us."

"Even if they do, they still can't land to pick us up, and without radio communication, we don't have any way to warn them about the ice, and they'll be stranded out here with us. When our fuel runs out, it's going to get freezing cold in here."

"How long do we have before that will happen?"

Tom looked at the digital readout. "Even leaving the engines at idle, we'll run out of fuel in less than four hours, and without heat, we'll be dead thirty minutes later. I'm sorry, Sonja."

Award-winning author James M. Corkill is a Veteran, and retired Federal Firefighter from Washington State, USA. He was an electronic technician and studied mechanical engineering in his spare time before eventually becoming a firefighter for thirty-two years and retiring. He has since settled into the Appalachian Mountains of western North Carolina, and has a fantastic view from his writing desk.

He began writing in 1997, and was fortunate to meet a famous horror writer named Hugh B. Cave, who became his mentor. In 2002, he rushed to self-published a dozen copies of Dead Energy so his wife could see his book published before she was taken by cancer. When his soul mate was gone, he stopped writing and began drinking heavily.

His favorite quote. "When you wake up in the morning, you never know where the day will take you."

In 2013, he met a stranger who recognized his name and had enjoyed an old copy of Dead Energy, except for the ending. When she encouraged him to start writing again, he realized this chance meeting was just what he needed to hear at the right moment. He quit drinking and began the rewrite of Dead Energy into The Alex Cave Series, and thankful for that fateful encounter.

Other books by James M. Corkill
Cold Energy. The Alex Cave Series Book 2.
Red Energy. The Alex Cave Series Book 3.
Gravity. The Alex Cave Series Book 4.
Pandora's Eyes. The Alex Cave Series Book 5.
DNA. The Alex Cave Series Book 6.
Parallel. The Alex Cave Series Book 7.
Impact Yellowstone

You can contact him at.
Jamesmcorkill@gmail.com

Movie script available from the author.